WITHOUT
A TESTIMONY

A NOVEL BY

Jerod Killick

Published by Jerod Killick on Amazon Createspace
Revised Edition, 2018

ISBN: 978-0987943910

"God is love.
Whoever lives in love,
lives in God, and God in him."

-- John 4:16

ACKNOWLEGEMENT

This book is dedicated to my husband, Johnny Killick, for his insights and encouragement. I also want to acknowledge the friends and family that supported the completion of this heart-felt project. Your editorial and cover art design feedback contributed significantly to the quality of this published work.

Part One

"The Bridge"

Chapter One

He balanced in the shadows on the railing of the bridge that ominously hovered on four concrete pillars, supported by a dark grey foreboding mist. He hung hidden in the shadow, beyond the orange and yellow cast of the bright sodium lights. In the depths of the darkness, green and red dots passed below, leaving behind the vague but distinct odor of diesel. The vestals sang their unforgettable eerie tune, carried up and drowned by the gusting of wind through the teeth of pine treetops along the bank.

He wore no jacket, only a t-shirt, jeans and sneakers. The negative wind chill bit deep at his core. Ice formed around his eyes while tears oozed onto his face, blending with the thick streams of mucus from his nose. The sudden rushes of wind carried droplets off his chin and into the blackness below.

His arms extended out with both hands on the cable running just above him. With each passing breath, his exhausted fingers loosened and tightened their grip around the icy steel, the pain unbearable. He struggled to feel the solid curved beam underneath the arches of his feet, holding steadfast with his toes tightly curled, trying to mold to the contour of its shape. His exposed ankles were raw with abrasions indicating fleeting moments of ambivalence and exhaustion.

The forces closed in around him, taunting for decision. With each passing gust, he recaptured his balance, his tired hips thrusting outward and then back in compensation.

The voices resonated in his head, the demons whispering incessantly, urging him to give in to impulse. Suddenly, he felt them from behind but was too afraid to turn. They came close, hissing their poison.

"Go ahead my Son, just do it. You don't really want to continue, do you? All this walking around, existing in the shadows of the living must be getting just a bit tiresome. It's too lonely existing the space between life and death. It has been far, far too long, don't you think?"

The whispers were right. And all he had to do was let go. Let go and then it would be all over. It would cease, the voices, the unbearable chattering from the corners of his mind. Yes, it would all stop, the flashes of sinful scenes, that that from a play of a morally failed life, the looming disappointment left behind in the letters from home, the silent paternal disregard, and the loneliness of his untouched skin. Peace was finally at a moment's decision if he simply had the courage to let go into the taunting blackness.

It started to rain, lightly at first, then with quick waves of needles against his face, piercing his cheeks, lips and eyelids. Water ran along his fingers that embraced the steel life support above, down into his armpits, and quickly soaked his shirt, causing it to adhere to his tight oily skin. He could smell his own warmth and taste the tears running into his mouth. His torso shuddered. He adjusted his stance, exhausted from holding himself, the blood in his arms sinking with gravity.

Suddenly, the slick rubber footing of both shoes gave from underneath. He tried desperately to pull back…the pain, the fear.

Then, a quick and forceful gust pushed him back. In compensation, his head thrust forward and his arms hyper extended, trying desperately to hold his stance. It was too late. His feet slipped off the rail behind him. Pain shot down his hands and into his arms. He couldn't hang on. He tried to pull up, forcing his chest forward. He looked down in horror at his feet dangle behind the railing, desperately grasping for any hope of footing in his final moment.

He lifted himself, pulling hard with his arms one last time. "No, I can't...," he thought as he forced his eyes shut, clenching his teeth.

He pulled up hard in one final attempt, letting out a high-pitched groan. His hands slipped. He fell forward, his chest hitting the steel support, bouncing him onto the roadside pavement flat on his back, just beyond the walkway. A rusty blue station wagon screeched to a halt.

Then there was blackness, a murky land of shadows without the supernatural. It consumed him, no peace, nor pain, only an absent void. He was alone, and it embraced him.

Chapter Two

Brad sat on the sofa, his hands dangling off his knees, looking down at the floor, trying to shake off the side effects of late evening sleep. He pushed himself to his feet, ran both palms over his scalp, and went to the clothing trunk next to the door, while pushing back the intrusive thoughts to go directly to his bed to finish off the day.

Brad knew what he needed. The unacceptable alternative was to stay put. However, what lurked in his desire for inaction, came with the unpredictable darkness in his dreams. It would certainly, and without invitation, return. The dream was becoming stronger, more vivid, and visiting his consciousness more frequently. And now it started hanging with him during the day, refusing to take rest in the presence of the sun. But still an ambivalent curiosity wanted to explore the reasons. Why, after so long, had the shadows returned?

Waking up required getting out of the apartment; a kind of starting fresh for the day, even though it was far past dusk and the nightlife had already consumed the street below.

He took his customary place on top of the trunk, the lid only slightly protesting, and pulled on his boots that were patiently waiting with their heels tight against the bottom edge. Brad pulled the laces snug against each hook, quickly leading up his ankles, and crossed the long string around his leg, and pulled the ends back around to the front. He tied them in a firm knot and wiggled his toes. They felt a bit tight, but he thought they would do for now, hoping, contrary to experience, that they would loosen up as he went.

Brad stood and lifted the lid, pushing his hands through the sea of magazines and clothing, looking for his usual outdoor accessories. He spent all day cleaning his apartment, and the trunk had been the dumping ground for everything that had no real good place otherwise. His friends commented on how clean the place typically was, but his best-kept secret was the trunk. Cleanliness was only what others could see.

He fished out the solid blue knit scarf and pulled it comfortably around his neck, crossed it in front, and tucked it into his campus coat without placing a knot in it. He rarely knotted his scarves, disliking the bulky feeling. Reaching back into the trunk, Brad pulled out the matching hat, let the lid of the trunk fall on its own, and went out the apartment door, leading into the dark poorly lit empty hallway. The yellow glow of old light fixtures hanging on the side of the walls, cast their usual peculiar shadow to the ceiling. Even from the third-floor landing, the top floor of the Moscow Hotel Apartments, he could hear the crowd of people below.

In front of him a flight of stairs circled right and to a second, slightly less expensive set of apartments. Immediately following was another flight leading onto the first floor that entered into an open smoky space with a lounge on each side.

To the left was the Main Street Bar and Grill. It was a relatively quiet bar for the small Idaho university town, entertaining the more sophisticated older crowd of graduate students and community members. In the center was the lounging pit with a couch built into the perimeter, and tables tightly packed at its edge. The bar was attached to a restaurant that had a sign obtrusively declaring, "Please Wait To Be Seated" to all who dared contemplate its cuisine. Few paid it much attention. Brad himself thought this was a little formal for the quality of food and services the grill had to offer. Both were without surprise or disappointment, and both did not matter if you started early with drinks at the bar; inadequate food and service were inconsequential on such nights.

To the right of the first-floor landing was the Garden Lounge, owned by the same merchants of the Main Street Bar and Grill and the Moscow Hotel Apartments above. Every night by eight o'clock, clouds of cigarette smoke could be seen billowing into the street from its side exit. The walls were darkened with yellow gummy residue from decades of student gatherings. Rumor had it the owners refused to paint the inside walls because the tar served as its own kind of marbled artistic rendition.

The building was always busy. The traffic between the bars was heavy, and many residents of the apartments above spent their off hours taking in an early morning smoke, or an afternoon lunch. Blue Monday was an event all of its own. It started at three o'clock in the afternoon, the only night of the week when patrons could order any drink on the menu for two dollars. Next to Saturday, it was the most heavily attended event.

Brad heard someone coming down the hall. He shoved his hand in his right pocket and pulled out a wad of tangled metal. Pulling the door quietly but firmly, as it usually took some force to catch, he slid in the key, quickly turning it to the left and a full rotation to the right, until he heard the bolt take. The head of the key was sticky, left over from the gummy residue of the aged price tag. Trying to rub it off his thumb, he found himself annoyed with the distraction. An urge to go back inside and wash his hands came over him. He resisted. "Fuck it. I'll get it later," he thought to himself, instead, forcing the skin between his teeth, attempting to work off the glue.

He dreaded anyone trying to strike up conversation. It took too much effort to give off a friendly air, a performance that felt ridiculously placed against his need to be left alone. He hadn't always been this way, yet he despised the typical phony encounters with others. But lately he hated putting on the usual social graces. Alone felt easier. There was a certain amount of guilt associated with this avoidance, a fear of coming off rude or inconsiderate. Nevertheless, guilt was more bearable.

He hurried to the stairs and tapped his way down, passing a couple sitting at the top of the second flight, where he then made a second hard left to the first floor. At the bottom, he quickly made another sharp turn to the right, and proceeded out the double doors and into Friendship Square. He tried to be as inconspicuous as possible, half believing he was invisible if he continued to move quietly, keeping his eyes down at the movements of his feet.

Friendship Square was the center of downtown Moscow Idaho. It buzzed with activity during the late spring, summer, and early fall months, the gathering place for political events, speeches, and the Saturday Farmer's Market. When Brad first moved into the Moscow Hotel Apartments, he spent countless afternoons at the slate bistro tables taking in academic conversation and drinking copious amounts of coffee with friends.

Brad's nose felt instantly uncomfortable, and he had the irritating perception that the mucous just inside his nostrils was crystallizing. He put the wool cloth of his sleeve to his nose, trying to break the frozen particles loose. But there was none to break. Was it the hair inside his nose freezing to his skin? Regardless, the sensation slapped him with the reality of how cold it had become in just a couple of hours since the sun went down. While taking the garbage out after lunch he didn't remember the people, or the cold.

"Shit, I forgot my gloves," he thought to himself. "Fuck it. Fuck it all to hell." He didn't want to run back upstairs and start the process over again. At any rate, the cold was a good distraction from the feeling gnawing at his gut. The dream, no more, he had to forget about the dream, put it away for now, just for a few moments.

"Why now?" he questioned. Brad wondered what subconscious script was to be revealed. It was all coming to a head. "But why now?" he went on. "Are you here?" He looked over his shoulder into the darkness.

He walked through the square, turning left onto Main Street. This was the corner street entrance to the Garden Lounge. A large frozen frantic crowd of people stood around the door waiting to have their identification checked. Every time it opened, an oversized bouncer forcefully directed another person in for screening. The loud beat of the music pounded out and into the street in waves directed by the rhythm of the door.

He walked past the crowd and quickly looked in his peripheral view on both sides, then crossed against the red light. He took a right onto Third Street without intention and unsure exactly where he was going. Was it the voiceless forces of his subconscious? If it was, he gave into its will without resistance.

The hard-crusted snow reflected back the orange tint from the periodically posted street lamps guiding the way. He walked quickly, moving farther and farther away from the activity of the town. Glancing ahead, Brad noted a man standing on his porch, bundled tightly, with the orange-yellow dot moving to and from his mouth. It smelled good. Tempting. There was something about the cold and cigarettes that went together.

The sweet smoke flashed on scenes past, the years living in the Third Street house, as its acquaintances fondly called it. He lived in the house for most of his years in school, only moving downtown since graduating. They lived there actually, on the main house floor, first two, then three, then one. Brad shook his head. The addition and subtraction all seemed so objectifying.

Brad looked up as he passed by, impossible to avoid. He wondered who was in it now. The windows were darkened, and no one sat on the porch. His mouth turned up and then down again, snickering lightly through his nostrils. That house could tell the story. It knew the secrets hidden in her walls like any old house could. "That is what old houses do," he thought, "sit and watch, taking notes that will never be disclosed."

When thinking about all the memories stored in the grain of the hardwood floor and the thick white paint of its walls, mixed feelings quarreled in his chest. He wanted to move on, leaving the days behind him. He played the part of doing so. He was also keeping one foot in, longing for what he had.

He walked on by, quickly, targeting the entrance to East City Park up about a block and a half now. He crossed the street, approaching the entrance of the opening at the corner of the adjoining street.

Brad slowed his pace taking notice of the humming power lines. Only the faint sound of a beat overshadowed it, the exact musical artist which couldn't be made out clearly, moved in the space around him.

He stared into the park, the icy clumps of snow making his footing uneasy. The bare oak and maple trees shadowed his movements along the path. His suspicious mind wondered if anyone was watching.

Suddenly, his hands flew back, and his chin contorted as he thrust his right foot back in reflex. He grunted trying to regain control, stood on defense, and caught his breath.

Collecting composure, Brad followed the narrow asphalt path into the center of the park. Before him was the large wooden platform. He had seen countless folk and garage band concerts, suffering the summer heat and unpredictable windy weather. Then it came to him. His subconscious spilled over into his awareness. Jordan! Yes! It was Jordan that filled his consciousness suddenly and without any warning. It was all coming back again. He longed to talk to him. He glanced over seeing them there, just about where he stood, but up a little farther just under the stage. They were dancing to a kettledrum band during Renaissance Fair.

For the first time Brad noticed his breath and how loud it sounded. He looked around, peering amongst the shadows, listening, and noticing again the hum of the lights. The moisture vapor from his breath slowed. The inside corners of his eyes watered. The wind pushed at his back, making him wobbly on his feet.

Brad looked back on the path he had come down. He didn't want to go back. He tried to loosen the tightness in his throat. He was angry with himself, realizing that he encouraged something he couldn't stop. Like a ghost it had come back in his dreams, and now it was working into his day.

Tensions stomped at his abdomen. He couldn't control it anymore. His breath pushed high up into his chest causing quick and shallow bursts. He remembered the day, the events that took place in the backyard of the house on Third Street. He felt dizzy and knew that somehow, he needed to get control. Bending over, his head hanging below his waist, Brad cupped his head in both hands and cried uncontrollably.

*****

Brad turned onto Main Street again, walking towards The Garden Lounge from the opposite side of the street. As he wove around the occasional body, he imagined he was the only person walking the streets of Moscow. It was a bittersweet thought knowing that he couldn't be without people, but one he enjoyed entertaining. Brad knew the risks of isolation, but frankly didn't care.

He was not ready to go up to his apartment yet, feeling the tug for coffee pulling at his veins. He decided to keep walking down Main. About three blocks up he saw the cluster of erratically parked cars along the street, some waiting with taillights lit.

Brad saw the oversized sign above the doorway. It had oversized calligraphic letters, mottled black and brown, pointing to the location of, "The Beanery Coffee Company". In college it was his favorite place to take in a café mocha and study in-between classes.

Someone jumped out from one of the cars and ran into the building with chin low and hands deep inside his coat pockets.

Until now, Brad blocked out the rawness on his legs. His knuckles were stiff with the bitterness of the air cutting through his campus coat. A hot cup of coffee would be a relief.

Chapter Three

He stepped through a heated conversation at the door between two under dressed, and poorly shaven, gaunt in stature men. He surmised they were students since the conversation was about some finer nuance of philosophy. It wasn't a conversation really, but more like verbal masturbation, each overstating their points of view, entirely missing the perspective of the other. Over the exaggerated inflections in tone, the paper coffee cups between tattered wool gloves remained safe as they carried on, only slightly pausing in an irritable manner, as Brad passed between them.

The line to the counter was daunting. A train of addicts stood before him, most passing time carrying on in similar debates and lecture spurred inquiry. Brad searched intently seeing if there was anyone he knew. Only a face or two was vaguely familiar. But no, Professor Brown sat in the center of the room, with a stained porcelain cup pushed against the edge of the table, graded papers. He methodically turned a page, took the pen from over his ear and marked a note on the paper. Then, he looked over, noticing Brad and returned without care or contempt.

"Good", he thought to himself. "What an ass."

On the counter at the head of the line was a digital thermometer displaying the relative indoor and outdoor temperatures in oversized black numbers. It read "73" and "34" degrees. A small blinking snowflake symbol hovered above the 34. Brad was unconvinced. The ice was brittle and air bone dry for the warm reading.

"The wind! Yes, that fucking wind! It must be negative fifty, man," he grumbled.

He pulled his shoulders up towards his neck, flaring his nostrils and shook his head with the thought.

The line didn't move. Obviously, there was some hold up keeping things stalled. The door opened behind him, blowing a gust of cold air at his back. He stood with elbows tightly inward, hands deep in his pockets, and started bouncing lightly on the toes of his boots.

An employee stood at the steamer with his back to the crowd, holding a silver canister up to the large rod coming out of the machine, slowly moving it up, around, and back again. The noise was piercing but a good distraction from the growing numbers beginning to crowd in.

"Brad…oh my God…Brad, is that you?"

He was startled but recognized the foreign accent. Before he could turn and find its source, two thick canvas arms grabbed snug around his chest, immobilizing him in position. He forced his head around and down. It was Elaina! Her eyes were wide with happiness and she wore the smile burnt deep in his memory from years past.

"My dear God!" Brad said, as he loosened his arms and held her in close. "Elaina! How are you?"

She laughed, twisting her body with joy while holding her ear to his chest.

"What in the hell are you doing in Moscow?" Comforting warmth overwhelmed his chest. It had been nearly three years since they last talked.

"Oh my God dear man! I'm great! I'm visiting friends before heading north to Quebec to see Cousin Anna. Thought I'd come through my old home and see who I might find. How've you been, Mr., "I'm a writer man living in Moscow after all this time."

Elaina used several unique idiomatic twists when speaking English. In particular, breaking the ice in any potentially sensitive situation, she used the following format: Act out in the first person beginning with "Mr." and make a statement about the person's behavior. Brad snickered remembering all the funny combinations she used, and how he made fun of it when he wanted a laugh with friends that knew her after she moved away.

"I've been good! God. It's so good to see you! I can't get over it though! I'm actually standing here talking to you!"

"So, catch me up. What's been going on?"

"I've never left, you know," Brad expressed with a flushing of his cheeks.

"Oh, Mr., 'I work all the time and don't know how to get out of this town.'" Weren't you moving to San Francisco after school? Yes, that's right," she went on. "And then there was that time you were going to visit London. You didn't go, did you?"

"Oh yeah, I turned down the job for the comfort of the university I guess. And Europe is another story. You know how it is."

"Well, so, what do you do now?" she continued in her chiding, inquisitive style.

"I'm supervising the campus paper. Been doing some freelance work on the side. No luck with that shit. Quite bored actually since I've been out of school."

"What can I get you?" interrupted the pale-faced man, with a dull air of annoyance, from the other side of the counter. He had a disheveled presence with loosely pulled back ponytail and oversized green marijuana leaf print t-shirt.

Without honoring him with a response, they fixed their gaze over his head at the artistically rendered blackboard, searching the menu. However, Elaina thought the man was distracting, finding it difficult to focus against his pressuring glare.

"Come on man, the line is long. Coffee? Hot chocolate?" he urged.

Brad's stubborn nature pushed back, thus ignoring the remarks and took his time in the face of being rushed. In an exaggerated gesture, he oriented towards Elaina. "What will you have my dear Elaina? It's on me!"

"Hot Chocolate!" She rushed, responding to the tightening atmosphere."

"Okay then." Brad looked up just a second longer, even though he knew what he was after. "We'll have one coffee, and a hot chocolate. Both the largest you got." Brad pulled out some cash from the front pocket of his jeans and tossed it onto the counter. "Keep the change". The man ignored the gesture, arrogantly turning to start the order.

Brad directed Elaina to the table hugging the back wall. It was a subtle endearment, acknowledging that it was likely warmer being away from the doors, not to mention the dozens of people piling in. Brad typically sought the edge of a room in public places.

They took seats across from each other, Brad facing the entirety of the room, Elaina looking at him with the whitewashed brick wall at his backdrop. Black and white pictures in sturdy silver frames garnished the boring opaque scene.

It was now that Brad secretly acknowledged his slithering anxiety. Sure, it was wonderful to see her. Yes, even though he would have preferred to be alone for the night, her company was unexpected and becoming more and more inviting.

But, he didn't know how much Elaina knew about the last three years. He sensed her questions. Her visit wasn't a simple drop in. And, how much was he willing to tell? The anticipation made his head swim, but he brushed it off, needing to focus on the immediate importance of her visit.

He didn't want to turn it into a self-focused conversation. She traveled a long distance and needed his artistic superficiality.

Elaina jumped right to it. "How is Lydia?" Brad sat back. It wasn't going to be easy.

"Umm…She's fine. I see her every now and then when she comes back into town." A short silence followed.

Elaina didn't let it stop there. She knew his vague methods and short curt antics. He had tools, brilliant, but ineffective at that, when he didn't want to talk about personal matters.

"Aren't you guys friends anymore? I thought you would have worked through stuff by now."

"I think so, but things change you know. Friendships change. It's been a long time since I saw you last Elaina. There was a lot we went through…a lot of stuff happened."

As much as he wanted to avoid the conversation, Brad also wanted her to ask. Everyone else was afraid of approaching the issue, acting like nothing had happened at all. "There is not a lot of trust there anymore," he led.

"I'm not surprised!" Elaina said, throwing out her own hook.

Brad picked it up. "She took a job in Seattle, living with her sister."

Seeing hints of surprise in Elaina's face, he surmised that this was the point her information sources abroad had dropped off. Obviously, the network of connections, the links between them, the information exchange through the international web, had gaps. And this held true. As far as Elaina knew, Lydia and Brad remained at least cordial for the time she and Brad roomed together.

"Hey, I wanted to tell you! I saw Henri in Amsterdam about a month ago on my way back to Brussels. I found him in the airport having a cigarette with some dude, apparently there partying for the weekend."

"Really?"

Elaina reported with exaggerated crescendo over her usual thick accent, "It was a total accident. Said he's working in a convalescence home in Switzerland. He looked great. Not drinking as much. Not so grungy. He told me life at the house got really crazy back in Moscow, but wouldn't go into it. I begged, but he absolutely wouldn't give in. Mr., "I keep secrets so fucking well."

Henri used to room with them starting in his sophomore year at the University. Henri was actually in and out of school, finding it difficult to acquire the necessary study habits and lifestyle.

He was from Switzerland, and like Elaina, went on exchange to Moscow High School, opening up the door for academics at the University. Most anyone that far away from home, finds them self inevitably absorbed in the educational opportunities abroad. In the end, due to homesickness and disillusionment with American culture, the typical student returns home.

However, Elaina and Henri fell in with a close group of friends in high school that established the bond necessary to stick it out, and then move into higher education at the university.

Henri loved big band music, dressed in the shabbiest of bohemian attire, and spoke near perfect English. His mother was American, passing on a softened style to his speech. He blended into bar conversation, only given away by the occasional misuse of English vocabulary.

Brad felt a fondness towards Henri and was sad to see him leave in the middle of his senior year, especially since it was when his emotions felt the most out of control. He wished it could have been a better leaving.

Elaina, on the other hand, returned to Belgium at the end of her sophomore year after finding out that the government would not grant her another work visa. Life was different after she left, and Brad willingly fell out of contact.

He shifted his weight to one side slightly and stared down at the steam forming off the surface of his coffee, suddenly flooded by memories of their years in college. He wished he could go back to that time. He wondered if he would do things differently. The thought was fleeting, but intrusively jabbing.

"I've lived a crazy couple of years Elaina," Brad said as he continued his fixated stare at the disappearing moisture. "I miss Jordan very much, but things are better. I'm absorbed in my new job, made a good life for myself here," he went on. He forced a grin without looking up. He hoped she bought into his deception, shocked that he even dared to bring Jordan up in the conversation.

"Did you know he was doing that bad?" She forced her eyes between him and the rim of the coffee cup, jumping at the opportunity.

"Damn!" Brad thought to himself, "She knows. She knows!" She had played him, acting like her old self, naïve and dumb, playing her cards with brilliance, likely holding all the aces, leading him like a witness on a stand, waiting for the flood of self-disclosure.

"I didn't..." he started and then hesitated. He began as usual, struggling to give a simple and clear answer. It was his curse his friends complained about at one time or another. Even the simplest matters were complicated for him to communicate; the more personal, the more impossible.

"It's okay Brad. I actually came looking for you...as if you didn't know! I've missed you...just wanted to know that you're okay." She reached across the table and put her had on his. He flinched but then relaxed, slightly embarrassed.

"I've left you out. I know that. Maybe I should have talked to you sooner."

"It's not like you didn't know how to get a hold of me!"

"I know," he followed firmly, pulling his hand from underneath hers. Pulling his head back sharply and sitting back in his chair, he had the urge to end it.

"You were so into life back then. You stopped spending time at home, and anyway, he was never my friend, he was yours. I just didn't think he wanted me budging in. Remember? You guys were always running around."

Irritation stirred, sitting deep in his stomach, but he knew she was right. After he moved in, their relationship became business like, each checking in and paying rent, simply living together out of responsibility. She was replaced by Jordan, Jordan and Henri both.

Elaina sat forward. Her voice was shaking. "I don't want to fight, to be even farther apart. Can't we go on from here? Look, I'm visiting for a couple of days Brad, and I really just wanted to hang out with you.

I wasn't sure that I could find you, and now I'm here with you at this dorky coffee shop. I'm sorry, don't mean to pry, but I just want to know that you're okay and to fill in some of the time. I don't want us to remain so apart Brad!"

Elaina sat back in her chair and crossed her arms. She looked down at her gloves sitting loosely on her lap. The conversations went on around them. The steamer screeched and sputtered in and out of the silence between them.

"You're right. I've left you out...out of all of it."

She sat inviting him to go on.

"Elaina, we're going back to my place." Brad sat up and started to pull his scarf around his neck. "I don't want to get into the details in a coffee shop." He stood, refusing to give her a chance at rebuttal. "Come on. I'm living just up the street at the Moscow Hotel Apartments."

He led the way past the full tables towards the door. Then, with an unexpected tug at his arm, he turned. Elaina pulled herself up to his neck, holding tightly, and whispered, "I'm glad to be sitting with you. I'm glad I'm home." Brad ignored the twenty sets of curious eyes and pulled her in closer, let go, took her hand tightly at his side.

Chapter Four

Brad and Elaina made their way down the street towards Brad's apartment. They got to the foot of the steps of the Moscow Hotel Apartments without slipping, despite the hard chunks of petrified snow and ice on the cement sidewalk. Entering the building, Brad felt relief from the warm air pouring around him. A bead of sweat instantly formed under his scarf.

"I'm up on the Third floor." He leaned his head to the right, guiding the way around and upwards with a quick start, with Elaina on his heels.

Elaina was puffing loudly behind him. "Fuck man, only on the third floor?"

Brad stopped and turned to look down at her. She was a half flight behind.

"Oh, Brad, can I smoke in your apartment? If not, I'll get a couple of drags and be right up," she said gasping for breath. At first, he thought she was joking.

Brad pondered if he wanted to wake up to the smell the next day, but the guilt picturing her shivering outside the building was even more overwhelming. And without doubt, he would have to stand outside with her because it was rude otherwise. Either way, he was going to suffer.

"Don't worry about it. It's too fucking cold! Hurry, my apartment is just up a couple flights."

She grabbed the railing. "Yeah, right 'Mr. athletic man.'" For the first time, he saw the weight she put on since he had last seen her. Sedentary adult life was setting in. Or was it? She had always been quite sedentary.

Waiting just inside the door was Marty and Sebastian, two cats with thick black hair. Brad paid a dollar each to a red headed girl standing outside a quick stop off the freeway on his way to Lewiston five years ago. Growing up, his father liked to give their house pets peculiar names such as,

"Brother", "Joan of Arc", or "Mary Magdalene". No one was able to match his father's sense of humor when it came to pets and his quiet affection for them. Never feeling that clever with names, Brad let friends name his cats when he had parties, a game that never produced bad results.

"Hi boys," he mumbled, as he stepped through them to the bench next to the door, leaving the door open for Elaina. He took off his coat and scarf and sat down to unlace his boots. Elaina came in, the heels of her boots dragging heavy on the matted carpet.

"So, you two beasts are still around. I'm surprised no one's been shot or eaten by the dogs." She bent down and greeted them. They welcomed the affection enthusiastically. Sebastian stood up on his hind feet, pushing his head against her outstretched hand.

"You menacing bunch."

Brad pulled off his boots and offered her the bench. She had already tossed off her jacket and was thumping her way into the living room towards one of the couches.

"This is nice. How long have you lived here?"

"Oh, about a year now. It's a lot different than the place up on third. Have you been up to see it yet, the old house?"

"No! You sure do reminisce," Elaina chuckled. She looked at Brad. He didn't seem to see the humor in it. "I do miss the guys though. Lots of great parties," she added.

Brad moved in with Elaina and Henri for a year before leaving back to Belgium. During that year, there were foreign students in and out of the house. It was always busy with company and overnight loafers. At one point, a group of acquaintances used the basement garage as a practice room for their band. Cigarettes and beer was the staple addiction with people in the house, at the top of the stairs of the front porch, and in the back yard sitting on cheap plastic lawn chairs.

"Those were good times, weren't they?" Brad's voice lacked excitement or validation.

"Brad, what the hell is wrong with you? You're just a little bit grumpy. Are things OKAY? Do you want a visitor? I mean...I'll come back tomorrow if you want."

"No, I'm fine." He hesitated. "You're right, things have been better. You're just here at the right time and also not. As weird as that sounds, I'm just not sure if I want to go into it." The direct confrontation made Brad soften a bit.

"But, I guess...if you really want to know," he paused, shifting his gaze to the floor, "I keep having this dream." His level of self-disclosure inched forward. He still was not sure how much he wanted to say, but he found a longing to tell her.

"Dreams..."

"Yeah."

"Come on, this is really getting annoying. You have me come up. You sulk and act all weird, and you're not going to tell me what the fuck is going on? You've changed! I don't like it!" Elaina started to get up.

"Okay, okay, but you have to listen. It is all so fucked up and needs explanation for you to understand. You have to hear me through. No doing this half way. And I don't need any judgments from you."

"That's fine. Spit it out."

"And I know you know more than you're fessing up to Elaina."

"I know some."

Brad was both irritated and relieved. She sat back down. He kept standing.

"It's this dream, about once a week or so for the past few months, that I'm standing on the railing of a bridge...I think it is the bridge down in Clarkston...but I'm not sure. Anyway, I'm hanging on and it's cold and windy. I can't hold on any longer, and then I feel this sensation of falling. I realize that I'm falling backwards onto the roadway. A car barely misses my head and I black out. The black seems to last forever, and then I wake up with pounding in my chest. I know it sounds dramatic, but I don't understand why all of a sudden I've been having this shit, haunting crap bug me."

Elaina looked at him, like he was a case study. He felt observed.

"Well, maybe you're dealing with some fear, something from your past, something you're running from. Maybe you're feeling some kind of guilt? Have you talked to anyone else about this?"

"No. And if you're saying a fucking shrink, forget it!"

"This situation with Jordan must have been serious. Yes, there must be a connection."

Brad found the statement raw. "Situation?" he thought to himself. Furthermore, he didn't like the connection. Why bring him up out of the blue? He questioned if he wanted to go on.

Brad didn't answer the question and attempted to hide his annoyance by looking around the living room, searching for something he didn't need.

Elaina pressed, "Are you going to tell me about this, Mr., "I'm being all elusive with my depressed fucked up life."

Brad bent over looking at a magazine cover on the floor. He turned directly to her and snapped, "I don't think you want to know. It's crazy fucked up shit Elaina."

Straightening his back, Brad started fidgeting with the buttons on his cardigan. They were undone and the button he was messing with appeared loose hanging with off color threads. This was a standard habit of Brad's when frustrated. He wore his cardigan all the time. It was typically an accessory under his campus coat, and he habitually put it on after getting out of bed during cold mornings. It was in average condition, with few signs of aging, with the exception of a hole worn in the right upper arm, small, but noticeable.

Elaina was getting through to him. She sat back waiting, pensively pulled out a cigarette, and lit it. The smoke circled just in front of her face. It smelled sweet.

"Can I have one?"

Elaina looked surprised. "Sure darling!"

Brad lit the cigarette from Elaina's and stood just to the side of her, taking in a long hard drag. It made him dizzy. His exhale was as long as his inhale.

"Do you want some tea?"

"Yes. And then, you can tell me about Jordan."

Brad held the cigarette in his mouth and went into to kitchen. From the living room, Elaina heard some pans banging against each other. One sounded like it fell to the floor. She waited, not wanting to interfere with the space he needed as he did his deepest formulating.

She walked around the dimly lit room. A lamppost with three bulbs directed light in different directions, one up and against the wall, and two down at an angle to the floor. Various black and white photos in metal frames were scattered on the cream-colored plaster. There were a few that she recognized from before, others that were clearly new.

At the farthest end of the room, just under the bay window overlooking front street, his old black mini hi-fi system from college had CDs scattered on top of it. Just below, a CD case was left open on the floor. Next to it a black marbled pillow. Apparently, he had been lying there earlier. She pictured him deep in the caverns of his mind listening to his music.

She knelt down and flipped the top of the case over. It was his exhausted jazz compilation of his college days. Together, they listened to this album many times before. Yes, smooth trumpet jazz, an old favorite pastime over cigarettes and beer.

She took the leather couch to the right of the bay window. The pillow was at her feet. She picked it up and placed it between her and the arm of the chair. She took a long drag off her cigarette, pulled the butt away from her mouth, and started picking at her nails.

"How did you afford this furniture? This isn't in a writer's budget," Elaina yelled, directing her voice into the kitchen.

"What? Oh…yeah, well, my mom was getting new stuff and said I could have it. I loved it, so said, "Sure". Hey, do you want honey in your tea? I think that is how you have it, right?"

"Honey is fine. Do you have any cream?"

"No, no, I don't. Sorry."

"Well, fine, Mr., 'I don't ever carry anything that any of my friends may want when they come over to visit me when I'm depressed.'"

Brad poked his head around the corner. He was holding the kettle in his hand. "I'm not depressed." He had a smirk on his face. He ducked back and continued getting things ready.

"Yeah sure…Jazz, the lights, walking alone outside in this hell for weather. You don't have me fooled. I think you've gone beyond the Beatnik thing and into hell itself." She took another long drag off her cigarette. The ash was getting dangerously long, but she didn't mind. "Hurry up and finish with that."

"Sure, little misses Bourgeois. I'll be just a sec." A pan dropped to the floor again. She heard him cursing under his breath.

Marty jumped to Elaina's side and lay down. Elaina looked at him with a sarcastic eye, "Oh, the cat is kind to foreigners now!" She heard the Kettle whistle and Brad clanking what sounded like ceramic ware. Then a cupboard closed against wood.

He emerged with two cups of hot water with string and a perfectly square piece of paper hanging out the side of each. He handed her a cup and pulled out a small glass ashtray from his cardigan pocket and handed it to her.

Elaina watched him intently with a smile. "What kind?"

"Mint."

"Thank you." She put it to her nose. It was too hot to drink.

Brad walked over to the front door and adjusted the thermostat. He was still chilled from his walk and hoped the tea would take the cold out of his toes. Leaning close to look at the gauge, the teacup came close to his chest. He felt the steam rising up against his chin. It felt nice. He moved the small plastic knob up until he heard the furnace kick on.

He pushed the wing-backed chair from the other side of the room to just in front of the coffee table and to the left of Elaina. He carefully sat down so as to not spill the hot liquid on him. An uncomfortable silence fell between them. Elaina appeared confident but pensive, and Brad focused on the steam coming off the top of his cup.

Brad and Elaina's relationship was not by historical standards intimate in nature. They had good times and the regular parties as typical sophomore roommates do. But when it came to paying rent, there was always trouble. Elaina was never able to do it on time. That kind of discord always builds resentment between people living together, not to mention the struggle of mixing friendship and business.

He once got into a drunken disagreement with a friend at the Garden Lounge on a Blue Monday night over the same topic. His stance was that roommates rarely end up being friends, because friendship doesn't have the commitment required when the business end goes awry.

The counter argument retorted that people always have good intentions, and thus roommates never purposely damage a good relationship with a business mistake, missing rent; there isn't always something rotten in Denmark.

Nevertheless, Brad had not told anyone about the details of the events that day in the back yard with Jordan. It made the newspapers and a short spot on the evening news, but he himself told no one about his personal experiences that day, refusing all interviews.

Much of the details were pushed so far back in his mind, that not Elaina, Brad's family, nor any other person in his life knew what actually happened. If anyone had an insight, it was Henri.

Brad took a careful sip of the sweet mint tea. It mixed well with the aftertaste of his cigarette.

"Elaina, it was a very complicated thing, the whole Jordan and me thing. I don't know where to start or how much you want to know." Brad stopped himself and looked away as if he were gathering his thoughts, sifting through the rubble.

"Maybe it would help to start from when Jordan and I first met, how we became friends."

"Yeah. That would be perfect. Start somewhere comfortable. I need a context. Do you mind if I keep smoking?"

He smiled. "Only if you share bitch!"

They laughed, lit a cigarette together, and briefly talked about the cats, which were also taking more permanent places on the couch, as they all slowly slipped into the milieu of the past.

Brad looked deeply into his teacup, as if looking into a crystal ball; he held it in both hands and leaned slightly forward. He remembered. He remembered very vividly the first day he met Jordan, the first day in the dorm. It was his first time away from home. Yes, these were good memories, safe ones he wanted to share, a good place to start his story.

Chapter Five

As you already know, I started my liberal arts education at the University of Idaho in 1991. I took a year off between high school and college because I wasn't emotionally ready for the big world that faced me, a story that I don't have time to go into in the short time we have. However, as I was soon to discover, the security of my soggy Southeast Alaskan Island did not prepare me for what I was to encounter in the first weeks of school. It was an exciting time, but also a difficult adjustment.

The first debate my darling mother and I had in my preparations for school was whether or not I should live in the dorms. If I had my way, I would have started off in my own apartment having the free space to study as many hours as I wanted without distraction. She was determined to have me on campus because of the introversion she worried about throughout my adolescence, and my tendency to isolate thereof. She was the classic extravert and successfully completed nursing school in Idaho at Lewis and Clark State College, convinced that everyone could make friends if they wanted; in fact, it predicted academic success. I rolled my eyes at such ridiculous commentary.

After long hours of grueling argument, I, of course, had to give in. A secret stubborn tendency, that she also possessed, plotted to secretly find an apartment after I got to school. But, this would require an elaborate excuse for why the dorms would become a disaster, not to mention that lying wasn't my strong suit.

In the end, the necessity to save money during that first year made my plight futile. Living off campus would arguably cost more, and I knew I didn't have the backing to make it happen. I was going to have to deal with social hells of having people around me, not merely by my choosing, but because they were living there too. I mean, it's not like I lacked the ability to be a team player and cooperate with others. I simply dreaded the idea of being forced to socialize.

I will never forget my first day, standing outside the entrance of the dormitory. I arrived in Moscow early that morning, via Seattle, by plane. The taxi dropped me into the center of a seething pool of confusion. Students were everywhere, suitcases and gear piled in islands between circles of conversation. The cabby curtly pulled my stuff from the back seat and the trunk, and after taking my cash, quickly drove off without even a customary "see you later" or "thanks" or "goodbye".

Standing hopelessly overwhelmed, I took out my itinerary with my mother's detailed description of tasks for my first day. In bright pink highlighted marking, I found the room number emphatically overwritten several times, and prepared to search the hallways for my room at my new home, Geordie Hall.

Leaving my belongings, I entered the building and followed the irregular flow of people. The hall was poorly lit and slightly musty. I counted the numbers on the doors as they climbed, a mass of rooms running down beyond sight on both sides of me. Finally, I found it at the end, the very end, beyond the shadows.

I stood in front of the tan door feeling slightly sick to my stomach. I couldn't believe I had actually made it this far. The excitement I had for going to college during the application process was beyond my mental reach. The dull feeling of anticipation combined with being alone hung on my back.

It was a tan wooden door with twisted grain. The embedded   plastic numbers read RM 164. The top part of the number "4" had been partly scraped off. A corkboard hung next to the door on the right wall reading, "Welcome Brad Norland & Jordan Anderson." My guts made a sharp twist up and into my throat. "Oh fuck. I have a roommate."

The room was empty. On either side of the room was a bed wide enough for one person each. The room angled back towards the window between the mattresses overlooking Sixth Street. Peering out the window, I saw a rugged dumpster against the dusty brick McConnell Hall.

Looking around the room, I noticed that nothing had been disturbed since it was prepared for students moving onto campus that weekend. Thus, my roommate hadn't arrived, and I used it as rights to pick my side of the room.

Thinking on it, I was happy that I didn't have to face the uncomfortable scenario of walking in the room after my roommate arrived. Now, he was going to be the uncomfortable one. The dominant card was mine, to be displayed with a warm welcome, only if he appeared nice. The automatic "one up" position quickly put my mind at ease.

The mattress was leaning up against the wall, so I put it down on the frame of the bed and put on the sheets. Sitting on the partially made bed, I stopped, putting my hands on my knees and looked onto the aged tiled floor, allowing my vision to blur. The sound of people rustling in the hallway prevented any sense of peace. I made it, my first full day out on my own. I was an adult for the first time, living in the real world.

On the sidewalk outside the building still sat the three boxes and two suitcases I brought with me. It was a skeletal amount of my belongings, but my mom said she would send me a few more things as I needed them. I needed to bring in the boxes, but I actually wondered if it would all fit. The room wasn't bigger than 14x12. I had no idea how I, and a roommate, were going to live in such cramped quarters.

I waded back through the masses of people and outside. The weather had turned sour. I was enjoying the sunshine through the high clouds all the way to campus in the cab. But it was clear that the weight of the rain was going to prevail. Rain started falling, and accordingly, the masses of students and parents broke free from their groups and started to move quickly inside. By my standards, growing up in Southeast Alaska, it seemed like a sprinkle. Nevertheless, rain was softening the tops of my boxes. Dark brown spots massed on the surface like ink does on absorbent paper.

Forcefully I picked up the two suitcases and waddled to the entrance. I remembered them being heavy at home, but I surmised that my mother must have slipped in a few items as well. I kept my eyes at the pavement as I struggled along, trying to avoid the beginnings of any social interaction. Someone was holding the door open for me. I looked up. He was about my age and looked equally as concerned but far more innocent.

"Thank you," I said with my characteristic half smile and constricted glance from the side.

"No problem." He returned with a shy smile on his face, holding the door with his back while cradling a pile of blankets. As I passed, they had the distinct and overwhelming smell of fabric softener. I certainly hadn't washed my blankets before my journey. I wondered if I should have.

I turned left and down the hall. He followed directly behind me. He was looking around at the door numbers, slowing, almost stopping every so many numbers, just as I had before. By the time we got over two-thirds down the hallway, I was convinced it was the guy I was going to be sharing my space with. When I got to the room, he stopped a safe distance behind and waited for me to turn.

"Oh, you must be Jordan!" He leaned against the hallway wall and took a deep breath. I felt immediately at ease. He was certainly non-threatening in appearance, dressed in a loose buttoned up shirt and brown slacks. Maybe it was the combination of his meek smile and quiet demeanor, but I quickly felt that I could be myself with him. I set down my gear and put out my right hand. He took it carefully but with intention.

"Yes. Jordan Anderson actually," he said in a quiet but firm voice. He looked into the room and walked around me into the small confined space throwing down his bundle. "Ahhhh…It looks like you got to the room first," he said as he turned and took my suitcases setting them next to my bed. "What is your name?"

"I'm Brad, Brad Norland."

This was all going far too easy. I had nightmares about fucked up roommate scenarios. Jordan seemed nice and I knew instantly that we would get along just fine. He was very hospitable in his action, clearly doing better than I to overcome his discomfort with the novelty of it all.

We stood there just looking around the room, both pondering to ourselves how the space would be worked out. He was equally as shocked at the small quarters, and the cooperation required getting along. After a prolonged silence, he reached over, flopped down his mattress, picked up his bedding and threw aside. It made a dull thump.

"I think sleeping on the floor would be more comfortable," I joked. He snickered and started out the door but then stood intentionally right in front of me.

"Hey, I almost forgot! My parents are outside waiting. They have the rest of my things."

"You mean this isn't everything you own?" I said sarcastically. He looked back at me with a half-smile.

"Can you help me? I only have a couple more boxes."

"Sure, I have three monsters myself"

Jordan leaned slightly side to side with hesitation and then looked directly at me. "Do you want to meet my parents?" I was about to be used as a distraction. It struck me odd that his parents were not helping him in the first place. And then there was his whole approach! He was shy and then suddenly begging for companionship. Regardless of the intention, I was up for the challenge of sorting out the mysteriousness of the situation. But first, I had to do my own probing.

"Why aren't they coming in? Are they sick? Couldn't they help? We could be done with this in a second with their help!" I said manipulatively.

"No, they need to get right back on the road." He looked down at the floor and suddenly back up at me as if he didn't want his thoughts to be noticed.

"So, come meet them and not keep'em waiting! Then we can get our stuff unpacked!" He was forcing an act of excitement now, one I would see many times in the future, one used to cover up his deepest emotional struggles.

His parents sat in an off gray Cadillac, looking forward at the road, speechless and ignoring the activity of students busily working around them. If I had to make a judgment based on their behavior, they were finishing up an argument, only pausing at an impasse. It was tension, pure tension.

Jordan went up to the car closely following behind me. He signaled for his mom to roll down the window. His dad looked over with a restricted frown at me, and then returned his gaze at the street ahead.

"Mom, dad, this is my roommate Brad, Brad Norland." His mother looked up at me and smiled sheepishly. There was a hint of relief in her face.

"Nice to meet you Brad. Are your parents here?" She looked at me in full and then honored me with direct eye contact.

"No, they couldn't make the trip, but my mom is coming down for Parents Weekend next month possibly."

"Oh, well that is nice. I hope she can make it. Are you boys going to get things set up in your room now?" It struck me that she didn't ask where I was from, or any other polite formal small talk, especially the new roommate of her son! It was sufficiently detached and frankly creepy. All along, Jordan handled it with a smile and filled in the uncomfortable gaps with small talk.

"Yes," Jordan answered. But regardless of his mastery of dealing with the thick air, it was clear that he deeply wanted her approval. He wanted their approval of me.

"Maybe you and dad can come for Parents Weekend. Then all of us can go out and eat and stuff. I bet we could find places for everyone to stay!"

She looked up at him and smiled sincerely and then said cautiously, "Yes sweetheart let's see what happens, okay?" Jordan shifted back on his feet and sighed. I couldn't tell if he was disappointed or simply expected the lack of determination in his mother's voice.

"Well, I better get going. There's tons to do!" He added a musical lilt and slight volume to his voice. "Will you call when you get back to Oakley?"

"Yes sweetheart, we sure will. Could be a few hours since we will likely stop for lunch along the way." She reached out and took his arm, pulled him in and gave him a kiss on the cheek. There were no tears or struggle from Jordan. It was scripted right out of a manual. I looked on, feeling out of place at the strange scene.

Throughout the entire process, his father remained stoic and silent. When it was all finished, I saw him reach for a switch on the dashboard, followed by a click. The trunk popped open. Jordan went back and took out two milk crate sized boxes and set them on the sidewalk. He closed the trunk and waived through the back window. The car pulled away. Jordan watched them leave, and turned towards me, not even giving the car a second look. His face was colorless, but he held a smile waiting for his feelings to match his expression.

He stood in the street, I on the grass at the edge waiting for the next move. Jumping right to the heart of the matter, I asked, "Were your parents pissed or something?" I was tired of the murky boundary about the relations I had just seen a snapshot of.

"He picked up one of his boxes off the ground, stood up and started for the entrance to the dorm. He looked back at me turning his head as far as it could go and said, "My dad doesn't want me at the University."

"Wow." That is all I said. If his dad thought he needed be somewhere else, why was he here? The hanging pieces were starting to feel like a soap opera, but I decided to back off anyway. Judging from Jordan's apparent, "fake it till you make it' approach, I knew I had an adequate amount of information for now.

I picked up his remaining box and followed. An estranged parent with a pipe griped between his teeth, held the door open for us. The tobacco smelled wonderful. He wore a lovely grin on his face and judging by his firm placement, he had taken the job of doorman, a definite strategy in order to avoid the hysteria inside.

For the rest of the day, Jordan and I worked on adjusting to our new surroundings. It was quite easy and there was little competition concerning taste. We liked the same music, enjoyed each other's wall hangings, and could have shared the same clothing if I was a little bit shorter.

However, Jordan did have a deeper flair for the arts. The books on his side of the adjoining bookshelf covered topics in dance, opera, clogging, and still life drawing. He stated that if we could make room, he wanted to bring his drafting table from home one day. Drawing was a passion of his since the beginning of high school. He further explained his obsession for drawing religions material. Was Jordan a Christian? The possibility added an even deeper

35

mystery to him. And the more that I thought about it, he did carry himself very properly.

The answer came to me soon after dinner. We had just returned from the cafeteria across campus, talking our time walking while making immature jokes about all the weird people we had seen. Since both of us were from rather isolated parts of the country, I from Alaska, and he from a remote part of Southern Idaho, we were a little shocked at all the diversity on campus. We had resorted to high school cruelty, using our clean-cut natures as the basis for judgments. We cracked comments for hours until the pain in my gut wouldn't allow me to continue my dinner.

It was getting late and Jordan jumped to his bed and took the packsack sitting on the floor by the book shelf. He pulled out what appeared to be a Bible. It was black anyway, and not hard covered, but definitely formal in appearance, so I guessed it had to be a Bible. With it also came a second. He set them on his bed stand, let out a quiet burp, snickered, noticed my curiosity and returned his attention to task.

"Okay, so what is that you are reading?" This was a stupid question for what I defiantly knew was not a novel. Nevertheless, I was shocked at my own poignancy.

"Well, if I tell you, will you leave it alone?"

"Sure."

"It's my Bible and The Book of Mormon." He said it firmly. Nevertheless, his face flushed. He didn't look over at me in an attempt to conceal his thoughts. "You're not Mormon, are you?" he went on.

"No."

"I didn't think so."

"Well, I guess I've met Mormons. There is this new Mormon Church back home. They're nice people I guess." I found myself being reassuring, but also a bit confused. I thought that I had the trajectory on his personality, but this was definitely a curve ball. Mormons weren't accepted in

Petersburg. People thought they were trying to take over the state with their masses. I was apathetic myself, but still thrown off now that I had a Mormon roommate.

"Idaho is the Mormon State, next to Utah that is."

"My family is Presbyterian, but we never go to church except for on Christmas Eve and all."

"Dissatisfied with my inadequate way of relating, I added, "Actually, I have learned a lot about Mormons. In Petersburg, when the Mormon Church was built, there was so much controversy. You wouldn't believe it…"

"Yes…yes, I would," he interrupted.

"…People were crazy over it! Ministers called it a cult! My mom is an E.R. nurse. She once told me a story about the Mormon missionaries that came in to see patients." I was watching Jordan intently, looking for him to notice my accepting words. I pressed on.

"She found them reserved, but rather annoying, always coming around to comfort their 'brethren', as they called each other. She didn't like the missionaries because they were always in the way and had to be told to wait outside the E.R. when members of the church were being treated. But she didn't think it was any different compared to a difficult family member in the way and all. That is what she equated it to. That everyone was like one big family."

I didn't get the sense that I was doing a good job relating to him and felt like I was insulting him more than conveying my acceptance.

"You never went to church?" Jordan looked at me directly, seemingly rescuing me from my own discomfort.

"No. We really didn't, not very often anyway. But my family has respect for all beliefs. We have every type of church, I guest most anyway, where I grew up."

"Well, okay then. I hope you don't mind these hanging around." He pointed at the books and glanced at me. "I can put them away if you want."

"No, it makes no difference to me. If you accept that I'm a heathen, then I can accept that you're a Mormon. Okay?"

He smiled. The connection had been made. I watched tension melt out of his back as he picked up the books again.

Clearly, Jordan was a very complex individual. Somehow, I knew more surprises were to come. Also, a darker conflict was creeping into the light. He was eighteen and involved in a very structured all-encompassing religion that, by what I learned from my experience back home in Alaska, infiltrated every thought and action of its members. But if anything, this made me want to understand him more. I wanted to understand the strange encounter with his parents, and the warm friendship we started to share together.

On a deeper level, what I secretly understood in our conversation that night was that being Mormon was not a simple matter of choice. For its members, it was molecular, separating it from all other religions. Bred by its indoctrination from birth, it becomes as much a part of the person as one's race. That meant that Jordan was Mormon at his very core and there was no competing with it, only trying to understand.

Chapter Six

The first week as a student was hell. I was an early bird by nature, but those days were gone. I pained myself into a daily routine of getting up at 6:30 a.m. since my first class started at eight. Late night conversations over copious doses of coffee, the fad of every entering freshman, made getting to sleep at decent hours impossible. There were mornings I would rather have stacked a cord of wood than pick myself up out of bed. The morning fix of caffeine wasn't optional. Crowds stumbled to the cafeteria by 7:30 a.m., like baggy eyed underweight opiate addicts, looking for a quick fix.

Furthermore, I absolutely dreaded the use of the shower room. This is why I made myself get up as early as I did. Rarely was there any other soul showering at that time. This gave me the privacy I needed. Even then, there were others that thought the way I did and were showered early also. It infuriated me. Showering in a group set of stalls wasn't part of the contract I remembered signing up for prior to enlistment.

One morning I decided it was too much to handle, standing naked, with a room full of college men. So, I bashfully put on my swim trunks and headed for an open showerhead. Being on swim team in high school, this was common practice; we all showered with our suits on.

That morning, two guys were already in their respective places. They look over at me as I stepped into the water, focusing their attention wide eyed directly at my waist. Their jaws hung wide. Either they thought it was the best idea in the world and didn't want to admit it, or figured I was a total and complete freak. The blood in my face pounded while I hurried with the soap, attempting to rinse myself off as fast as I could.

We shared the space in silence, I in an obvious haste to escape the uncomfortable situation. I mean, I could have taken the trunks off, but then that might have seemed kind of seductive right? Well anyway, their reaction was far too obvious for me to ever attempt modesty again.

But then, there was this one guy who lived just a few doors down the hall from Jordan and me. I think his name was Michael. He was quiet, way too quiet to be considered sane, rarely saying a word to anyone the entire year I lived in the dorms. One morning, only an hour after getting to sleep at about four o'clock, I had to get up and piss. I went into the adjoining bathroom and heard one of the showers running.

"Fuck man, who would be showering this early?" I thought to myself. I had to see! I finished and didn't flush so whoever it was wouldn't know I was there. I slipped my head around the tile divider separating toilets and the shower area. It was him, Michael! He stood directly under the showerhead with water streaming down his body. His eyes were closed, and he faced the drain between his toes. I was sure he couldn't hear me.

That weekend, I heard rumors about Michael from some whisperings next door. The consensus was that he was either an engineering major or deaf, evidenced by the fact that he had a room by himself and never talked. As the semester went along, I hardly saw him on campus. He intrigued me to the point that I woke up early another morning to see if he was in the shower room at that unusual hour. I wasn't sure why I wanted to find out more, but as luck would have it, he was not there, and the tile floor was dry as bone.

Yes, that first week had its challenges, and its mysteries, but the adjustments felt minor after time. Jordan, on the other hand, was struggling. We were at the end of our first week in college. Friday! We both looked forward to our first full weekend together and the plans we could make with our new freedom. I got up that morning feeling in a groove. I got up early and ate, but when I returned, I found Jordan in a crying mess.

Closing the door behind me, I stood helpless with my wadded bundle of clothes under my arm, not knowing what to say. He wouldn't look at me.

"Jordan, what's wrong?" I said carefully, setting my stuff on the floor and sitting next to him. He was in his bed with the covers pushed down to his feet. He had his new pair of pajama bottoms on, not the ones he went to sleep in, and was facing away from me, staring at the grey cinder block wall. I waited for him to say something, but he kept on.

"Hey, I'm really worried man. Will you tell me what's going on?" I hesitantly put my hand on his shoulder tucked high against his ear. He pulled himself closer to the wall, avoiding my gesture.

I quietly stood up and put away my night clothes, while he remained locked in his self-imposed torment. I wasn't sure what to do, but he absolutely wasn't going to respond to me with words.

I slipped out and headed for the cafeteria. Instead of finding my usual quiet place to sit and start my morning reading for the day's classes, I charged two muffins and two bottles of orange juice to my meal ticket and started back to the room. I wasn't gone more than a few minutes. And when I returned, he was gone.

That is when it all came together. He didn't expect me back. That was clear. I never came back until late in the day and he must have figured I had given up on breaking through to him.

His bed had been carelessly pulled together, and his pajamas from the night before were now on the floor. I hadn't noticed them before. He attempted to hide them, maybe keeping them tucked into his side while I sat next to him. But now they were on the floor open and exposed for me to see. The problem was clearly visible. Semen lined the inside of his bottoms. Did he have a wet dream?

Next to his clothes was his open Bible and a small threefold pamphlet. It read, "How to Stop Masturbation: Father God's Plan for You." I didn't bother picking it up, feeling instantly disgusted at a teaching so distasteful. Could someone actually be this upset over jacking off? How could any religion support this kind of guilt and self-hatred? There had to be more to it.

I stood in a daze holding his breakfast in my arms. Now I had to plot how I was going to deal with this! It wasn't in my nature to see a friend suffer and simply act like nothing had happened!

My first inclination was to leave, but no, I had to take the risk, even if he would feel the embarrassment. Instead, I put one of the small white plates with the muffin on the open Bible and the two bottles of juice next to it. Then I sat on my bed and had my extra breakfast. He would come back eventually and see that I was there, see the gesture, understand that I didn't care and still thought he was a great guy.

The whole religious mystery started to perplex me. And ultimately, I felt bad for him growing up in it. I, myself, never remembered crying over masturbation. He held himself to a standard I did not understand but was determined to probe. Jordan was now my project, the person I wanted to figure out. He was the person I wanted to change.

*****

The days were getting shorter, and the leaves on the ground gathered into bigger piles up against the sidewalk edges, only subjugated by the bursts of rain fall at night.

The Palouse wind carried the rich odor of tilled soil and damp wheat, and the heavily lined maple streets, released a powerful overtone as the season approached fall time.

One remarkable aspect of academic life is the perception of time. Before I knew it, the first month of classes was complete and we were headed into October. It was my favorite time of the year.

Yes, life felt great, and Jordan and I were getting along, but we still hadn't been to any public events outside the classroom or dorm. Chatting with people in the hall had become routine and I frankly needed a break from the same faces. I knew Jordan wasn't going to take the risk of getting out, thus it became my mission to seek out an adventure.

And you wouldn't believe it, but the solution immediately fell directly into my lap. I was headed back to my room after my 3:00 p.m. Psychology class, when two guys from the hall literally ran into me as they were leaving. They flew out of their room laughing uncontrollably and yelling at each other to hurry up, failing to notice the traffic.

"Whoa," I said, holding my arms out defensively with my head back.

"Oaaah, hey dude…sorry about that man," he said coming to a jolting halt. "Hey, you're Brad right? Don't you live down at the end of the hall?"

"Yeah, me and my roommate Jordan. Why, what's up?"

"Hey man, a friend of my sister who is like a senior, invited us to this party at Sigma Chi. They said to invite people, man. Anyone we want. Wanna go?"

"Sure. What time?" I kept my composure, but in that very moment could have jumped up and down and run into the next passer by myself!

"Anytime man, but we are headed out at nine." Then, a malicious smirk took over his face. "Oh, and feel free to bring your honey, um, I mean, roomy." I stood awkwardly not knowing how to respond.

"OKAY dude, well anyway, see you there okay?"

"Is this a 'come as you are' deal, or do we have to dress up?"

"Fuck, where are you from? Stop with the pretentions girlfriend! It's a frat party man. We're drinking to get fucked up and puke and get fucked up some more."

"Cool." They rushed past me and out the door before I could say much more. On their way the second guy blurted, "We're going to get some goods. Will stop by your room at nine. If you're not there, you're on your own man!" he yelled pushing through the entryway doors.

I headed down the hall and Jordan came out of the room. He overheard the interaction.

"Hey there guy," I said in my usual inviting manor, a style I developed in dealing with him. "How's your day going?"

"Good I guess," he replied passively.

"The guys down the hall…"

"Jake and Matt?" he interrupted.

"Yeah, I think that is their name's. They invited us to the Sigma Chi party tonight. They're coming to pick us up around nine." I didn't want to give him an option. "Let's go! It'll be awesome!"

"…I have math homework…" He started to walk past me and then hesitated, looked back and then paused, while nervously chewing on the end of his index fingernail.

I stood in silence putting on the pressure. Then he looked directly at me taking in a deep breath and said, "…no, I'll to it tomorrow."

I was relieved. The last thing I wanted to do was spend time with those guys alone at a huge party with a bunch of people I didn't know.

"Is there going to be drinking?" I was surprised at his naiveté.

"Yes, I'm sure of it. And you better not drink! You're underage son!"

"Good. I want to drink!"

"Hey, when you coming back?"

"In just a sec," he yelled. "I need to mail this letter to my mom."

I went in my room and fell onto my bed, propping my head up with my hand, looking out the window at the red brick building facing our room. I felt a need to nurture my friend. I felt a need to protect him. I wanted to understand him and his past, and I was going to make sure he knew that he had me to rely on. He didn't make friends easily because he was so quiet, and people certainly made fun of him. Although I hadn't heard much of it myself, I knew it was going on; people didn't say much around me because he was my roommate. Maybe they thought I was weird too. I didn't care.

Now, don't let me detract from my story, as it is true that I easily go on tangents. So, as I was saying, I was not only surprised, but dumbfounded that Jordan wanted to go to the Sigma Chi party. Was he going to drink? I didn't know, but I was planning on it myself. The fraternity crowd was not my style, but worth trying once.

When Jordan returned, I was still deep in my thoughts and entangled in feelings. He jumped up on the end of the bed, pushing himself up against my feet. I pulled my knees in, giving him room and repositioned my elbow so I could look at him more directly.

"Brad, I'm hungry, and totally sick of the cafeteria. Let's go get something to eat. What would you say if I said that I had some money my parents gave me for stuff and that we should use it for going out?"

I smiled and replied, "Sure. I don't know of anything good around here though. Never even been off campus man. You?"

"Jordan snickered. "No."

Looking outside the dorm window, a light overcast was moving in. I dressed accordingly with windbreaker and hood, and a comfortable pair of jeans. The reported temperatures were in the sixties, but the winds made it feel much cooler. I was accustomed to quick weather changes and never felt under prepared. Jordan, on the other hand, grew up in southern Idaho where extreme shifts were not common, and thus people did not prepare for anything more than dry summers and cold winters. Seeing that he would be soaked with his cotton University of Idaho sweatshirt I lent him one of my water proof pullovers.

Heading out of our building we took a left onto Sixth Street toward downtown Moscow. Coming toward us was a man in his sixties walking alone looking down over his glasses at his paper, smoking a pipe. He wore a fine wool suit and bowtie loosely at his neck. His shoes were well kept, but old from years of use. His hair was gray and unmanageably wavy.

"Excuse me, sir?" He jolted to a stop and looked at me as if I had just shaken him out of a deep sleep.

"Yes?" he exclaimed stepping back, nearly off the curb. He pushed his glasses up closer to his eyes, tucked his paper under his arm and folded his hands loosely in front of his belt.

"We are looking for a place to get something to eat, and maybe some coffee or something. Could you suggest a place downtown for us?"

"Oh, ummm, well," he cleared his throat, "You're students, right? Well, there is a nice little coffee shop that serves sandwiches and the like just down on Main Street." He spoke with a thick Maine accent, but very refined. He turned and pointed down the street. "You must stay on 6th now, then go right to the corner of Main. It's just across the street young chap. It's called The Beanery. I think you will find it to your liking."

"Thank you," Jordan said as he put out his hand. The man graciously accepted and shook. And then, without another word he turned, pulled out his paper and was off again.

Jordan quickly set the pace ahead of me as a light sprinkle started to tap at our Jackets. We crossed one light at Jackson Street, and up ahead we could see The Beanery directly on the other side of the next block.

The exterior was decorated in an old motif. Potted flowers were meticulously placed around the outside social area, and old vines grew up the edges of the stucco style building. A table and chairs in dark wood filled in a hexagonal space focusing on the entryway at the farthest edge. Each table sat two, making the settings quaint.

We found ourselves on a natural path leading around the outside edge of the tables. Despite the wind and light on and off sprinkling of rain, people sat outside, and the door to The Beanery was propped open with a large granite stone engraved with the words, "Welcome All Lovers of the Bean".

As we entered, I was overtaken by the artistic atmosphere. The spices, the darkened corners with whispered conversations, the Picasso style table tops with orange, red, yellow and lime blocks and swirls. It was a Mecca for personal expression and nothing I had ever experienced before.

The mixture of people scattered about the room was equally as diverse. Some were doing homework, others sitting alone reading books, and still others seemingly in deep debate over political or philosophical topics. There was a tabletop made into a chessboard, and two guys sat intently contemplating their moves. In the center of the room, a woman tuned her guitar.

We went to the counter and ordered drinks and the soup of the day, clam chowder. I got a twenty-ounce coffee and Jordan asked for water with lemon. We stood off to the side waiting for our order when the server turned and said, "Go ahead and find a seat anywhere. We will bring that right out to your table. Okay guys?"

He was feminine in appearance wearing a short well-groomed goatee, glasses and an offset black barrette matching his shirt and slacks. In white solid lettering the words, "Da BEAT Daddy" ran up his right sleeve.

We sat down close to the window at the end of the room, a preferred place for me as I liked to be able to see people come and go and not have a room full of people at my back.

Jordan pulled his jacket up and over his head, put it on the chair next to him and sat down. I left mine on.

"Don't you drink coffee Jordan?" I asked inquisitively, finding it odd not to take in every opportunity of the artistic environment and at least have some eccentricity other than lemon water.

"No, I don't," he looked back at me directly with a hint of irritation as if he didn't want me to press further.

"Have you ever tried one?"

"No, it is best I don't."

"You don't think it's best?"

"No," he said, now looking at me, eyes tense, stewing with irritation, a warning, and a direct warning that an argument was just around the corner if I wouldn't let it go.

But I couldn't. He'd always played the weak soul. Seeing the emerging attitude as a challenge, I pressed, deeply wanting an intellectual game of cat and mouse since he wasn't going to just come out with it.

"Is there something like inherently wrong with drinking coffee? Are you allergic to it or something? Or is against your religion?

"No, it's against the Mormon faith, as a matter of fact," he said raising his voice and leaning forward, "to drink it."

"What?" I sat back trying to hide my surprise. The game was over in one quick session, and I was pissed with the answer. Wisdom said to apologize and let it go, but at that age, I was full of nothing but passion for momentary emotions and defending them.

"Ah...so I get it now. You're going out to a party to drink alcohol tonight, but you can't handle a cup of coffee or even a fucking mocha in a stupid coffee shop? That makes a lot of sense."

"No...," he said clenching his jaw, looking off into the distance, searching for what to say next.

"Okay," he continued, "I'm going to drink. Is that so bad?"

"Fuck no Jordan. Actually, I think it's fucking great. I just don't get the inconsistent moralistic approach.

He folded his arms and sat back, refusing to look at me. "I have some reprogramming to do."

"Reprogramming? What the hell are you saying? Dude, you say the weirdest shit sometimes!"

"Yeah, reprogramming! I hate my religion. You can't know what it is like being this way. It's the first time I've been away from it Brad."

Jordan relaxed, looked at me without defense. The sparring had come to an end.

"My ethics class for instance. I love it! I'm getting the easiest 'A' I have ever gotten. And do you know why? Because I'm dying to understand how other people live. For the first time I'm being challenged to think about other ideas, whether we are born good or bad, the important stuff. Brad, I mean look at you. You don't have a religion, or at least you don't profess to be active in it. You're just fine. You don't seem to go around thinking people are bad and need something external to make them good. And you know what?"

I sat back in my seat. The floodgates were cracking. "What?"

"I haven't met a Mormon since I've been here. I feel great. No one is trying to keep an eye on me to make sure I'm staying clean and make moral choices. Frankly, I'm sick of going around feeling guilty all the time and would rather believe I was born a good person and can make my own good choices. The water thing. That was just a habit and you caught me at it and I got defensive. I've just never tried coffee, and someday I will. But, when I'm ready."

"But Jordan, don't go overboard man."

"I won't, but don't bug me about the stupid stuff okay? I don't know what I believe right now. It is all confusing." His voice became louder and emphatic again, but this time he caught himself, aware that I was accepting what he was telling me.

The waiter approached on the other side of Jordan with our drinks and soup. He held the platter high overhead, skirting around two book bags at the table next to us.

"There you guys go." In a twist of his arm, the platter came down swiftly, and he place the orders in front of us, turning to give Jordan a noticeable smile and quickly stepped away, only looking back to say, "Enjoy."

"What about your parents? Are they going to freak out?"

"About what? There isn't anything to tell them. I know they are worried about me going to the University of Idaho and all, cuz it isn't a Mormon school, but oh well. I don't plan on telling them much about my life. That's how it's been anyway. So, whatever," he added, as he picked up his soupspoon and played with the surface of his chowder.

"Well, okay. Just keep me informed Jordan."

"Don't you think I am?"

"Yeah, but certainly you're acting a whole hell of a lot different today than I've seen so far. It's kind of freaky. I don't want to think that I caused it."

"Oh my God! Get over yourself Brad."

With that, Jordan just smiled, proud that I noticed his change, and focused on his meal. I would see in time that in no uncertain terms was our conversation a decision point for him, one of discovering and affirming his own personalized belief system. Instead, the edge was being honed, with one side of the blade his participation in intellectually challenging classes, and the other, his devoted study of the scripture. It lent itself to many interesting conversations between us. But on other days, dissonance took him over.

Chapter Seven

Historically, I've not been good at the chore of waiting, especially when work separates me and the anticipated. Jordan cracked open a textbook immediately and started working math problems on his legal sized yellow narrow lined note pad. I went right to the astronomy reading for the weekend, giving up brief but painful effort, and finding myself on my bed staring at the ceiling. Reaching back, I felt the bookshelf for my tattered leather hacky sack. I tossed it up and caught it dead in the palm of my hand centimeters from my face. The obsessive trance of boredom took me over. Jordan focused relentlessly working problems.

"Okay, okay," Jordan blurted with a huff, it's 8:30! Shall we go?" He pushed the pad into the pages of the book, marking his spot, and slapped it shut with annoyance.

"I can see you're not going to try getting anything done," he snarled, exaggerating the importance of it all. "You're acting like a damn head case with that thing. How about I just save us some time...yeah, I'm going to call and have you taken to the loony bin."

Without looking, I flipped it at the ceiling one last time, catching it with a forceful overhand, and then jumped to my feet, bouncing on the bed. My loose white socks grabbed at the duvet cover.

"Let's go." I said with eyes crossed, placing my thumbs under my arms, flapping my elbows hard. "Come on man, don't you like me being the true me; a fucking nut?" He stared long and emphatically, holding a tight frown. Then he broke with a half-smile shaking his head.

"Man, you are weird."

I turned and flopped myself onto my mattress. To my surprise, he jumped on me! I was off guard and didn't move fast enough to get from between him and the wall. He forced his knee into the center of my chest. I tried separating it, but all effort was futile. His brown corduroy pants were slippery. I couldn't get a grip. I reached up at his chest, finally getting a nipple firmly between my thumb and index finger. Giving it a hard twist, I clenched my teeth and growled with him. His knee slipped off to the side, leaving him straddling my chest.

Just then, the room door flung open revealing Jake and Matt. Jordan turned and looked through his messy blond hair and I lifted my head to see who it was. We were out of breath and disoriented.

Jake took a moment to pull his chin back, and then thrust out his hip and flapped his hand loosely from the wrist. "So, I can totally see we have interrupted something! We just came by to see if you two giiiirls were ready?"

Jordan quickly jumped to his feet. I sat up on my elbows. "Fuck you guys, don't scare us like that!"

"Whatever! We're cutting this joint in two minutes. So, are you going to stay home and play your little game of grab ass, or are you coming along?

"Hey...," I started, and then realized the ridiculousness of the defense. "Yes, we were just getting our clothes on...um...no, I mean...our jackets." Jordan looked at me with a jerk. His mouth was wide open, in silence asking why I was being antagonistic. I started to snicker. They looked at me blankly. I was shadowed in silence.

"Well then, let's get to it," Matt said with a sharp bark! Until now he remained quiet but intensely tuned in. "We don't have all night!"

We took the jackets from the door hook, pulled on our shoes and followed. They were already half way down the hall when we closed the door. Catching up to them on the street, Jake briefly acknowledged us and pushed ahead, whispering and laughing with an occasional backwards glace. "Don't be looking at our asses now giiiirls," Jake blurted, covering himself with his hands.

The night was off to the worst start. How much worse could it get, and could we trust the morons we were following?

Jordan watched the ground in front of his feet. I nudged him with my elbow, but he didn't respond. We could fall behind and go back. We didn't have to go.

The Sigma Chi house sat on the southern end of campus. It was mixed in with other Greek houses on a road looping back around to the University Stadium called the Mega Dome. It looked like a beer can tipped on its side buried half way into the ground. Apparently, a beer company actually wanted to advertise its product by dressing the dome with their logo for a game. The University declined.

We cut directly up the hill leading to the center of campus. Passing the library, we angled left of the Administration Building and up past the Hampton music school. We were now on the heels of our leaders.

I was going for the sole purpose to party my ass off. The Greek system wasn't one of the campus cliques I was interested in. I saw the members as part of the immature masses, an extension of the high school mentality I happily escaped. But everyone talked about their parties. Jordan was committed to drinking, and clearly had to see that through. Oh and, how dare I sound so altruistic...I wanted to see for myself what it was like on the inside of a Greek house.

As we got closer, the heavy mix of sounds came to a crescendo. I heard it first on the approach to the Administration Building. The heavy thud from the music came first. Then the distinguishable sound of guitar and keyboards, soon mixed with the voices of people talking over the noise. Anxiety disappeared as my heart matched the low dull rhythmic thuds.

We rounded the corner and then realigned our scope to the lawn littered with partiers. I looked over at Jordan again, this time he returned the gesture. He held his hand on his chest grasping at his breath; sweat beading around the base of his neck. He was just as drawn in as I was. I glanced over. We exchanged a mutual secret smile.

Weaving our way through the grouped conversations, people hardly took notice as we walked up the cement path to five oversized steps and past the large doors into the foyer. What I saw next absolutely amazed me. In a small but open ceiling room, people packed in by the dozens. It was very tight. At center, in front of a large stone fireplace was a cluster of chairs and couches piled with people. Large galvanized steel barrels were positioned at each corner of the room, each full of ice and packed with small bottles of wine and beer. A table with liquor and bottled juices of ready-to-grab premixed concoctions was left of the fireplace. Not much was left with splotches of sticky purple juice at the base of the bottles.

Jake and Matt pushed into the crowd, leaving Jordan and I on our own. I scanned around looking for anyone I might know. We were in the company of strangers, from the poor side of the tracks, blessed by the Gods for an invite.

It was the land of perfection, the sea of collectivism. The guys wore tight jeans and t-shirts with thick black belts. Some sported flannel shirts, the guys who looked older and bigger than the rest. They clearly had authority.

The women dressed in loose fitting blouses that came down just above their belly buttons, supported by designer jeans and plastic sandals. They were a much more colorful group, obviously believing summer had not taken leave.

I leaned into Jordan's ear, pulling him in close. He warded me off, a slight resistance, overly cautious in a crowd of people that didn't even notice us. "Hey man, I think I'm going to puke on all the perfume!" He rolled his eyes in agreement.

"What do you want to drink?" The music forced me to scream.

"I don't care…just something sweet."

I started toward the barrels closest to us in the left corner next to the fireplace. I felt a brief tug at my shirt. He let go and followed. I reached through the ice and took two bottles of white zinfandel, put them under my arm, and then turned to the coffee table taking two cups with premixed drinks. They were purple. I sipped and forcefully pushed the cup back, sharply turning my head away…"Vodka." I signaled for Jordan to take the zinfandels and I sheltered the cups from intrusive elbows and hips. He led the way to the door.

A girl walking past me, grabbed my arm, bobbing her head without control. The drinks sloshed onto my hand. I pulled the cups in close and looked up to find her nose nearly touching mine. I initially stood back to see who she was. I didn't recognize her. Nevertheless, she was stunning! She had blond hair pulled back into a tail with the most striking green eyes. Her skin was without a blemish with the most beautiful soft brown hue.

"What is your name?" she said with a hiss. Her intoxication explained the welcomed intrusion. The dense mass of bodies made it impossible for anyone to fall over, and clearly, she was using every point of pressure for support.

"I'm Brad."

"So, hey, who is your friend?" I looked ahead. He made his way for the door unaware I wasn't behind him.

"That's Jordan, my roommate. We live at Geordie Hall."

"Geordie Hall, eh? Pity. Well regardless, he is fucking gorgeous!" She swayed back on her heals and then readjusted with the help of an arm on the other side of her. Her head followed, swinging back into my face.

"Yeah, he's a great guy. I guess you want me to see if he wants to talk to you?"

"Yeah darling! You're sweet. You're cute too." She snickered, snot dripping from her nose. "Can you get him for me like really fast?"

In a circular motion her head swung down and back up again. The smell of partially digested beer filled the space between us.

"I'll be right back, darling," I exaggerated. "Just stand right here and I'll bring him to you!" I lied.

I found myself outside scanning the area for Jordan. He was sitting at the bottom of the stone steps in the shadow of the oversized oak tree. The drinks were next to him while he patiently waited. His hands were clasped in front with his arms resting on his knees.

"God, I'm glad you came out. It's out of control in there. Have you ever seen anything like it?"

"No. I don't think I've ever seen that many people packed into such a small place. Are you freaked out!

"No no, I'm cool. It's like a bus station but everyone looks the same. Did you notice they even talk alike? Like clones? I stand out like a sore thumb," he shivered.

"Nah, we just look a little lost, nothing that this shit can't fix." I put the bottle to my mouth.

I sat on the steps next to him and handed him one of the cups with the purple vodka drink. He took a sip and set it down on the other side of him where I couldn't see it.

"Hey, before I forget dude, this girl stopped me and demanded I bring you back in. She thinks you're fucking hot man!" Jordan looked at me with a funny grin. His face blotched pink against his soft untouched tan skin. The discomfort was an invitation for me to press on.

"Well, what do you think man? Do you want to go back in? Come on, she wants you! This could be a really cool night...drinking...girls..."

"Umm...no...no thanks Brad. I have a better idea."

"What's that?"

"Let's…"

The sound of familiar voices came out from crowd and onto the long approach to the oversized stairway. It was Jake. He was with two well-built guys, clearly older, most likely seniors. They looked uncomfortable in their large barrel chests and thick necks.

"There you guys are…Yeah dude, that's the two little flowers I brought!" Jake balanced himself against the red brick building. He was uninhibited and looking for trouble. We remained fixed to the cold concrete steps, frozen, hoping it would end as quickly as it was starting.

"These are the boys we caught playing with each other at Geordie." Jake was now talking very loudly, attempting to attract attention. People standing out on the porch and walkway stopped their conversations and looked back at us.

Then, one of the guys walked up to me. He put out his foot and nudged my leg. He quickly pulled it back to get his balance. "Hey, little dudes. Checking out a Greek party, eh?" He uttered staunchly with a southern accent. Well, little fellows, we know you're not Greek. We accept that guys, but I do hear from my friend Jake over here that you're…like…*that*. You know what happens to little guys like…*that*…don't ya?"

I stood and looked directly into his eyes, holding my glare, waiting for the first swing.

"No," I snapped! Jordan breathed shallow and fast, it was his time to make a run for it. He leaned away and looked out onto the lawn past the oak tree. Unfortunately, disassociating wasn't going to help him at this moment.

"Well, if you were…you know…a fagot, you woooould have to…"

A guy watching from the walkway by the street edge shouted, "Hey Frankie, leave them alone. They're just kids dude." I resented the remark but welcomed the support.

Jordan stood up behind me. The mammoth swayed on his feet and looked down at the voice echoing from the street.

"If you were," he drew out, "a couple of those…sissy faggots…I keep see around campus, I guess I'd have to kick your little fem bitch asses!"

He sneered and turned back to the party inside. Jake was laughing quietly to himself, bent over holding his guts. With distaste I glared at him until he turned to follow his friends.

As soon as it had started, it had ended, but not soon enough. People watching returned to their conversations as if nothing had happened, and no one paid attention to us standing like petrified statues, unable to move our feet out of position. Nothing sounded better than to get the hell out of there.

We didn't move at first, but the longer everyone didn't seem to notice us, the greater the force pushed at me. I took one deep breath and bent down and took the two cups. Jordan was in front of me leading the way, cutting across the lawn and onto the street. He stayed several steps ahead until we arrived at the dorm. I didn't attempt to talk about what happened, just tried to keep up without the drinks sloshing on me. He was carrying his open bottle and the other one poked out of his back pocket.

"That was fucked up," Jordan said out of character.

"It's over dude. All I want to do is get drunk!" Jordan didn't argue, marching quickly down to the end of the hall.

I put the cups on the floor and we sat down leaning against our beds, legs outstretched in the narrow space, facing each other. We took a deep breath and in tandem took a large drink in silence.

Jordan finished off his wine, then mine, and resumed gulping the purple juice and vodka punch. He needed it more than I. He was quiet and contemplative. I watched his glassy eyes develop and his shoulders relax. He looked up at me revealing the deepest of thoughts swimming in his head. The grimacing from the strong purple liquid subsided, and the drink went down easier the farther down the cup we got. He took a deep breath looking down at the level on the cup and then he smiled at me.

"I'm no longer a virgin." His teeth and wet pink lips glistened purple in the orange hazy light of the room.

"Well, I guess not for booze!" I laughed and raised my bottle in the air in a cheer. His knee slid over and touched mine. It felt good being close to him. Then it hit me. What they were saying at the party had validation. His conflicts weren't entirely spiritual in nature.

The more I thought about it, the clearer it became. His mannerisms and the information he omitted from conversation gave him away. Yes, that was it. He didn't act like other guys. I sensed that about him but wanted to protect him. Fear was a waste.

Jordan looked at me and bathed in pride for loosening up that night, risking the dangers of a Greek party, drinking alcohol. But then, the mood in the room took a sudden turn. Out of the shadows, a thick tension emerged. He pulled his knee back to himself and looked away.

It was difficult, but he was stressing, and I wanted him to stew. He was stuck in a blank stare at the wall behind me; the odor of alcohol and the psychological freedom it lent mixed and marbled conflicting thoughts. Then he took another drink, a very deep swig. He looked up at the ceiling and began to speak.

"You know about it don't you?"

He was crying, not bitterly. He looked at me directly taking another solid drink, holding onto it as if it was the security getting him through.

"Jordan, tell me...what is it?"

"I'm not like you Brad."

"Yes, I know."

"I don't even understand it, so, how can you? Those jerks saw it. I haven't willingly let anyone see it Brad. It's like I'm this sheet of Plexiglas I keep scratching into so people can't see what I am."

"Jordan, you don't have to hide from me. I have a gay uncle." The word had taken form, unleashing a complicated river of fear and bitterness. He took another drink. I reached over giving him my cup.

"I hate that word. It is such an ugly word."

"Jordan, you don't have to hate it. That's as bad as hating yourself. I love my uncle, and Jordan, just like him, I believe being gay makes you stronger. Don't let those fuckers take you down. My uncle is probably the best human being I know. If I could be as creative and open and loving as he is...but I'm not." This wasn't about me. I had to be careful.

"Brad, you don't understand, I can never be gay!"

"What?"

"If my parents find out, I'm excommunicated." Brad pulled his knees in sheltering them with his arms and rested his head. I moved over leaning against his bed and pulled in next to him. He didn't resist my arm around his shoulders. I started to cry. He was trapped.

We sat on the floor, the place that would become the sacred space of future thoughtful conversations and shared those painful moments together. Answers escaped me, nothing could be said to relieve the pain.

When the moment was right, I quietly got up and crawled into my bed, and he into his. We didn't bother to take off our clothes or put on pajamas.

I pulled the string on the reading light, flipped the switch on the radio at low volume and looked for the public news channel, a familiar habit to redirect our minds.

Jordan rolled over to face the wall, but before doing so, he took the two familiar books from the space between his mattress and the wood side board, setting them next to his head.

Chapter Eight

While Jordan was battling with the shadows, it was clear that my role was defined as supportive, secondary to none.

I missed home, feeling trapped in the realization that I was going to make a career of the University for at least the next four years. The excitement of being the tell-tale 'College Student' had worn off, leaving me hopelessly lonely and no one to talk to.

I was happy with the University of Idaho. The atmosphere was exactly what I dreamed of. The virulent ivy on the rusty-crimson red brick buildings, the challenging intensive liberal arts courses, the profile and diversity of the student body, all had the potential for these to be the best years of my life. However, the longing to be back in the familiarity of my native Alaska raged in my heart.

Three days after the fraternity party experience, I escaped unnoticed after my roommate fell to sleep with his face in his books. I waited, lying on my bed wearing my jeans and a light sweater, reading a book, waiting to hear the gentle rhythmic breathing of his dreams. I carefully got up and slipped into my shoes, choosing not to lace them until I got on the other side of the door. I took the green windbreaker draped on the chair in front of the desk at the end of my bed. Embracing the frame of the door to assure it would shut quietly behind me, I tip toed out into the hall.

"Shit," I said, realizing that I had made the worst mistake in my haste.

My keys were still lying next to my bed. "Fuck," I said, giving the doorknob a gentle turn and push. Yup, it was locked.

I went down the hall trying not to be noticed. As I steadily pranced unnoticed, I saw a door ajar on the left.

Quickly passing I glanced in and saw Michel, Michel from the shower room. He sat at his desk and looked at me without expression. He had his glasses on, so I almost didn't recognize him. His eyes were obnoxiously oversized.

"Hi," I whispered. I heard the door squeak behind me. He was standing in the doorway watching me make my getaway. "What you doing up so late," he said back in a whisper? I turned and struggled for a response. Why had he taken the sudden interest in me?

"Ummm, I'm going out for a walk."

"Be careful out there," he warned.

"Yup!" I said politely as I turned and left.

I went down Sixth Street about half a mile and turned into the Student Union Building. It was past 10:00 p.m. and few people walked about. The parking lot was nearly empty with only a couple cars parked up close to the door. On the outside wall next to the entrance of the building was a pay phone. I saw it earlier and remembered its place. It was discreet with only a bank machine along the wall for company. I looked around inconspicuously. No one approached or was coming in that direction. I took the calling card out from my front shirt pocket, dialed the numbers, and waited for an answer.

"Hello?" I heard on the other end.

"Hi Mom." The tears filled my eyes and ran before I could control myself. In the excitement of the first few weeks of school, I talked to her only once. It was impossible to understand how I could have waited so long.

"Hi honey, how are you?" she said with her calm stable voice. She heard my distress. I could only talk about how much I missed her and wanted to be home. I told her about my classes, but that I didn't know if I could stay, that every day was unbearable, and I wanted to go home. Her voice turned shaky as she listened, giving me support and then firm again.

"Now Brad, you're going to be fine. You stick it out and things will be just fine."

"But mom..."

"I know it's hard. You just stick it out and everything will be okay."

Despite her own pain, she gave a steady flow of encouragement. It was the most difficult moment of my first semester. We were close. We spent more than two weeks packing for my departure, allowing time for us to process the upcoming change. When I talked hesitantly, she spoke decisively. There were many moments sitting on suitcases and cardboard boxes in my room sharing funny stories and tears.

It was a relief to hear my mom's voice. She didn't tell me how she was doing, and now I understand why. She was in her own pain, but knew she couldn't express it, that being the sacrifice of the best parent.

We talked about my classes and teachers, and then the basics on Jordan. We looked for a natural close but couldn't find one.

"I have to go mom," I broke in.

"Okay sweetheart. You hang in there and I'll be thinking about you." We said our goodbyes and then she added, "Oh Brad, did I tell you about the car accident out by the airport. It was..." We started again and went on for another half hour, finally ending abruptly.

I hung up the phone and pivoted to head back to Geordie but noticed lights in the building. Was it still open this late? The partially peeled letters on the glass revealed, "Doors locked nightly at 11:00 p.m." I was relived, yet ready for bed.

The room opened into a large sitting area. Students were sparsely scattered about, some hunched over books and others involved in tight conversations. The Student Union Building was a popular study and gathering arena.

There was no music on overhead, and the lighting was good for reading.

I went to the far edge of the room and sat on one of the cloth couches. It was deep and comforting. Putting my head back, I looked up at the grey and white-checkered drop ceiling, mesmerized by the intermittent splashes of glitter. My mind focused on the sprinkler heads. I imagined the resulting mess of students if they were to go off. My mind darted aimlessly like this from visual subject to visual subject, connected only by the numb mood that carried it.

"Excuse me, but are you okay?" I lifted my head, jerked out of my haze, a bit startled at the female voice now standing in front of me.

"I'm fine." I shook my head and pulled myself to a straight sitting position. "I must have been on some cloud in Amsterdam." I know it sounded stupid, but I didn't know what else to say.

"Amsterdam? That's interesting. I could have sworn that was the look of a guy on a cloud hovering over the coldest corner of Antarctica." She smiled and put out her hand.

"Hi, I'm Lydia, Lydia Richards." She held me firm and gave a steady shake.

"I'm Brad Norland." She gave her last name. I was honored to give mine.

Lydia was all class and confidence, not artificial as if trying to sell something. Her authenticity was overpowering, confident, a relief. I quickly became self-aware and embarrassed at my appearance. I had stubble on my face. However, it didn't seem like she cared but I was sure she noticed.

Lydia had long dishwater-blond hair. She was of average height, thin, and wore slacks with a ribbed shirt. Her shoulders were covered by a long but thin black cardigan. She had on dark flats without socks, revealing ankles as beautiful as her thin delicate hands.

"I hope I'm not bothering you. I just saw you alone looking like you had just completed a marathon; wanted to see if you were going to be able to get out of that chair."

"No, no," I blurted! "I'm very glad you're here. Thank you." A short silence fell between us while I searched for what to say next.

"So, what is your major?" She sat in the chair adjacent to me and leaned forward with her hands cupped together and looked directly at me. There was no detectable shyness in her. Direct. Yes, a very admirable quality.

"I'm studying English, thinking about going into Journalism, Mass Communications."

"Cool. I'm in the Environmental Science program. Transferred from the University of Oregon. Spent my first two years there, and then moved to Moscow because of the program.

"What year are you?"

"In my junior year. Entered the program last summer to get ahead. Been living in Steel House. So how about you? Do you live in the dorms?"

"Yup, Geordie. It's a total blast," I said sarcastically

She had drawn me in, made me feel comfortable, showed interest, and had a knack for keeping a positive spin on the conversation. I was drawn to tell her things, important details, facts, everything about me. She was warm.

"I like Steel. It is one of the better houses I've lived in so far. The people are really cool. We are all kinda hippy like, you know, the dreaded, 'earth first' freaks." She made exclamation marks in the air in front of her.

"I don't know much about environmentalism? Did you say that you went to University of Oregon," I redirected?

"Yes. It's a good school, in Eugene actually. I call it my little liberal Mecca of the west. I found it hard leaving, but Moscow has worked out as a pretty cool place." She bobbed her head with exaggeration, agreeing with her own statement.

"I've developed apprehensions."

"What do you mean?"

"My roommate is from Oakley in Southern Idaho. Idaho has to be the Mormon Mecca of the nation. My roommate is Mormon. He's all messed up cuz of it."

"Yeah. Mormon country it is. Actually, Utah is the Mormon state, but some must have decided that Idaho was better. There is not as many up here in northern Idaho, but I have had a couple Mormon friends since living in Moscow."

"I'm originally from Oakland California and never met a Mormon before myself. They are different, that is for sure. Good ideas about family I suppose. Nice people on the surface, but I really couldn't connect with them overall, strange walls in the end, with the couple I've known anyway."

"Boy, you can't know how nice it is hearing that. My roommate struggles."

'Anyway, I'm from Alaska. Petersburg Alaska. I miss it. I mean, I'm glad I'm here. There's so much I like about the outside world, but I do miss my family and stuff. You grow up knowing everyone so well. There is no way to travel easily in and out of town because it is an island, so you have to take a plane or ferry. Really, it doesn't seem like anyone knows each other at all or even cares to. Everyone is so cautious. In Petersburg, it's like, we don't even lock our house or cars when we leave." I was starting to ramble and stopped myself.

"It's hard getting used to being on your own Brad. I missed Oakland very much at first, and sometimes still do, but it does get easier! Believe me. Feels so good to just do it, do it on your own. Know what I mean?" For a brief moment she reminded me of a Fraggle, you know, off that show Fraggle Rock in the 80's, but only in the cutest way.

"Yes, I think so."

WITHOUT A TESTIMONY

"Tell me about your classes," I said inquisitively.

For three hours we sat and talked back and forth, learning about each other's history, where we came from, and our struggles to adjust. She had more experience than me in the art of being "on your own." I was curious what it was like for her and how she became independent and enormously confident. It went beyond big city attitude.

The exchange of energy that night was remarkable. It was not sexual like with other women I had met previously. The meeting was held on a whole other level. She interested me intellectually. She was mature but not dismissive.

We talked ourselves into exhaustion, carelessly ignoring the drowsiness we would feel the next day in class. The doors had been locked to the outside, and only the most manic conversations and students remained studying.

Walking out into the parking lot, we shook hands, exchanged numbers, and went in opposite directions. She asked for my number first. I was assured that she wasn't simply taking pity on a pathetic homesick boy.

Chapter Nine

That week I thought about Lydia constantly, especially during monotone moments sitting in bed tossing my hacky sack or walking alone through campus. I wondered where she was and how she spent her time. Was she in classes, eating lunch with friends, having nice conversations with other vulnerable guys like me? I returned to the Student Union Building hoping I might run into her again. But I was never satisfied. I became obsessed. She got to me, asking direct questions, but careful, not too personal, she was sensitive. She knew how to walk the edge of the provocative, not physically but intellectually. I found myself intrigued by her mind. She captured my soul.

School was now in full motion. Midterms were the next wave and Jordan spent hours in our room in silence, tightly bound between the pages of his books and notes. My newfound obsession and the fact that I didn't possess the most remarkable time management skills, was remedied by discipline and verbal floggings to stay on track. He studied non-stop and took courses that I found boring, most likely because they were simply above me. During his first semester, he tested directly into Calculus II, challenged the first two semesters of German, and took sophomore Ethics and Psychology. He made the rest of us look like asses.

After a tenuous explanation for the millionth time on the difference between prokaryotic and eukaryotic cellular systems, I begged Jordan to go out and have a coffee with me at The Beanery, and take up studying there, arguing that a change of atmosphere would desperately help me. He rolled his eyes, accusing me of procrastination while pushing his arms down into the tight sleeves of his jacket. He was out the door and down the hall before I even had my shoes on.

When we arrived, it was already dark. Equinox had long since passed, signaling the onset of cozy evenings and hot chocolate conversations. If I could have read the local Idahoan's mind, it was the onset of depression and hell. But for an Alaskan, it was a time for celebration. Regardless, even if a man comes from the north, staying warm is critical. Like an idiot I neglected to bring my jacket. By the time we got to the counter, I was convinced that hot chocolate was going to be my savior. To my surprise, Jordan ordered himself a mocha.

"Hey…"

"Don't say it…I want to try one, so shut up. Do you have a problem with that?" There was very little sarcasm in his voice, only the complete muting of my dramatic intent.

I ordered without another word from the large breasted woman behind the counter with the t-shirt that read, "I fucked your mother." I think we caught it at the same time because the mutual innocent moment took us both as we crept away with our drinks.

The usual table we jockeyed for, far off to the back and enough away from others, was open. Jordan took out his notebook, put on his glasses, sat back and started to read. I left my biology notes in my folder, looking at him, and waited.

"What?" Jordan said looking over his nose with a groan.

"Damn, do you ever veer off the predetermined path of perfection?"

"No."

"God. You are too much. I'd love to pick your little arrogant brain. You really are full of yourself, aren't you?"

"I want to get this reading done okay?" He looked down at his yellow notepad again trying to ignore the challenge presented.

"This is studying Jordan. Oh, come on. You must like a good debate!"

"No."

"Oh…"

Shooting a glare, he interjected, "I don't care about academia or sociology or any other kind of stupid debate. I have to get the good grade Brad, and that's it! I have a quiz on Monday, so if you wouldn't mind?"

I leaned back and waved my hand at him in a gesture to blow him off. He shifted his eyes back to his notes, apparently unfazed.

"Hey, do you like your mocha?" He slowly closed his book, took off his glasses and leaned into the middle of the table.

"Yes, I do. So, now that you have my undivided attention bored little one. Let's get it out of your system. You're looking to get at me. So, what is it? My sinful consumption of caffeine?

"Uhmmm…"

"Okay, so just shut up with that before you get another word out. I will have to do some counseling with the bishop and repent for my sin I am sure, but does it really look like I give a fuck?"

"Bishop…fuck?"

"Yeah, we have Bishops that we confess our wrongdoings and repent to. But it isn't as if I have much to do with that these days! Haven't you noticed? Isn't that what you're after? My righteousness?"

"No…"

"Yes it is…you're after me…what do you want?"

"Jordan, I don't want to fight about it. But I do have my questions."

"So, spit it out."

"Okay, so, don't you have Mormon friends you've met?"

"No. I don't want them. And as a matter of fact," he said, leaning in further, "I'm not even sure what I believe anymore Brad. You know, my mom was right. She said that if I went to school in Moscow, I couldn't be faithful. And deep down, that is why I demanded I come to Moscow. I wanted to see something else. Remember how quiet my parents were when they dropped me off?"

"Yeah."

"Well, deep down my mom knows I'm 'different'. Jordan used both hands to make quotation marks between us. "At one point they demanded I go to BYU."

"BYU?"

"Brigham Young University. Anyway," he leaned back and relaxed, "...that is where all good Mormons go. It is sometimes called the 'Lords' university. When I told them that I wanted to go here, they were pissed, but gave in and said it would be an experiment since there were more programs here. The bishop actually helped out on that matter actually. They talked to our bishop back home and he said that wherever I went, I would find my way back to the gospel."

"It sounds like you're not following the Mormon plan of action."

"No, I will always be Mormon. A cup of coffee and bad language doesn't change that. I'm just trying to figure things out right now for me. Getting away from my family has been nice."

"What about your sexuality?" I anxiously took my cup in my hand and watched for a reaction.

"That is something I can never be."

What could he possibly mean by that?

"Never be? Like you have a choice in the matter Jordan."

"No! That is where you are wrong. I do have a choice. I will get married one day and follow the gospel. You can't understand, nor do I expect you to. There is no way a Mormon can be both gay and follow the gospel. To be gay means rejecting the faith."

His words were more than decisive but grave in conviction. For anyone dealing with a budding sexuality, talking out the issue was normal. However, he had a schema, a template he followed, overshadowing it that was completely solidified and unbendable.

"Do you feel guilty for having gay thoughts? I thought you told me that you were dealing with it."

"Guilty? No. I have the moral agency to choose my life. And this is not a life I want."

"You don't even know anything about it." Tension tugged at me to figure him out, to rescue him from the obscure delusion. There had to be self-hate and an unhappy person behind his rational. Therefore, he could be fixed. I saw it as my job to break through it.

"Look, I want to forget all that. I'm not going to give into being a homosexual. Being rebellious about a drink is one thing, and questioning my beliefs is part of that, but being a homosexual is not an option. It is my affliction."

"Affliction?"

"Yes affliction. Let me finish…those afflicted with homosexuality, were in heaven once and considered very noble and honored beings. We are taught that souls are born on earth to be tested. If I choose the life, I go to a place absent from God for eternity. And anyway, regardless of what my church says, the choice is a dangerous one. I overheard once that the average age of mortality for homosexual men is 41. You think that is safe?"

"That is a bullshit statistic. People have been filling your head with total crap. Is this the kind of shit you have been thinking about since you came out to me? That you're going to hell and are going to die an early awful death? They are scaring you straight."

"Take Jake and Matt for instance."

"What about them? And what do they have to do with your statistic, Jordan the pragmatist." The sarcasm went unnoticed.

"Since the fraternity party when those assholes accused us of being a couple, they haven't let up! There isn't a day that I don't worry about their threats and name-calling. I don't want to live that way."

He was right, but I didn't want to admit it. Jake made jabs about my androgynous ways, stood wide in the hallway and purposely knocked me in the shoulder on more than one occasion. The atmosphere of threat was present in the Hall. He never stayed in the showers if I came in.

Jordan continued, "It is dangerous Brad. If you think for a second that people would simply embrace it, you're totally fucking nuts. I can't deal with the rejection of my family, and certainly not my life!"

The depth of his belief was intense and therefore impossible to argue against. His convictions gripped deeply inside of him and shaped his motivations. He was decisive and had clearly spent many hours thinking this through. We were still just getting to know each other. But nevertheless, the conversation created a divide.

After a short tense silence, he added, "Look Brad, I'm sorry for fighting with you. You see the inconsistencies. So do I. So, guess what? I don't even have it all figured out. I just can't be both."

"I'm trying to take it all in. And really, the best that I can see, either way, you choose hell, hell for living dishonestly, or hell eternity. Right?"

"Yes, and that is my choice to make. Do I live for now or later?"

"With what I would determine the same result."

"I wish I was more like you."

"I looked at him blankly.

Then, I felt a gentle hand on my shoulder. I turned to find Lydia standing above me.

"Hi!" I stood up and gave her a hug. I was disappointed that she was here in the middle of the intense atmosphere, but happy to see her.

"What are you doing here? It is so cool to see you! This is like my favorite hangout. Isn't it so the best?"

"This is our second time checking it out actually. But hey Lydia, I want you to meet my roommate Jordan."

Jordan stood up and took her hand. His face was relaxed as he smiled politely, almost as if it were a fresh new day. The loose end created hung on my back, but there would be time to pick up the string another time.

"Yes, nice to meet you. Now who are you?"

Jordan looked at me inquisitively. "I'm sorry Jordan, this is a friend I met the other night at the Student Union Building. Remember when I went for that walk, locked myself out of the room? Well, I ran into Lydia there."

"It is very nice to meet you, again. Do you want to join us?" Jordan offered.

"Yes, I'm not intruding? I hope you guys don't mind." She rested the tips of her fingers against her upper chest, begging for an invitation.

"No, not at all." I gestured for her to take the chair next to Jordan and sat down.

"Just a second, I need to get something to eat. I'll be right back." Lydia went to the counter.

Jordan took his seat again. We looked at each other for only a second before he asked, "She seems nice. How come you didn't tell me about her?"

"I didn't think it was that important. Hey, are you okay with were we left off?"

"Yes. I'm fine...sorry if I got a little animated."

"Can we talk about it later though? We need to pick this back up, alone Jordan, Just you and I?"

Lydia returned with a cup of coffee clasped between her hands. "Jordan, so, tell me about yourself. What are you doing in Moscow?"

Chapter Ten

Lydia, Jordan and I got acquainted by talking about the eclectic atmosphere of The Beanery and our individual acclamations to Moscow's student community. We talked about our hometowns and both how horrifying and fresh the first few weeks away felt.

Lydia told us about Oakland and her parent's work. The small-town atmosphere gave her a newfound expression, finding that the city hid her away in the shadows of others.

Jordan engaged immediately, and his body moved into curious pose, seeking out her insights, just as drawn in as I, the first time we met. Without hesitation he put his notes away and was entrenched, carefully holding his cup with his fingers, while sitting back in his chair slightly pulled away from the table with his legs crossed, one knee over the other. The typical apathetic nervous style was nowhere in sight.

It began light, the mood comfortable, Jordan ever intrigued with Lydia, and I hopelessly relieved that my friend approved as I would want to spend more time with her.

But it was the flash a seemingly insignificant piece of jewelry that took us into the depths once again. Lydia leaned over into her cup, tipping the hot rim to her lips. The flash of gold momentarily sparkled in front of the bone above her small breasts. I hadn't noticed it before, but it hung clearly now, revealing another complexity of sweet Lydia. Jordan spared no moments.

"Are you Catholic?"

"Yes, yes I am." She was slightly taken off guard, gently took the metal between her fingers and pushed it against her chest. "I don't attend mass very often, but I guess you can still call me Catholic."

"That is a saint isn't it?" Jordan continued.

"Yes, Saint Andrew, the Patron saint for fishermen and single women. My grandmother passed it on to me. She was Scottish. She lost her husband to a fishing accident. It was common for Scottish women to wear I believe."

"Why don't you attend Mass anymore. Are you against it?" he led.

'Well, I don't believe in it much at all. It isn't very kind to women's choices and the current pope is very conservative. I have spent much time in pursuit of philology, and I definitely lean far enough to the left to almost fall over. I like some parts of the church, but can't seem to find a balance as of yet because of the politics of the church. But that is just my view. There are liberal Catholics as well. That is one thing about being Catholic. You can be a Liberal Catholic and not be cast out. So, I'm just following my family in tradition and always willingly looking at lots of avenues. Everyone in my family does. But, I think my dad is still involved in the church; he attends Mass every week."

Jordan's face lit up with curiosity. "Do you believe in God?" he asked quickly, before I could get in.

"I don't know."

Jordan flowed into the conversation with ease. "I'm taking an ethics course this semester. We talked about Karl Marx last week. He has some interesting views on religion."

"Yes, I think he is great, at least to talk about. He pushes a lot of buttons for me. Coming from a religious background, that philosophy is considered heresy."

"Fill me in. I've not taken any philosophy yet," I muttered, feeling left out.

Jordan turned to me and said, "He preached that religion was a kind of drug, specifically an opiate for all of society. He thought that it was a tool for governments to control people. And for that, he hated the concept of God. It is a crazy way to think about it."

"But brilliant I think. He thought religion was used to keep oppressed people from revolting. Marx believed in revolt, and he believed in money being distributed evenly. In the dark ages, before the enlightenment, revolt meant the rich could lose their place. The poor were kept poor through the state religion," Lydia added.

The premise was making Jordan uncomfortable. "I don't know about that. Religion comes from God. It doesn't come from people."

"You don't believe that governments used religion to keep people oppressed? I think governments use religion now to oppress. But now the religion is the media and the media are the drug. Don't you think that the media is used on us as a form of control, information as a form of control instead of organized religion?"

"I'm lost." Jordan sneered.

"Don't you think that economics to the government is more important to them than us sitting having this conversation? They want to stay in power. One way is to control what we think and that is through the media? We buy products cuz they tell us to. We vote on what information they feed us."

"No. The government would never seek to control its people for economic or political gain. Anyway, what does religion have to do with this?" I asked.

"It's all about control. Many forces control us. Think about it. How many decisions do you make that are truly your own?" Lydia added.

"You should talk. You're Catholic. Aren't you controlled by your religion?" Jordan prodded.

"I'm not a believer in an organized form of the Catholic faith anymore Jordan. I go when I feel I need to. The basic tenants are important to me. I don't feel I'm saved by going all the time or keeping myself pure."

"I see people going to church and forced by their families to believe in all the dogmatic bullshit. That's fucking sick. If there is a God, he only wants us to be kind to each other. He doesn't care about our skin color, sex, attractions, or politics. He wants us to be kind. Anything beyond that is just people controlling us. He is definitely not that petty, keeping some kind of scoreboard in heaven of how often we attend church or how righteous we are. It is about loving each other. People buying into perfection out of submission, are brainwashed and mindlessly controlled, no different than the government controlling opinions and values through the media."

"That is where I disagree. I'm a member of the Mormon church, if Brad hasn't already told you that." He glanced over at me with a hint of a glare. "I believe in my Father God. I believe that he gave me a choice to follow him or not. You have chosen not to believe."

Lydia took time to absorb the robotic words, and said, "Jordan, I'm a good person regardless. So, let me ask you this…if you didn't believe in God, would you still be a good person and love?"

Jordan was clearly stumped by this question. "Father God teaches us how to be good."

"Jordan, do you think you have choice about whether or not to believe in God?"

"Yes. And I do believe in God." Then she stopped. She set her coffee cup down and looked directly at him, only slightly leaning forward. "Jordan, I'm not trying to be a bitch. I just see a person who is really cool sitting in front of me, and I don't think it has anything to do with God."

"I do. If I don't believe, there aren't any good options for me. True happiness is only with a belief in God and following the Gospel."

"I'm sorry to hear that, because I'm happy, and I don't believe much in your Gospel."

Jordan sat quite for a minute. Then Lydia turned to me.

"What do you believe in Brad?"

I anticipated the redirect, and it wasn't a shift I wanted. "If you can choose to walk away from the religion you grow up in, can you just walk away? Like that?" I snapped my fingers in the air.

"Why not?"

"I don't know, it just seems to me that if you're brought up in a lifestyle that attempts to control your every thought and the social structure around you, can you actually stop living that way? Isn't it kind of in the back of your head forever, kind of organic?"

"So, St. Andrew, the patron saint necklace, is it a reflection of the permanence of my Catholicism? You're saying it's like a branding of sorts. I don't know..."

Then, out of sheer excitement I interrupted, "...I think growing up with a religion as institutionalized as Mormonism, or Catholicism in your case, prevents you from ever really having choice. You can choose not to follow, but don't you have parts of you that worry you're wrong for leaving?" Jordan looked on intently.

Lydia was puzzled. I pushed her in a quandary. "Well, I suppose I have to say that there are some doubts. Some parts of me feel like a religious failure I suppose, but we don't lose our spirituality for not going to church and looking around at the world. The church does not even take a hard stance on evolution. There is a lot of choice. The issues that made me walk away have more to do with current social policy, actually, so this is where I disagree. Mormonism isn't as inviting of diverse views.

"I walked away from the church, but still cling to ideas. However, I always have a home to go back to. My political views are mine. I would have to completely become an atheist I suppose, and hate the concept of God, for there to be a problem in the eyes of the Vatican."

"You're right," Jordan stepped in and said, "I don't have much of a choice about what I believe. I said I had choice, actually I don't. The consequences are too great. My parents would disown me. I would be excommunicated from the church. When that happens, your name gets taken off the books as a member if you don't repent after a period of time. That's not really a choice."

"So, maybe that's better in the end," I said with resolve.

"No, you get erased because you have made a clear choice to not follow the gospel. And that means not going to heaven."

"Now, wait, don't you have several levels of heaven? I thought you didn't have a hell in your religion," said Lydia.

"No, we have a hell. The ones who go to it renounce the gospel, commit murder, or sexual misconduct." Jordan's words sped up and increased in volume.

"Jordan, I hope you aren't mad. I'm just really curious why you believe in something so clearly discriminatory towards race, sexual orientation, and women, when you are clearly a very bright guy."

"You can be bright and Mormon. And as for the discrimination, it is what the gospel says, and that is what we believe. Plain and simple! Didn't you know that we are bigots too?" The humor took the punch out the intense moments. Lydia followed it with a sincere laugh.

Nevertheless, she didn't let it drop. "I know you're not, but how can you believe in the rubbish about women having their proper place in the home. I mean, don't you glorify motherhood. I see that as a tool to keep them in their place."

"We're not the only religion that does that."

"Easy for you to say when you're a guy. Now, what if I had a penis. That's it, a girl with a penis. Wouldn't that be cool? Then I could control the world, corporate America maybe? Or maybe I should just drop out of school and piss children from a slit in my crotch, stay at home and raise brats for my man?"

Her language was jolting. Jordan threw himself forward, setting his cup on the table while letting out a loud laugh. Lydia followed. Suddenly, the contagion took us all, not caring if anyone in the room heard, or that we were being obnoxious.

"Hey guys, I have an idea," I said with my right-side aching, noticing that we were about finished with our drinks. "Let's take a walk to the Administration Building. It's a brisk night out."

Jordan stood up taking the lead, already putting on his jacket.

Lydia stood up and smiled. "It is so beautiful up there at night. The lights are so orange when you stand in the middle!"

"The middle of what?"

"Let's not tell him Brad"

"Agreed."

I watched him light up with curiosity and head for the door. Lydia and I stood at the table. For that instant, I looked up at her, at the straight lines of her hair leading to her shoulders, feeling a pressure in my stomach, wanting to pull her in close. Before I knew it, we were standing outside, walking down Sixth, the coffee shop now only history.

"Just a sec Jordan," she said, pulling at his arm, halting him in place. "Are we cool? I mean, we didn't like totally piss each other off in there did we? That was just a little bit intense."

Jordan stood with confidence. "No, no, I'm fine."

As time would tell, our friend worked out a battle we could not possibly understand. His sexuality raged war like peasant against knight, with his religious upbringing. As his struggling identity developed, he was going to have to revise his religious beliefs, or could he? In time we would see which was the softer and which was the harder of the two, wax vs. stone, sexual identity vs. religious identity.

When eternity and family as the anvil were brought forth, could a battle be waged? That was to be seen.

We walked up through campus, up the steep hill leading past the Health Center that leveled off, leaving us under the large clock tower of the Administration Building. We turned up the walkway and veered through the trees to the center of the large grass lawn.

Jordan and Lydia slowed down, waiting for me to catch up. Without any of us agreeing to do so, we slowly walked into the center of the circle of trees. Our heavy breathing mixed with the humming of the orange lights. A moist mist surrounded us, shadowing us from the rest of campus, encasing us amongst the star like pattern of maple. In perfect synchronization we stopped, turned and looked at each other, formed a triangle, and took a hold of the others hand.

We stood simply noticing the moment. We didn't speak. Words couldn't capture what took us over. Everything slowed down in that union of three. The heat of our breath clouded the inner triangle. Then, in a ceremonial smile and guided by something greater than ourselves, we tilted our heads up. Jordan gently whispered, "Wow," and we peered through the branches around, with their snowflake pattern, supporting us with leaves underfoot. The familiar constellations from childhood fixed statically in the sky. It was warm, quite warm, and we were one.

Chapter Eleven

"Hey guy, aren't you awake yet?" I pried my eye lids open, squinting bitterly at the oncoming light, feeling the interrogation of the morning, trying to keep the phone to my ear with my shoulder, too exhausted to keep my hand on the receiver.

"Lydia? I fumbled with my lips."

"Yessss. Get up, I have a great idea!" There was nothing that couldn't wait until noon.

"Okay," my voice squeaked with morning cotton. I rubbed my eyes with the knuckles of my left hand, taking the phone in the other, forcing myself to sit up.

"Don't you want to know what my idea is?"

"Yeah, but what time is it?"

"I don't know. It's early. Come on Brad, it's Columbus Day weekend. Three days off."

I looked over at Jordan. His arm covered his eyes and he was on his back. He was oblivious. I stepped closer to see if he was awake. My foot landed on something. It was the Book of Mormon open on the floor. Some pages were creased. "Fuck!"

"Fuck what? Brad, lighten up!"

"No, not you."

"Anyway, I have a sister in Seattle. I've been dying to see her. Let's go! We can go to a club, just have fun, and my God, get the fuck out."

"But, there's this one little problem. A car!"

"I have a VW Van silly. We can stay with my sister, play our asses off for the weekend and be back in time for class on Tuesday. What do you think?"

"Sure, why not. I'm sure Jordan will go." My body was loosening up. The challenge was convincing the studious roommate dead to all existence, but he could be successfully coerced.

With some initial hesitation, Jordan stirred. And to my astonishment he jumped at the chance. He got up with a shot and we showered, put a couple of bags together, with plenty of time to hang around waiting for the ride.

Lydia took longer than expected, a fashionable kind of late, irritating as it was, and extremely frustrating to my mate. I ignored his huffing and put my head back down on the pillow with my shoes on ready to launch. My deep thoughts led me into a momentary haze that was quickly interrupted by a loud pounding at the door. I flew to my feet, my body more exhausted than before. Lydia came in and walked directly over to Jordan and shook him alive again.

"Let's go boys. I'm ready to roll!"

Jordan and I stumbled down the hall with our belongings under arm, out the door, and into the van's first row of rear seating. The goal was sleep. I attempted to claim it for myself to be closer to Lydia, but Jordan's head hit just next to my thigh before I could claim it. I jumped back the next row, not before putting a wet finger in his ear. He barely noticed.

"Fuck!" I thought, realizing that the air was icy. Again, like many times before, I neglected to remember appropriate outerwear. My jacket remained on the hook next to the inside of the door of our room. I started the stumble back to the room, realizing halfway I didn't have my keys. Lydia rolled her eyes impatiently.

We started the drive at 10:30 a.m. Columbus Day travelers swarmed around the obnoxious vehicle of antiquity. The forest green VW van made the way in the slow lane with cars passing us in an irritating manner, not to mention the loud sputter of the engine and smell of gasoline. Nerves ran tight with nausea.

The swerving of cars around us, the inability to enjoy a decent conversation, and to make things worse, Lydia's bad habit of looking back for extended periods to carry on conversation, caused me to slip into an ongoing state of panic. I stayed put knowing my life had a better chance two rows back, than in the passenger seat next to her, should we hit something.

Seven hours later, we were in Seattle, and Jordan remained oblivious.

As we approached the exit taking us up Capitol Hill, I couldn't believe the volume of traffic and the sudden gush of rain. It beat any amount of downpour I experienced in Alaska.

We turned hard right onto a gradual hill that from my estimation went on into oblivion. Along the streets were tons of leaves, some fully deteriorated, some still clinging to form. A path was cut through them along the sidewalks showing signs of city life. They were heavy in clumps and soggy with rain.

Then we made three seriously sharp turns, too fast for comfort, causing even Jordan to sit up with a grunt, jumped a curb, back off again, and then to an abrupt stop.

"We've made it!" Lydia exclaimed, as if transported in time, chipper with no signs of exhaustion from the drive. She turned off the motor; it struggled, then choked and was silent. My ears were sore.

"Okay boys, let's get out of this heap." Lydia's eyes were wide. Her delicate arms came down off the wheel, clasped in the air as if to signal, "Hurrah", something you might see at a British polo game.

Before we had our packs over our shoulder, a loud shriek came from above. I oriented. It was a woman just as dainty thin and deeply resembling Lydia in stature and facial structure. I wondered about which parent had the strongest influence on their genes.

"Oh my god, you made it!" the voice came down in a high-pitched uncontrolled excitement.

Lydia ran, meeting her sister on the stairs. They hugged quickly and kissed each other on opposite cheeks. They came down the stairs toward us standing ready at the van.

"Susan, this is my friend Brad. Brad this is my sister Susan." Our hands met. She looked me deep in the eyes and smiled. "Nice to meet you Brad." She kept her fixated look and said to Lydia, "So, this is the boy you've been telling me about." Heat slid up my face, terminating at my ears.

"Yes." I think Lydia was equally as embarrassed.

"And this is Jordan, Brad's roommate." Susan reached out her hand and Jordan met with his. They shook hands quickly. Jordan didn't look up, continuing to pull out the few things left in the car.

"Jordan," Susan directed, pushing to get his attention, "I've heard a lot about you too. You're from Southern Idaho I think Lydia said?"

He stopped, realizing he was being rude. "Yes, Oakley. Southeast Idaho actually."

"I had a friend from Boise when I was in college. She loved it there. Really conservative outside of the area, as I understand, but liked it nevertheless. How about you?"

"I'm not very close to my family," Jordan said in a definitive tone. This immediately got my attention, his random honesty with strangers.

Susan looked at him inquisitively. "I'm sorry to hear that."

She disengaged, put her hand on Jordan's forearm, instructing him to follow Lydia up the stairs. She stayed behind.

"Go on up guys. Let Lydia show you around. I'm going to get my mail. Be right back." She walked around the van and towards a large metal cluster of mailboxes.

My impressions of Susan were very positive. Lydia and her sister had a lot in common. They both had dishwater blond hair, although I could tell that her sister was growing out a hair coloring from the past. Their gentle and concerned nature was also similar. Susan was equally adept at making personal contact with strangers without fault. They both carried this deliberate quality, the characteristic in Lydia that drew me in from the beginning.

Nevertheless, there was one major difference that set them apart, and I was left puzzled trying to figure out what exactly it was. My intuition failed me. Besides the obvious ten-year age difference, everything was like looking at a clone. But there was something different about the way she moved and her presence that I couldn't connect with.

We walked up the stairs and into the living room of the apartment. It was casually decorated, almost cluttered, with many pictures on the walls, prints of famous oil, pastel and watercolor paintings. Down one hallway there was also a variety of black and white photos in hand made mats, personal pictures of people, a few artistic.

While walking around, following Lydia as she showed us around the small apartment quarters, I searched for family photos, anything that would give me a clue as to what Susan and Lydia's home life was like. With this initial sweep, I didn't see anything significant with one exception; it was sitting on an oak stained end table in the hallway leading to the bedroom. Susan was pictured in a small 5x7 photograph, sitting on a porch with a black lab at her side holding a stick in his mouth. From what I could tell, there was no dog now, so I surmised he had passed. But still, there were no pictures of Lydia, nor anything of their parents.

Lydia showed us to our respective sleeping arrangements. Lydia wanted to sleep on the couch in the living room. I agreed to share a room with Jordan, allowing him to take the bed, and I the floor. Susan's room was at the end. After some initial polite disagreement about Lydia taking the couch, we settled on the arrangements amicably and went to visit in the living room.

There was a large sized couch and love seat off to the side. I was surprised to see no TV. However, there was a stereo in the center of the wall next to the outside door leading downstairs. The apartment had plenty of windows, but it was still situated in the center of the building with apartments on either side, thus restricting the light. Jordan took the love seat, and Lydia and I sat next to each other on the couch. Susan walked in at that moment. She had a bundle of magazines and other assorted mail under her arm. The latent odor of tobacco followed her.

"Sorry guys. I got talking to the neighbor. So, did you find yourself what you needed for sleeping space?"

"Yes," I said with relaxed joy, "Thanks for letting us stay."

"No, thank you actually, it is nice to have visitors. I'm happy you're here. Are you guys thinking about going out tonight?"

"I wanted to show them around," Lydia answered.

"I have a date with a friend this evening. I hope you don't mind if we go our separate ways tonight."

"We're fine. We don't have to be back until Monday morning, so I thought we would party tonight, and then maybe have a dinner with you tomorrow? I didn't think you would want to go anyway. You know. The club thing?"

"Good call! That club scene. It's for the young."

"You act like you're over the hill Susan."

"You get over the club scene Lydia."

"I suppose," Lydia said with annoyance.

"What you want to make tomorrow?" Susan said shifting topics. "I wouldn't mind that pesto you made for us last time." She went into the kitchen as she was talking. I heard the refrigerator open, followed by, "What do you guys want to drink?"

"Any kind of pop is good," Jordan immediately jumped in.

"And you Brad?"

"No thanks, I'm fine. I was hoping we could go out for a coffee later."

"Yes, that sounds good to me too," Lydia agreed.

"I know this nice little place in the Pink Triangle district just up the street," Susan added as she gave Jordan his pop.

He looked up, "The pink Triangle?" I was sure he had to have some idea what that referred to.

"Well yes, my dear Jordan, this is a big gay city, not to mention you're in the gay district of Seattle. It is very open. You should like it. There are tons of cool shops and gay couples everywhere."

I was surprised at Lydia's blunt words. I told her about Jordan's sexuality, but failed to inform Jordan I revealed his secret.

Jordan blushed. Lydia realized her infraction. A long silence followed as Susan stood looking around the room at all of us. She quickly figured out the dilemma.

"I've loved living here. This has been the best apartment situation for me so far. I have never felt more accepted and at home. The gay community in Seattle is huge. Every gay person should have a place to call their own, and Capitol Hill is it for Seattle."

Was Susan a lesbian? If she was, she sure didn't fit the stereotype of short hair, black oversized boots and the gruff masculine overbearing attitude.

Lydia looked down at her hands clasped in front of her, hesitating. "Jordan, I'm so sorry for letting that out. You need to be in control of what you tell people. Please don't hate me." Jordan's shifted his glare to me.

"I'm sorry." I was so nervous I couldn't hear myself breath.

"Well, I'm still not okay with it and you put it right in my face. All I can think about is how I can't go on and live this way. Who can?"

Susan looked down with eyebrows turned in. "Jordan, you can say that kind of self-intolerant bullshit to yourself elsewhere, but in my home, we practice tolerance to each other and ourselves." She walked over to his side and put her hand on his head, pushing the hair out of his face. Jordan kept his eyes down. "I like you Jordan, and I don't even know you." She put her arm around his shoulder. "Being gay isn't easy. Hang in with it little guy."

"We are here for you Jordan." Lydia added.

"I have an idea, you guys get your stuff unpacked, and I will do some cleaning up in the kitchen. As soon as you are ready, we can head up the street and get that coffee."

Jordan jumped to his feet and I followed him to our room. He sat on the bed and took out his toothbrush and extra clothing. I fussed with the sleeping bag leaning against the wall. Susan had placed it there before our arrival. Jordan went into the bathroom across the hall. He took his toothbrush with him. When he returned, I was sitting in his spot on the bed.

"Are you mad at me?"

"No, just a little numb. I didn't know anyone else would have to know. I kinda expected it, just caught off guard. You would be too."

"I really do apologize."

"It wasn't a secret I asked you to keep Brad."

"I will be more careful Jordan. Just with my uncle and all, I forget it is difficult for people."

"Well, I'm not sure what I'm going to do about it yet. I may never be open with it Brad. I must live in free agency, remembering that I don't have to act on it. That is what I believe so far."

I felt a level of frustration building in my chest. "Jordan, there is nothing wrong with being gay. Look at Susan and she looks great!"

"How do you know that?"

"Fuck, can't you tell. Didn't you hear what she said? She virtually wrote it on the wall with neon marker out there."

"Even if she is, even if everyone is, I don't have to act on it. It is a matter of my family and my church. You can never understand that and never will." He sat on the floor, leaning against the bed. "If I want to have a testimony in my church, then I can't live a gay lifestyle. It is that simple. You can't build a philosophical case for me to see it differently so stop before we get into an argument about it."

"I'm sad for you Jordan, sad because that shit is dishonest, dishonest to yourself and your church." My voice was tense. Jordan looked down at his clothes sitting in front of him and continued to rearrange.

"It may be, but I have to choose between them, and you don't."

"There is no choice Jordan,"

"You're right."

I left and went to the kitchen and met Lydia and Susan. Jordan stayed behind for an hour while we talked about school. I wondered if they sensed my lingering irritation. I imagined myself a great actor and could hide it well, putting on the appropriate face for the situation.

Finally, Jordan came out. He joined in the conversation without effort and was welcomed. I pondered between thoughts wondering if he felt sad on the other side of that wall. Did he hate himself for choosing his own hell? Did he hate me for putting it in his face?

We talked a little more and then took Susan's lead out for a walk-up Broadway to the Pink Zone.

The gay district of Seattle was amazing. The Pink Zone was a mall setting midway up the street with several clothing, novelty stores and eating establishments. Inside was two floors full of lingering people, many shopping for everyday necessities, others freely holding hands with their partners and visiting friends. I was not in my element, but I felt entirely comfortable with the scene. I had never before seen two men or women open with their affection. It was a safe place where I was now the minority.

The scenes on television I watched growing up were suddenly diffused. There were no crude acts of exploitation or gay people fucking in public. It was the most artistic and expressive atmosphere I had experienced. Susan led our pack through the shops to a central café where we took a seat at one of the many open-air bistro tables.

"So, Jordan, is it what you thought it would be?" I asked, seeing the bewilderment on his face.

"No. This is so cool." Then, like clockwork, two guys walked by and kissed each other on the cheek in front of us. They said goodbye and, "See you at home", and went their separate ways. One was dressed in a fresh pressed white shirt, black slacks, and an apron pulled tight around his waist. The other wore a long black leather jacket and turtleneck sweater with black corduroy pants. Jordan watched the exchange intently. A contemplative smile formed on his face. I swore I could see him daydream.

After deciding that coffee wasn't enough and that we were famished, we ordered sandwiches and soups and ate a relaxed lunch. We returned to an earlier conversation on academics and moved on to how much we thought the Greek system needed to be done away with; it was an extension of high school therefore, allowing people to never grow up. By the time we finished our food, it was almost seven o'clock. The evening had moved upon us quickly. We started back towards the apartment. It was noticeably cooler with the night quickly approaching.

"I'm thinking that club idea is right up my alley."

Lydia turned back towards me and put her arm through mine, pulling loose the crossed tangle protecting me from the cold. Her body next to mine felt warm. "Awesome! I am going to take you to 'The Ornate'. It's downtown under the space needle." She turned back looking at Jordan. "Very open hang-out and great music, the perfect dance club." Ever been to one Jordan?"

Jordan stepped in and grabbed my other arm. "Nope, but sounds like fun to me." He had a skip in his step. I was being carried off to jail by two wonderful officers.

"I love to dance," I said. She kissed me on the cheek.

"Well, you girls," Susan said, "go and have fun. I have a date with a beautiful woman from Tacoma. It's our second time. I'm jacked."

"Congratulations Sis. I hope you bring protection!" We all laughed as we walked back to the apartment. Like an idiot, I didn't have a jacket, so I appreciated the warmth coming from the warm bodies on both sides of me.

*****

The line outside The Ornate was daunting, leading down the sidewalk several yards. We stood in line, none of us wearing appropriate clothing for the cold, advice by Lydia because we were going to sweat too much from dancing and that there was no place to leave extra clothing without it getting stolen.

It was about an hour before we stood in the darkened foyer at a window with a girl sitting on the other side of an extra thick sheet of glass. She wore black-rimmed glasses with a small diamond on each horn, a black oversized dress, far over reaching her fragile body, and black painted nails. The dark red lipstick was hardly visible in the poor lighting.

"Eleven dollars each," she slurred. I took out a fifty before the others could pay and gave it to the girl. Up above her head was a sign that read, "This Club is Family Friendly. No bigots or homophobes." She smiled and methodically handed me my change through the arc at the bottom edge of the glass. The music was too loud for either Jordan or Lydia to give me an argument. Lydia's face protested. "You can buy me something to drink," I shouted.

We walked through a short hallway that turned a quick corner and then once again into an open sitting area. Up front was the dance floor, already full of people deep in their own worlds. Two cubes were on each side of the floor. One of them had a girl and a guy dancing on them together. On the floor guys were dancing together, girls as well, and boy and girl couples shuffled in between. Lydia took my hand. Jordan stood behind, frequently looking between us at the crowd. Then suddenly, without any prompting, he darted past us and disappeared into the mob. We found our way down to a comfortable spot. I pulled her close to me. She smelt good. I was not prepared for what was about to happen. A force moved in the crowd. It slithered in the air among the glistening bodies, moving along the hardwood floor and up the walls and took me.

We moved out further together, never being that close before, and slowly found ourselves below the cube on the left side of the dance floor. We danced closer, conscious of our discomfort, but becoming ever more absorbed in the diversity of sounds and techno beats pushed by the bodies around us. I moved away, and back again, looking at the floor, back up, both of us sometimes looking down at each other's bodies. The progressive rhythms separated me from the floor. Then the music became louder in my head, a rum effect soaked my body. Sweat formed in the middle of my back, a drop fell off my nose and hit the floor. I watched it as it hit and spread out below me, almost as beautiful as the woman standing in front of me. I moved in closer, taken in by her, our bodies joined in a musical union. The opium like trance blended us together.

I looked up at a guy dancing on the cube above me with unbuttoned jeans and no shirt. His hair was bleached blond on spiked tips. He looked into me. I felt a wave hit my stomach. Lydia looked up. He didn't adjust his gaze, only smiled with his glazed eyes. I looked at her, my girlfriend, and smiled. We kissed in a sweaty embrace, pulling her breasts into me, without even a thought. I felt myself swell. I grabbed the small of her back and pulled her in tight. We moved together as I passed my lips down to her neck. She tipped her head back. Then I let go, moving away from her a few feet and then back again, taking her in even closer. She held my face and kissed me deeply. The music was louder, pounding through us, joining us as one.

I looked up again. The guy had his pants down. There was no underwear covering him, just his cupped hands. He put his tongue out licking the air, looking into me again. My groin felt hot. The tension was overwhelming, Lydia feeling me and pulling herself in with all I could do to pull my gaze off him. I turned and walked towards the bar. Lydia stayed on the floor unaware. I sat down, ordered a soda and turned my stool around to watch her, my trance broken finally in control. But did I want to be? She was standing next to me now, her hand on my shoulder.

"Hey, isn't this place wild? I love it. I'm so glad I was able to bring you guys with me!" She took my hand off my knee and squeezed it tight. We both watched the people in the crowd. I wondered if they experienced the music as intensely as I.

"It's way cool, but where is Jordan?" We looked around the room together, didn't see him at first, and there he was, a couple layers of people back into the crowd. His hands were crossed above his head. His yellow-black striped shirt stood out among the rave style clothing, soaked with sweat around his neck.

Then we noticed what he was doing, both stopping to take in what we saw. From below another body moved in closely with Jordan, sliding up his abdomen, then his chest where they met cheek to cheek. He wore a tight white-purple glittered shirt and sleek black plastic pants. He was about the same small proportions as Jordan.

His head moved to his mouth, Jordan smiling with his eyes closed. They moved to the beat of the bodies and sound around them. The guy was teasing him. Their lips almost touched and then he slid to the other side of his face, breathing on his neck, but not taking him into his mouth. Lydia looked at me. I think we were both confused and excited at the same time. Would Jordan regret it, or was this the beginning of his ego syntonic development?

Their lips met. Jordan took the back of his head with both hands and pulled him into his face. The kiss was hard, long and deep with the edges of their tongues exposed. My breath was shallow again.

"Hey, I need a cigarette. Want one?" Lydia said loudly in my ear. She saw the look on my face.

"No, I don't smoke, but..." She took my hand and led me to a back door opening into an alley where several people were taking part in the same nicotine pleasure.

"Hey, she shouted. "Can I bum a cigarette from anyone?" A stately broad-shouldered gentleman approached her with a pack, took one out and lit it for her. "Thanks darling," she said kindly.

"Want anything else?"

"No thanks. We're cool. The cigarettes are enough. You're great man. Thanks again."

"No problem lady."

Lydia handed me the cigarette. I took a drag. My head buzzed as I handed it back to her and blew out the smoke.

The people and brick building across from me became crisp with the nicotine moving around in my head.

"Wow, Jordan is really doing well in there."

"Yeah, but I hope he isn't going to regret it. He confuses the fuck out of me, oscillating between being a homo and that fucked up religion."

"Coming out isn't easy Brad. My sister had a very difficult time," Lydia said as she looked off into the distance, taking a drag from her cigarette, blowing the dark smoke into the air.

"If it wasn't for his religion, I would agree."

"He is fragile. I think he will be fine given some time and good friends like us."

"I hope." I leaned my head over to give her a kiss. Our lips met briefly before taking another drag of her cigarette. Without finishing the whole thing, she took my hand and led me back into the building. The icy air was starting to freeze the sweat on my back.

We continued to dance with very few breaks, enjoying the music and each other. It was about 1:00 a.m. when Jordan found us resting at the bar. He was smiling and soaked with sweat. His cologne was actively perfuming the air. It was overpowering, a smell I came to remember him by.

"I'm beat," he said, taking a stool and pushing it up next to Lydia, throwing his head on her shoulder."

"I'm ready to go" I jumped.

"Yeah. I don't think I will be able to move tomorrow. I have never danced so much in my life."

Lydia asked, "Who was that guy you were dancing with tonight buddy?" Jordan's face reddened.

"Oh, that's Jim."

"Well, did you get his number?" she rushed, breaking any pause in the action. Jordan reached into his sweaty pants and pulled out the damp piece of paper with the name written on it. "Yes, I did," he said with a glow.

Lydia gave him a hug. "That is so great! I'm very proud of you Jordan! You must call him as soon as we get back to Moscow." Then, with little delay, Lydia stood up. "Guys, let's get out of here." She led us towards the door, looking back to make sure we followed. "It is cold, so we better run."

We rushed into the van, started the engine and suffered in the cold night air only for a short couple of minutes to let the engine warm up enough to take off. Lydia gave it an exaggerated rev and pulled hard on the wheel, u-turning in the middle of the street, simultaneously shifting into gear and burning up Broadway.

When we got back to the apartment, Susan was sitting on the couch reading a thick yellow stained novel that once must have fallen into water, leaving its marks with overly wrinkled pages. She cradled it and a cup of tea on her knees, curled up in an afghan. She pulled off her glasses and looked up with relief.

"I was getting worried about you. We never agreed on a time that you would be back, so I was thinking about heading down to the club to see if you were still there. Did you guys have a good time?"

We sat in close to the couch and talked about our evening, especially Jordan's new-found friend. We were pumped with excitement, but it didn't take long to come down. Jordan was drifting to sleep, giving us the clue that it was time to cut things off.

Going to bed I gave Lydia a hug and told her thanks for the evening. She took her place on the couch and I headed to the guest bedroom. Jordan was already in the bed and asleep. I made myself comfortable in my mound of blankets on the floor and drifted away, heavy and exhausted.

The next morning, I awoke to the most peculiar experience of the entire trip to Seattle. I knew it before I awoke I suppose, and as my awareness brought it into consciousness, my body into the next morning, I settled there next to him at first in shock, and then comfort. I awoke to his smell. His back was turned, his neck tucked down, only the smallest amount of his blond hair for me to see. I have no idea how long we had been there together, but I held him, tucked in close.

Carefully, I rolled over on my back. He didn't notice, only quietly stirring, a shift in his breath, and a movement in his arm. What had happened? Was he aware of where he was? I doubted it. I enjoyed it. I wanted to stay. But didn't.

I got up into the bed and looked down at him, wondering how he could be in such a sad place, completely unaccepting of himself. How could so many love him, and he miss it. I drifted off again, heavy, into the depths of sleep's sweet embrace.

Then, I stirred, startled, jerked. I jumped up. I was alone. I heard voices coming from the kitchen. The scent of coffee floated in the air. The spitting of a coffee pot sounded the near finish of a fresh brew. I rotated my stiff shoulder. I looked through my bag and took out my pajama bottoms and one of the t-shirts I brought along. I walked across the hall and stood in front of the toilet and took a piss. Passing by the mirror, I caught a glance, something I typically avoid in the morning, and saw that my hair was all over the place. I took a minute to make myself presentable and then walked into the kitchen.

"Hey guys," I said with a raspy voice. Jordan and Lydia were sitting at the kitchen table with cups already in their hands. Jordan was taking to coffee quickly. Lydia stood up, walked directly over to me and put her fingers through my hair. I pulled to the side. She didn't let me get away and ruffled it up before I could move again. She kissed my forehead saying, "Good morning sunshine." Susan flipped a pancake at the stove and didn't look up until I almost ran into her trying to get away from Lydia.

"Well hey there sleepy head. Did you do okay on that floor? I forgot to tell about the mattress in the closet. Sorry. Maybe next time." Lovely.

"No, no, that's okay. It was fine. I didn't wake once, "I said putting my finger in the air. Slept so deep, I didn't even hear you guys get up."

After breakfast, Lydia interjected, "I thought we would go down to the fish market at the pier to get some halibut. Susan wants to make us deep fried fish for dinner. We decided against the pesto."

"Cool. What time is it?"

"It is almost 12:30 in the afternoon dear sleepy man," Lydia replied as she took her seat again. I pulled out a chair and sat down as I rubbed my eyes. Lydia stood back up and went to the cupboard, took out a cup and poured some coffee and placed it in front of me at the kitchen table. I put the hot ceramic rim to my lips and sipped. It felt solid in my hands and the steam rising to my face moistened my skin.

"Are you going to have sex with that cup Brad or just drink the shit?" Jordan poked. I looked up and didn't return the gesture. Lydia snickered.

"He needs another cup."

"Yes, I do."

"Well, okay then, let's give the grumpy boy his space," Lydia retorted. She got up and put her arms around my shoulder and moved behind me putting her cheek on mine and then ran her fingers through my hair again. It was irritating. Jordan looked on enjoying the fact that he knew I was holding back.

The pancakes were great. I ate my fill, a then some. Susan prepared far more than the four of us could eat in a week. After breakfast, Jordan and I did the dishes while Lydia took the first shower. Each of us followed in turn agreeing to keep it very short since there was not enough hot water for everyone. I don't think Susan took one at all.

I borrowed a pullover from Susan. Our drive was quiet as we weaved on and off streets, much of which confused me. I was mostly locked inside my head, still drowsy and slightly irritable, questioning the lingering scent of Jordan skin that I couldn't shake. Did he know he was sleeping next to me last night? Did he think about it as much as I did?

We went to the Seattle Fish Market and picked up five pounds of Halibut, a substantial amount for the four of us, but Lydia argued her sister could freeze what we didn't use. Then we toured the shops in the area among the light crowd of Sunday shoppers. I walked in the back most of the time, with Jordan and Lydia up front in heavy comical discussion. I was feeling ignored, but also wanted to be left alone in my thoughts. The longer this went on, the quieter I got until Lydia pulled me between them.

"Okay senior Brad! It's time you snapped out of your shit ass mood. We head back tomorrow...I want to enjoy this last little bit. If there is something you want to talk about, can we get to it now before the rest of the trip is ruined?"

"I'm fine."

"No, you're not."

"I don't know...I'm just so tired from last night. I'll snap out of it. Be patient with me...okay?"

The truth was that I was used to playing the caretaker of Jordan and felt jealous of Lydia and his newfound friendship. The reaction felt awkward actually. I was falling for Lydia, and hard, feelings that I was concealing as long as I could, because of Jordan. Yes Jordan. What would he think? But logic said he knew. Were my affections for him paternal, or was it something I couldn't touch or understand?

As we walked in and out of record, book, and designer clothing stores, sharing our thoughts on what was good, bad and simply outrageous in those categories, my mood improved. The variety of people on the street also started catching my attention, and I commenced by making remarks about the clothing and odd ways people appeared. It was remarkably immature and led us directly back to the van and up the street and to the apartment.

When we arrived, Susan was sitting listening to some music. She immediately stood up.

"Hi guys. Did you get the goods?"

"Lydia gave her a quick peck on the cheek, "Yes darling, we got five pounds."

"Fuck, five pounds? That is way too much," Susan said in a burst.

"Well, I suppose you can freeze what we don't use, yes?"

"Oh, good idea. What do I owe you?"

"You're cooking us dinner. You don't owe us anything. I got it." She took the package and disappeared into the kitchen. Jordan sat down on the floor in front of the CD collection sitting against the wall. I sat down next to him. We quietly looked through the selection of artists.

"Then a voice rang from the kitchen, "Do you guys want some wine?"

"Sure," I replied as I continued to explore the pile.

"Jordan?" Susan asked.

"Um, well, maybe just a little." I was getting to the point where nothing shocked me anymore. Jordan was flexing his independence muscles.

Susan came in with four tall oversized glasses and a green slender bottle with a dark wine within. Lydia emerged from the bathroom and poured herself a glass.

"Love the Cabernet ware. Is this some of the same we had the last time I was here?"

"No, it's a Merlot I picked up down town the other day. The guy said it was really good." Susan poured herself a glass as she stood next to Lydia. She took a sip. Lydia followed. "Oh wow," she said, and then paused, closing her eyes and then swallowed, "I like it. Good find I must say. I bet dad would love it." She proceeded to pour Jordan and me a glass, carefully handing the quarter filled crystal to our hands.

I sat with Jordan as he examined the glass with his nose. "Jordan, have you ever tried wine?"

"No." He took a sip. A sour expression possessed his face. His eyes squinted. "I'll get used to it," he grimaced.

"Merlot is a bit strong for a first timer."

"No, it is fine. I will get used to it," he persisted.

Then, in the middle of the next free flowing conversation, his glass found itself empty, begging for another splash. On the third glass, Susan ignored the indirect plea.

He clung to her like an older sister, standing in the kitchen next to the stove where Susan was preparing some peas, wobbly with his face bright red against his blond hair hanging in his face.

The dinner was perfect. Jordan talked incessantly about a guy he thought was good looking in his philosophy class, and remarked over and over how good the fish was. Lydia and I watched him enjoy the open environment while we held hands under the table. The evening was perfect. We laughed with Jordan and found his newfound experiences warming. During a short lull, I shifted focus to our host.

"Susan, you tell us about your night. How was your date?" I said, looking at her sitting across from me.

"It was nice."

Lydia never let a short answer end a conversation. "Nice. Okay. Well, what did you do?"

"We went out to Sandy's across the West Seattle freeway and had dinner. You know, it was just nice. Drinks, talking, and stuff. No loud lesbo bar or anything."

"What does she look like?"

"She's beautiful, but..."

"But what?" her hesitation this evening separated herself from the hours before.

"Oh, I don't know, not quite my type I guess. I mean, she has short black hair, too hippie."

"Now Susan, that's kinda shallow of you."

"Lydia!"

"Well, you have been on, how many dates since...?"

"A lot."

"And don't you think it's time to move on?"

I shot a look at Jordan, suddenly feeling uncomfortable and out of place. The jazz station in the background took front stage in the long silences in between. Susan stood abruptly, putting her plate in the sink and went into the bathroom. Lydia sat in place like stone. She bit her lip. The scent of candles and sound of jazz filled the space with darker tension.

"The wine was good," Jordan quietly mumbled, looking over at my plate.

"Yes," I whispered with a phlegm filled gurgle. Susan came out of the bathroom and took her seat. The music played back in the foreground until she spoke, then stepped immediately back.

"I'm sorry. I know I'm being negative, but I hate to see you like this Susan. It's just that you haven't said anything about your evening, and I wished all night you were out having a nice time, and you're just shitting on your evening now that you're asked."

"I know. But I miss her." Susan looked down at her plate fighting back tears. Lydia stood up and went around the table and put her arm around her sister.

"She was nice, but I just can't get Brandy outside my head. Every time I go out, it is just so hard."

Lydia looked up at Jordan and I. "Brandy was Susan's partner of eight years. She left her for someone else one night while she was at work. Took everything, everything...EVERYTHING, except pictures and their truck. We haven't seen or heard from her since."

"I'm sorry for being a boob guys. The last thing you needed is to come and see me act like this." Jordan held a strained expression wondering how he could help. He couldn't. Sometimes you have to let people sort through their pain.

Chapter Twelve

Seattle burned a permanent impression on my soul. In the following days, the moments I was able to get alone, I contemplated the changes it meant for our relationships. However, a growing mystery, an indefinable shadow took shape between Jordan and I, in the hours after dark. It was said without words, only spoken with glassy eyes between our bunks. Revealed by moon light, I looked over at him watching me. Painfully, I was also feeling closer to Lydia than ever.

The semester quickly moved by, and the relationships grew. We spent every free moment together after school. Surprisingly enough, there was no sense of competition between us, and never a moment's jealousy. We got private time to ourselves, with each other, and as a threesome. Lydia took on a maternal role with Jordan, matching my own subconscious paternal pattern that we both became more cognizant of as time passed.

Lydia encouraged him to attend the gay and lesbian club on campus, GALA, which is, the Gay and Lesbian Alliance. At first, he refused, saying it meant the beginning of the end. He stood by his decision, and before we knew it, the call was placed in front of Lydia and I one evening and he set up a ride with a member to his first meeting.

Of course, it wasn't that easy. He was terrified. The morning of, he was up, showered, and in the cafeteria before I had wiped the goop out of my eyes. I met him in the dining area later and asked what the rush was about. He repeated that he couldn't believe he was going, and if his parents found out, he would be pulled from school immediately. My thoughts spun with possibilities, settling on the only explanation; he had to be exaggerating.

"Jordan. Fucking relax! There isn't anyone at the University of Idaho that knows your parents to nark on you okay? Dude! You're acting like a mental case."

Then came the knock at the door at 5:30 p.m. I purposely missed the prime rib dinner hour to see him off. The cafeteria food would be picked through, but I feared that Jordan would suddenly back out and hide out at the Governor's Cup if allowed the time to think about it.

We sat on our beds looking at each other. I felt as nervous as he looked. Nevertheless, I kept my composure insisting to be the rock before his departure.

"Jordan, aren't you going to answer the door?" I whispered in a forced raspy breath leaning into the space between us. Without a word, he lunged to his feet, turned and pulled the knob. Standing at the door was a short heavyset Hispanic guy with a goatee.

"Hi. I'm Tim. You must be Jordan?" he said nervously. His complexion was far from perfect, splotches moving up past his eyes. Sweat visibly dotted on his forehead.

"Yes, that's me," he said, reaching out his hand. "Come on in." Tim slid past him and introduced himself to me. They both looked as nervous as any mouse that had entered the den of a wild cat. I didn't feel better after this scene. I pictured an assertive body building limp wrist guy in his late 20s at the door. Tim clearly lacked experience, likely even more than Jordan.

Regardless, after they left, I watched them get into a car joining two other people in the back seat. They took time to introduce themselves, with the gay splendor of it all, effeminate and overdressed, except Jordan. The car pulled away, not before I reached to call Lydia.

Before my hand touched the phone, it rang. It vibrated at the tips of my fingers.

"Hello?"

"Hello. Is Jordan there?"

"No, he is out. Can I take a message?"

"Yes, this is his mother."

"Oh hi. It's Brad, his roommate. How are you?" An uncomfortable silence followed.

"Okay. Well, can you give him a message for me?" she said, cutting off the conversation.

"Sure," I responded in monotone.

"Tell him that I finally got to talk to the Bishop of the 11th ward in Moscow. He wants to see him before the weekend. If he has any questions to call me as soon as possible."

She gave me the number, asked me to take it down twice.

"No problem Mrs. Anderson, I have the number and will get it right to him."

"Thank you." She paused and then added, "Oh yes, and tell him I sent a letter. It should be there shortly," and then there came a light click followed by silence.

"Bitch," I sputtered through the end of my lips at the receiver and hung up.

What was I to do now? This would totally set him back. Mormonism was the wall in front of everything good.

I immediately called Lydia and told her what I was thinking. We agreed the best thing was to let Jordan deal with the pressures of his church. At least then he could own his decisions.

But he was vulnerable. We rationalized that it wasn't necessarily his church, but his mother that was turning up the heat. His mother felt he had gone astray and needed to keep him roped in.

Lydia and I sat on my bed. We sat on my bed and snuggled, talking about what Jordan must be doing. It was almost 9:30 when he walked in the door. We lay there silently looking at him with small grins disclosing our excitement for information. Jordan walked to his bed and leaped onto his side. He started laughing hysterically.

"Oh my God, Oh my God, Oh my God." We watched on with curiosity, not knowing if we should laugh or not.

"What Jordan, what happened? Was it cool?"

"Oh my God," he said in one last schizophrenic craze of laughter rolling on his back, his feet off the side of his bed. "It was so wild. I mean the dance club was cool, but this was awesome. I never thought there were so many of us."

"What do you mean?" Lydia led.

"Man, oh man, there was like 23 people there. I thought I was going to shit my pants when I walked into the room. Everyone was sitting on the floor in a big circle. They were doing introductions. I found a seat between two big old lesbians. It was so scary. But they were so nice."

"Any drag queens?" I knew it was a stupid question when I asked it.

"No. I didn't see any drag queens," he added sarcastically. "If there was, they sure looked like chicks. It was really cool Brad. I want you guys to come. Friends can go too, even if you're heterosexual."

Lydia stood up and gave Jordan a hug. "Congratulations friend. I'm so proud of you." His face was bright with excitement. It was a new proud beginning for him.

Jordan left the room to go to the bathroom. Lydia sat on his bed looking at me.

"Do we tell him about the phone call?" she asked with a worried expression, placing the tips of her fingers over her mouth.

"Let's wait. I don't think it will matter right now."

Jordan returned with his hair combed. He picked up his jacket. "I want to go for a walk. You guys want to come?"

We took our jackets and headed out to tour around campus. We went through the center of campus, past the Administration Building and through town before the chill of the night forced us to return. Jordan shared the finer details of his evening; my head swam with shadows of the secret we kept.

*****

A week went by and Lydia and I failed to disclose the information, taking it from a message from his mom, to information that was building immense power the longer we withheld it. It circled in on itself. Every day we held the secret, it became virtually impossible to tell him.

It was the following Monday when I was laying on my bed reading my biology text. Jordan walked in holding the letter in his right hand. His jaw was tight, and he moved quickly about the room.

"This is fucked," he said between his teeth, "This is completely fucked. I'm hundreds of miles away and I can't get far enough from this shit."

"What's wrong?" I asked rhetorically.

"My mom writes me this letter and says that I have to join a ward. The bitch doesn't even suggest or ask. She demands! That or I don't get to stay in school. What in the hell now?"

"A ward? What are you talking about?"

"Church Brad. I have to go to church. If I don't, my father said they would stop paying. Like I said."

"Well, she can't prove it if you don't."

"She has already contacted a local bishop who I am supposed to say 'hi' to the next time I go, meaning that I'm to 'report' to the bishop so he can confirm that I am attending." He made quotation marks in the air to emphasize his point."

I contemplated the implications of telling him about the phone call with his mother, knowing that without Lydia there I was in trouble. She was much better on her feet than me. But I couldn't. I had to. I had no choice.

"You got a phone call the other night." I stood my ground.

"A phone call?" Jordan looked directly at me, "a call from the bishop?"

"No. A call from your mom. She wanted me to have you call."

"What? My mom called? What did she say?" His voice was emphatic.

"Again," I started defensively, revealing my guilty conscious, "she said she wanted you to call, and that the bishop would be calling some time."

"A panicked look took over his face. "When did she call?"

"Last week."

"Last week?! What is going on here? You don't forget shit like this. I'm so fucked Brad. Thanks a lot. She probably thinks I'm leaving the church and has sent the elders to come check up on me. Thanks, a whole fucking lot. I don't just forget to call my mom back you ass."

"What do you care? You don't want that fucked up religion anyway. I thought you were over that shit?"

Jordan's eyes took over his face, and then they reduced to a direct glare at me, leaning forward as if to take me at that very moment. He stood leaning panting with the letter in his hand, waving it in the air above his head in my direction.

"Don't you get it? I will have to quit school if they cut me off. I can't afford this on my own," he yelled.

"There is always financial aid."

"Where are you going with this? This is about you not giving me a message and now you're giving me suggestions for survival? You don't know what it is like having to talk to my mom. You don't know!"

The phone rang. Once. We stood breathless. Twice, I picked it up hoping it was Lydia.

"Brad and Jordan's room."

"Is Jordan there?" his mother said in monotone. I handed it to him. He took the receiver, the color disappearing from his face and closed his eyes. He brought the receiver to his ear and turned away from me.

Jordan said nothing at first. I could hear his mother talking to him and he confirmed everything with an occasional 'okay' and 'yes I understand'. Then he hung up. He paced the room and then suddenly but quietly left, not returning for over an hour by which time I was in bed. I heard him come in, but was too afraid of what would happen.

Chapter Thirteen

It is important at this point for me to tell you in detail the organization of the Mormon Church. It was by no accident that the following events occurred. Luck did not play its hand. Fate did, having Lydia in my life and her connection to a suspicious but willing professor to share what he knew. It is difficult to gain the knowledge I am about to disclose, as people of the Mormon faith rarely tell these details.

"Our troubled friend slipped deep into the dark quiet of his mind several weeks following the call from home. We forced ourselves to keep distant, hoping he would come around.

Then, Jordan made a move neither of us anticipated. Acting most calm, he hid all forms of bitter emotion and put forth a strongly determined happiness. He read the Book of Mormon more often, and started going to church on Sundays.

Now, I remember church as a kid, and it was an hour at the most, and two if my parents made us go to Sunday school. But Jordan was gone most of every Sunday morning and sometimes into the late afternoons.

Phone calls from the church inundated the message machine reminding Jordan of Church meetings throughout the week. On occasion people came to the room to visit him, always dressed in the same Sunday white button up shirt and plain tie, regardless of the day. The intrusion was absolutely irritating.

He didn't attend another GALA meeting and blew off the suggestion. There were a couple messages from the GALA president reminding him of dances and wondering why he had missed meetings. The second time, the disappointed voice said, "I haven't heard from you in a while and just wanted to hear your voice again. If you get time, you have my number."

Lydia and I commiserated on a plan of action. He was withdrawing more all the time, and I was getting sick of his constant phony, joyful yellow, 1950's façade. He became unrecognizable.

A cosmically endorsed gem landed straight in our laps. In conversation, Lydia discovered that her Environmental Science professor was Mormon, that he practiced years ago, and had removed himself from the church. She said he was very approachable, and that we should talk to him. After class, she inquired. He hesitated but curiously agreed, saying, "Sure, I guess. No one's asked me to discuss this before privately, but sure."

What we were to discover would emboss a dark hollow image of Jordan's situation, marking a pivotal point in our understanding.

"Good evening Dr. Brown," Lydia said as she walked into the room, holding the door for me coming in behind her. He rose from behind the dark oak desk and reached over and took my hand with both of his. It was about 8:00 p.m. An oversized ceramic coffee cup had seethed fresh with steam on top of a stack of papers to his right. On both sides of him were stacks of books and papers out of obvious order. The mark of his cup was on several papers, dried with a dark ring, old from days gone by.

After we introduced ourselves, he pointed to the chairs in front of us, and sat back in his dark swivel ribbed chair.

"Now, how can I help you. You're Lydia from my section eleven class, yes? You said you had a friend who was Mormon and that you wanted to learn about the church?" He waited no time getting to the point. He seemed pleasant but not one to waste time.

Lydia shifted in her chair, leaning inquisitively on her right elbow. "Yes. Our friend is struggling, um in trouble really, and we wanted to know if you could help us understand something about the faith?"

"Oh, I might have misunderstood. You want to help him with his faith? Well, I can't help you much with that. I'm on the other side of that fence now. I don't believe in the church and am excommunicated by my own request. I can't help you...help him...with that."

"No sir, I'm not being clear. He grew up Mormon. We are not Mormon at all. He's been moving away from the church. Is actually doing fine since being in school. He is challenging his what he has been taught. I think he is making progress and feeling better about himself.

"Feeling better...?" The professional inquired.

"But suddenly, he went back full-on into the church, and we want to understand what is going on in his head. We thought that by asking you, we could get some perspective on things, maybe understand this fucked up situation."

"Oh okay. I'm not sure I fully understand what you're asking for, but I will try to answer your questions."

"What do you want to know?" He quickly stopped, looked at us puzzled and asked, "Wait, before we go on, there is something more isn't there? I sense it. What is really the issue? Why is he questioning his beliefs? It can't be simply the academic environment at the University. This is a conservative area in itself. You must be leaving something out? You have to lay it all out for me to help."

He sat back in his chair and placed his fingertips of both hands together in front of his chin, with his elbows resting on the arm of his chair. It squeaked loudly as he went back.

"He is gay," I whispered. Dr. Brown's eyebrows rose high onto his forehead.

"Oh, well, that makes this a different, a sad, very sad case."

"We know. That is why we thought you could help us with it."

He leaned forward again in his chair and placed his clasped hands in his lap.

"I can try, but really all I can do is to help you understand the churches position. Gay men certainly have no real place in the Mormon lifestyle. Unless you grow up within the system, it is difficult to understand. The structure does not allow for singlehood, let alone being gay. Maybe it would help if I started with the basics. Then let's build."

I looked over at Lydia and nodded, and then at him, "That's fine. It is really all quite confusing. I hear people call it a cult sometimes in classes, you know, making fun of the polygamy practices with underage wives. It's hard to know what's true and not. With that kind of rumor, we certainly can't approach our friend about it."

He chuckled and rocked slightly in his chair back and forth. "I wouldn't classify the church as a cult, but certainly some fundamental Christian organizations have. As for polygamy, that is not acceptable in the church anymore. You see, the church has heavy political prowess. Polygamy was one of them. Early on, the government stepped in and told them they couldn't continue with it. The church authorities quickly accommodated, although, there still are polygamist groups that profess the Mormon tradition. The Mormon Church denounces them, having no association at all."

"You're saying that the church changes based on political climate? That sounds weak."

"Yes. Some of it is good too. They responded to the energy crisis in 1973 by rearranging their Sunday services. The original long church day required many trips back and forth to the chapel. So, it was decided that shorter services were better so less gas and power was consumed. I suppose the church sees this as their 'accommodating' the world's needs, but after you understand the importance of the structure of the church, and all its systematic ritual, it is remarkable they accommodated at all. Polygamy is easy; it is simply against the law. Still, for a religion to give up its beliefs for political purposes is indeed remarkable."

"Our friend, he has distanced himself from us, and is attending church after coming out of the closet. It is as if he never admitted to being gay at all. We can't even bring it up out of fear of how he might act. He gets phone calls to our room from members, informing him of church activities all the time. I'm not sure he remembers us or his old life at all."

"If he is getting pressure to return to the church, and he knows that is where he is going to be safe, then he will virtually forget you in order to be consistent with it. It is the only way to deal with his dissonance."

"Look, your friend obviously is in deep internal turmoil about his sexuality. He simply can't live the lifestyle and remain a believer in the Mormon gospel. Your friend has two opposing forces pulling him in opposing direction, neither of which can coexist, and he is going with the path he knows best. I mean come on; being gay is hard enough right? I have gay students in here all the time trying to deal with their family's rejection. Can you imagine having eternity held over your head?"

"Aren't most religions the same way?" Lydia asked holding her crucifix dangling in front of her.

"No. In the Mormon faith, you have no way of progressing into eternity without getting married and supporting the family structure. For most, that means having children, unless you can't of course, due to being barren, etc. They have other ways of dealing with that issue. But basically, for gay Mormons, they don't get married unless they choose to be dishonest, as I see it, and therefore don't have children.

"Mormon children start their training very young. You can compare it with going to school. They have 'grades', so to speak, that they progress through, all the way to the point of going on a mission. Every Mormon boy is trained from very young that the ultimate honor is his mission at about the age of eighteen. When they return from that mission after two years, they immediately start looking for a wife to fulfill their heavenly requirement. Children are not passive recipients in the religion, simply going to church every Sunday and then that is that. They participate as early as possible."

"You see, the structure that is placed on them is designed to control them, control them so they don't stray from the faith. The guilt associated with deviating from this path is extreme, affecting anyone who makes a conscious decision to leave. You can compare it to any kind of 'culture' that people grow up in. A person with a strong cultural identity has an ingrained scene of habit and beliefs that are predictive of the person's behavior. Furthermore, they create exclusivity, meaning that you can't date a non-Mormon because you might fall in love, and they might take you away from the church.

"Allow me to go back. Remember what I said about the structure of the church? Let me give you an example. Starting at the equivalent to the freshman year, kids start to attend seminary school. They complete four years, each year studying different parts of the Bible and Book of Mormon. Kids attend before starting public school and attend for about an hour. I can't remember exactly, it has been a long time, but the point is that this goes on every day, five days a week. In fact, it used to be that in Utah, there were breaks in the regular school day where this also took place."

"Anyway, if you take that, and add a rigorous Sunday schedule of services including sacrament and public speakers, plus if you are encouraged to only have Mormon friends, your time is totally filled up. Kids also are encouraged to participate in church choir practice if they want. Simply put, it is a hectic regiment of activity."

"Oh yes, and not to mention, that Monday nights are reserved for families. The sacredness of the family is their backbone. I hinted at this earlier, but I can't minimize it the least." The professor put his elbows on the desk and took a drink of his coffee."

"Men are commanded to support the family and be the traditional provider. Mothers are like stagehands. They make all the parts fit together, keeping the household up and raising children. Women are encouraged to stay home. It is a deeply patriarchal religion. They are taught that it is honorable to be in that place, in my mind a fucking brainwash. Sure, some are getting an education now, but not sufficient when you consider that they still end up at home for the rest of their lives raising children serving their husbands."

"So, people can't just leave it behind?" I interrupted. I glanced over and saw the intensity in Lydia's posture. Her mouth was open.

"No, not that easy. You can choose to leave, but people generally keep some ties with the church. To be taken off their books, you have to request it in writing, a monstrous feat to accomplish. I know...I tried. It took me twenty-two years."

"Your behavior can also lead to being excommunicated, a truly shameful act in the eyes of the church and the shame reaped by members. Adultery, homosexuality, murder, the basic bad shit, are some. They can re-fellowship you, which means that you have to repent, and then recommit yourself to the church. It is not an easy process because they make it a big deal.

"Another nuance of a member's belief is the power of personal testimony. To have a testimony means that you believe the church is the one and true church and that you follow it faithfully. Members profess monthly their testimony in the church and precede it by a short fast showing their commitment. If you have a testimony, you are a dedicated follower of the church, a true believer in the gospel. You have found your place."

There was a short silence as Lydia and I struggled to catch our mental faculties. "So, what happens with gay people in the church? Elaborate on that some more," Lydia asked.

"The church sees it as perversion. The only thing that can be done is repent and find a testimony."

"Perversion?" I blurted.

"Yes, although, I've heard the point debated. I remember from my upbringing fairly clearly that a practicing homosexual was denying truth in the faith, and therefore would go to the *Sons of Perdition*, the Mormon equivalent to Hell. It is a special place that is said to be absent of God, reserved for people that deny the churches' teachings and continue to live committing sins clearly outlined in the churches' doctrine as problematic. They are people that once knew the truth, but then chose to deny it decisively."

"There is this belief in a 'preexistence.' That is, there is a place prior to coming to earth where souls exist. As children are born, a spirit comes down and enters the child's body. I've heard it argued that anyone with an affliction, such as homosexuality, was once a very righteous and powerful soul, now afflicted as a test from God. I'm not totally sure about that, but I once overheard a conversation between bishops indicating such. If this is the case, it sets the stage for an interesting psychology of the homosexual Mormon."

"What do you mean?" Lydia pushed.

Dr. Brown yawned. "They're not accepted, and therefore must struggle through it to move on to a higher heaven."

"How do they do that? Does the church actually encourage them to get married?" Lydia pressed.

"It used to be so, but the leaders started to notice unhappy marriages and broken families, and all other kinds of expressions from repressed living. I mean, the dishonesty alone would drive me crazy. Anyway, they now encourage celibacy. But still, as I said before, that does not work, because in order to move higher in spiritual perfection, one has to support the institution of marriage. The degree of heaven that you make it to depends on it."

"Degree of heaven...," Lydia led.

"Well, there are three levels of heaven, the Telestial, Terrestrial, and Celestial. Telestial is the lowest heaven, similar to earth. The better you have followed the faith, the higher up you go."

"Well, this is getting confusing. When it comes to our friend, is there anything we can do? I don't see any way that this can work out from everything you said. It's like he doesn't have a choice...wouldn't you agree?" Lydia asked with hesitation.

"Wait, I don't agree with this 'not being able to choose shit,'" I added forcefully. I leaned farther forward in my chair and looked directly at each of them. "He has to choose to be himself. Like you said, there is no place for him in the church, and I think denying he is gay is eating at his integrity. I subscribe to, 'choice' because I believe we are all striving to grow and to develop integrity. Without choice, how can one have progress? I think Jordan is exercising his right to stay stuck!"

"I'm not quite sure what you mean. But if I follow correctly, you're proposing that he has a choice in the matter, a choice to walk away from the church?"

"Yes," I confirmed.

"Well, choice is an interesting idea. I chose to get away, to leave, but deep down I still have a paranoid node or two in my brain, telling me I'm wrong about the choice I made. It is inescapable. You have to remember, that his sense of identity, and therefore integrity, is wrapped up in his religious upbringing. Don't forget the idea of culture that we discussed. There is nothing shallow about the word. He really has no choice about the culture he was brought up in. The only thing he can do is de-program himself, try to reshape. But, I'm not sure it is entirely possible."

"Again, you did it. Paranoid or not, you did it."

"Yes, but I'm not a homosexual. I have a wife and two daughters. I can always go back without much consequence or punishment. Little shame comparatively involved for me if that was to happen. Maybe deep down I reserve that option as a kind of safety. If he sets out to live congruently with his sexuality, he doesn't have that liberty. So, who is he congruent with, himself or religion?"

I looked over at the oversized stack of books on the radiator below the window blocking the view. It was sinking in, the weight of his shadows he lived with. I felt it all over my body. What was there for Jordan? The realization was beating me over the back.

"Well kids, I have to get some more grading done. I hope you don't mind, and you are welcome to come back again another night. I pity your friend."

"No problem. Thank you, Dr. Brown. You have been a great help. As I have ideas, I wouldn't mind running them by you. I'm not sure about all this, but I suppose that my roommate is trapped in a way. Maybe it is hopeless, but I do want to try and help him."

He looked at me curiously and then walked us to the door.

"He has to help himself." He put his hand on my shoulder and then retreated back into his office, closing the door behind him.

Chapter Fourteen

We met at The Beanery on the first major cold blistery night of the year. Finals were approaching fast. Students studied with their faces buried deep in books and hunched over, vibrating with central nervous system stimulants, desperately trying to get an edge on the approaching competition for grades.

I left a note for Jordan to meet us. Lydia and I met early to talk about how to approach him. The meeting with Dr. Brown shook my belief that a passive approach, waiting for him to get his senses together, was the correct approach. We needed to speak our mind, tell him that he was our friend and that we wanted him back. Furthermore, the longer we didn't take up the issue, the firmer he would become and the deeper he could hide within his religion, for it was the path of least resistance.

"I'm getting myself some cocoa. Do you want anything?"

"Sure," Lydia replied. "Just have them make it with two percent instead of whole milk this time, k? I don't think my stomach can handle it."

I made my way to the counter, ordered, and stood waiting. Then unexpectedly, from behind came the palms of two icy hands on my neck. I spun around quickly with a sharp glare.

"Hey. You guys here early." Jordan laughed. When I realized who it was, I tensed up even more.

"Yeah. Left the cafeteria a little early. It was really crowded." I felt the presence of his honesty contrast with my deception. I didn't know what else to say.

"So, where are you guys sitting?" He looked around the room until he spotted Lydia. "Would you mind getting me steamed milk? I forgot my money."

"No problem," I said trying to conceal my anxiety. I waived my hand and raised my voice, trying to interrupt the server over the steamer rod. He stopped. I added to the order despite his obvious irritation.

Lydia and I were not going to be able to prep. We didn't have much to prep for except I wanted some emotional support building up to the confrontation. I had to deal with this. However, I still did not know what angle Lydia wanted to go, easy or head on.

The server passed me the drinks along the top of the counter. I pulled them to me, one in each hand, and the third balanced in-between my fingertips. I weaved my way carefully to the table trying not to trip over exposed backpacks and outside gear.

"Here you guys go." I placed the steamer in front of Jordan and handed Lydia one of the hot chocolates. They were already deep in the subject.

"I don't know why you guys are so concerned?" Jordan said seriously, looking up at me. "I've been wondering what you wanted all day. The note was just a little over the top. It's not like I'm dead." He looked up at me innocently and smiled. "I thought it was about classes, and now you're saying that you're concerned about how I'm doing? I'm doing just fine. Does it look like I'm not doing fine?"

I sat down carefully next to him, aware that if I sat next to Lydia, it might be perceived more oppositional. I let Lydia take the conversation.

"We've just noticed you haven't been around much," she said, lowering her head trying to catch his diverting eyes.

"I've been busy with school. That's all. What's the big deal?" Irritation was building in his voice.

"And church, right?"

"Yes. I've been going. What does that matter? I hope that isn't the problem."

"No. The problem is we don't ever see you. You stopped hanging out with us. What have we done? Are you mad at us? It's like right after we got back from Seattle, you disappeared into this cloud of white button up shirts and ties."

"Well, yes, I am going to church again, and I need to. You know that. My dad is going to stop helping with school if I don't. Don't you remember?"

"That's fine, but it still doesn't explain why you aren't with us ever and you are seemingly always doing something with your church. Are you avoiding us because we don't subscribe to those ideas? Do we have to join the church to see you?"

"I don't know what you mean. You're both acting crazy. Like, you're not Mormon. I wish you at least knew more about it so you would understand. I'm just busy with the church. That is all. Don't take it so personal." His voice took on a monotone irritable quality.

I turned and faced him. "Why haven't you been to any of the GALA meetings? Your friends from the group call all the time wondering if they scared you off. I cover for you, but...,"

"But what?" he huffed.

"But wondered if you actually were scared yourself."

"You said what?" Jordan's voice rose. People turned and looked at the approaching conflict. "I'm not scared."

"Yes, you are," Lydia added. "Maybe you don't understand some things about yourself my friend."

"And what would that be?"

"That you're scared of yourself. You're afraid what your parents might do, and the probability of losing everything for being what you are, gay."

"Being gay is a choice, free agency. I know you don't believe that with your sister and all, but I can't choose that lifestyle." His fist went to the table. "It isn't an option. I have been given a choice to live the gospel, and I have to, and you don't have to understand. So back the hell off."

"Oh, is it really a choice Jordan? Well, try telling that to my sister who battled with the Catholic Church for the majority of her life over her being a dyke. You tell her it is about choice Jordan. I think you're the one with problems and understanding. Failing to understand yourself, is the greatest tragedy. You are choosing away your happiness with that shit. You want to live a lie?" The tone of Lydia's voice was violent with anger but controlled.

I realized for the first time that this battle was not a simple concern for a friend. It was a battle with an institution that once stole from someone she loved, and was now stealing from another. However, the Mormon Church was a far bigger beast, one with a much more powerful and dominant infrastructure, and one with no tolerance or flexibility. Lydia's anger faced an impossible mountain of counter logic.

Then she added, "Religion should enhance a life, not make a ghost out of one. You're on your way to becoming the walking dead. Is that what you want?"

Jordan sat silent momentarily before turning to get up and leave. We followed him out into the cold air of the vestibule. He jolted to a stop and suddenly turned, causing me to almost run into him.

"You have no idea. Don't you see?! This is my only option." Fierce anger raged through the wrinkles on his face. His fingernails gripped at the air, his teeth bared with every word.

"I have to choose my church, which does not include you, or being gay. There is no in between. You try living the options Brad and dear-dear Lydia, and then tell me what you would decide."

"One big problem friend," Lydia added. "You can't choose gay away!" She stood on her toes pointing with her index finger inches from his face. "What is this shit about you not having a choice? One minute you say you do and the other you don't. Get it right."

"If you actually believe that bullshit, that there are no options, then you're delusional! You are stuck with being a faggot as much as you're stuck with that fucked up religion. It is a choice, a choice between living for your parents versus being honest with yourself. I see that the only option is honesty with yourself instead of this fucked up lie you've started. Fucked up Jordan, it's fucked up!" she yelled.

"No, I'm not going to tell them, and if continuing a lie is the only way, then I guess that is what I'll have to do. They will never know."

Jordan turned and walked away, leaving only the visible signs of his breathing in the cold night air trailing behind him. Lydia and I went back in to our table and sat down. Both of us were breathing hard from the conflict-pushed adrenaline.

"I'm sorry Brad. I got out of control." She was crying. "He is stuck in a place he may never get out of, blind to the reality within him."

"I can't believe he is so fucking ignorant. He can't run. He can't run." I shook my head looking at the grain in the varnished wood table, mesmerized by the sinking reality of what happened. We came on too strong, driven by the love we felt for him, mixed with the fear of what we knew was inevitable. Things were never going to be the same between us.

"We can't save him," Lydia said sorrowfully. "Jordan knows we're here. He has to come to us now. There will be another chance at this. I know this isn't the end."

Lydia stepped over to my side of the table and sat down in Jordan's place, pulling the chair close. She put her arm around my shoulder and played with my hair. We talked about Oakland, Alaska, and the approaching Christmas, and how lonely life was going to be living with the ghost of someone we once knew.

Part Two

"Coming Forth"

Chapter Fifteen

Elaina sat back absorbed deep in the leather couch. Her pillow had shifted to her lap. She took a long contemplative drag from her cigarette. Brad straightened his back and adjusted his sweater. Two empty teacups stared at him on his side of the coffee table. Butts, some with exposed tarred ends poked out from the pile in the ashtray. The sweet smell of smoke filled the room, adding a mild haze to the lights along the wall.

"So then, Jordan chose to walk away from his newly found gay life. That is sad. He had no chance against that religion," Elaina said, breaking Brad's swimming eyes.

"He had no other way since his birth. After the failed coffee shop intervention, I continued to struggle. I have never understood religion as a trap. If you don't like it, empower yourself to find another expression of your spirituality, right? Look at Lydia. She had her struggles with the Catholic Church. And she allowed herself the room to explore other beliefs and even attended the local Unitarians in the final year we were together. So, it was very difficult for me to understand why Jordan couldn't do the same, just pick another belief."

"He was brain-washed Brad."

"Yeah, but if you say that every Mormon is brainwashed, you're kinda overstating the matter. I don't want to say they are all freaks or something. He just needed to get out of it and didn't. He fought opposing forces that could not coexist. Furthermore, he took the weak way out. I've met other Mormon gay men since. Everyone says the same thing Elaina. That deep down they are morally wrong for making the lifestyle choice, but being honest about their sexuality is the only one they could make."

"So, what made Jordan choose the other side, the church?"

"Well, there was one part of his history I have left out. The sphere of sexuality was not new to him. Pain was nothing new, and he used to be very self-destructive. It sounds like he had a very difficult time with depression as well. Whether or not the spiritual conflict caused his mood problem is unclear"

"Wow. How did you find out?"

"One evening when we were talking, I noticed some scars on his wrists. They were old scars, probably from years back. I asked. He told me he did it in high school when first recognizing his budding sexuality. I guess the conflict was too much, growing up realizing the curse of attraction to guys. He told me about waiting in the hallways watching guys he had crushes on and his overwhelming guilt."

"Do all gay Mormons struggle like that? I'm sure there must be some out there that are at least partly adjusted, not walking around with some kind of fucked up guilt."

"I don't know. I'm sure that Jordan's way of coping isn't the rule. Some must choose the church and others sexuality, and without any conflict one-way or the other. But then there are people like Jordan who can't deal with the heaviness of the conflict, and simply are pushed over the edge."

"I don't totally buy it Brad. Lots of religions don't accept homosexuals. I think you're talking about fundamentalism."

"Yes, that is exactly what I'm talking about. Fundamentalists live in a black and white world, advocating non-acceptance of homosexuality. Most believe that homosexuals are going to hell. Worse yet, families reject their own children for their religious beliefs. It is unnatural. That is where I draw the line."

"I'd not be in the religion."

"What if you were brought up in the religion and believed through elaborate upbringing in this particular church that you had no way to express your spirituality, but through this one true church?"

"I don't know, I really don't know. I don't think that question can be answered until we were both in that position."

Elaina sat forward and lit another cigarette. She flicked the first ashes in the tray and cupped her hands together, holding the cigarette between her knuckles. She needed time to process the weight of the information.

"What happened after the meeting at The Beanery?"

Brad got up and poured another cup of tea for the both of them, pausing to stretch his arms high above his head, then out and back to his sides.

"Jordan put on this superficial attitude, acting like nothing happened. He continued to involve himself with the church, and after Christmas break he became especially devoted to his nightly Bible reading activities. His circle of friends changed, broadened, all of them exactly like him religiously. He was gone every night studying with his Mormon companions or attending Mormon singles group. It didn't take me long to get over being angry, and I knew that I couldn't stay in that emotional place. That is when I met you in our Communications 201 Class. Remember?"

"Yes. That was the shittiest of all classes. Remember that short frump of a teacher? She was bad, very bad. And Chris, my boyfriend? He hated us spending so much time together. And of course, there was Henri and his entourage of friends. Yeah. There were some cool parties. I even remember the day you got those two beasts."

Sebastian and Marty held each other close, curled up tight in the bay window hanging over the street. They spent many hours watching traffic and the occasional passing dog. When they weren't sleeping with Brad, this was the chosen location for rest.

"Yeah. Those were good times. I'm sad it all ended so quickly. The past few years have not been the same."

"But what ever happened to you and Lydia. Things really seemed so crazy before I had to go. Were you able to remain friends? I thought you guys were going to try to go to London. What happened there?"

"Yeah. We were going to go and visit one of my mother's cousins there."

"So, then you didn't?"

"No, that is where life got complicated. There is a lot I still have not told you Elaina. Lydia and I worked through some very difficult issues. Up until you left, the relationship was getting way serious. But, we also had no contact with Jordan. Umm, well, he just absorbed himself in this church."

"And that was our party year!" She added, not seeming to notice the slip of his comparison.

"Damn those were the days. Tell me, why does life have to get so heavy, almost darker as we get older?"

"I don't know. I wonder about that sometimes too. But hey, get back to the story buster."

Brad adjusted his sweater again and sat back to relax in his chair. Before going on with his story, he asked for another cigarette from Elaina, and again lit it from hers while taking several long slow drags. He tried to collect his thoughts. There was so much he wanted to say, so much that required explanation.

He pulled his right leg up from underneath him, leaned over to flick off the first ash into the tray, and began.

Chapter Sixteen

The semester ended in late May. Having already packed my oversized collection equating to six boxes of books, clothing, and memorabilia from just one full year of college, Lydia helped me move to the house on Third Street.

I loved that house. I can still smell the heavy painted walls and hear the whispers of the rusty pipes inside. Those days remain burned in my mind. I continue to romance that house, having the privilege to live among the walls, and feel a bittersweet sadness when I walk by there at night. Oh, how beautiful was the rain stained cedar siding.

The freedom and innocence of college life dances in my heart even now as I recall it. Life seemed to begin then, nothing approximating it since. The fiscal responsibilities of adulthood are daunting. I am exhausted at times over the pressure to perform in a work world that does not recognize hard work or quality. No one told us it was so Machiavellian.

In school, I was in complete control of the outcome. If I studied enough and spent time with my head in the subjects, I got the benefit of the grade. In the work world, I find that ultimate control is in the corporation's hands, the buyer's choice, not based on my hard work or quality.

Anyway, Lydia and I decided not to live together. The relationship was budding, and we did feel close with trust, but neither one was willing to take that step. A deeper wisdom spoke, one deeper than we could know at the time, a truth that events would tell.

She had a good living arrangement in her dorm. It was wise to not leave to start living the off-campus world. She said, without necessity, for I did not need the convincing, that everything was close, and it was ultimately a money saver for her. At least by me having an apartment, she now had a place to stay when she wanted escape.

WITHOUT A TESTIMONY

I settled in fast. Henri and I became instant friends. I was intrigued with his Swiss background and magnetic open personality. My elbow supported my heavy head in classes from previous nights of intellectual conversation with Henri. We covered it all. There was very little he couldn't relate to. It was his gift.

The true magic was seen in his ability to listen. He drew information out into the open like a syringe, interested in perspective, sharing just enough to keep things going. Henri was a guy who had nothing to prove or argue. He loved to take it all in. We talked about cosmology, what our lives might look like in the next ten years, and of course, spirituality.

Jordan on the other hand, returned home for the summer. In the final days moving out of the dorm, he became a stranger. The more he involved himself with his church, the less room there was for outsiders. Discomfort led to avoidance, and avoidance led to a complete communication shut down. Neither of us knew what to say anymore. The entire semester was awkward.

The day I moved out, he was not there. I hesitated about whether or not to stay to say goodbye, but instead wrote a note with my new phone number and address.

Lydia and I were now free to explore our relationship. However, not having the common focus of another's troubles brought out several problems of our own.

But, before I digress, it is important to first explain the spiritual exploration that Lydia and I embarked on. It was a foundation from the beginning. We became consumed with spiritual conversation. And in our quest for answers, Lydia found an answer of her own.

It also reflected the kind of relationship we nurtured, largely intellectual with us both attracted to the other's thinking process. We did not focus on the physical aspects of the relationship. We had a sexual relationship for a few

137

months, but it didn't keep me up at night wondering when we were going to have sex again. Nor did sex between us satisfy my core. I attributed it to the intellectual complexity in the relationship, not realizing that the infrequent intimacy was becoming problematic for her.

One Sunday morning, soon after moving in, Lydia called and asked me if I wanted to go to church.

"Hey there big guy. How are you this morning? I hope you're not still sleeping."

"I looked over at the clock. It was 8:36 am. I flopped my head back on the bed, resting the phone on my ear. My hand found comfort between my knees where it was warm. My eyes closed hoping more drifts into the oblivious. "No, I'm here. What's up?" It was hopeless to hide the irritation in my demeanor.

"I talked to my friend Sasha the other day and she was telling me about this really cool church. I was wondering if you wanted to check it out."

"Church? Now? You thought of this when? What the hell are you talking about?"

"The Unitarian Church. It is just up the street from you on Polk. She said they are…"

"Unitarian?"

"Yes, they are a hip open group that is not really Christian or anything really. Just a group of cool people I guess."

"A cult?"

"What?"

"Kidding. Okay, what time?"

"I'll pick you up at quarter to eleven."

"Sure," I moaned.

"Now be ready Brad."

"I will."

I pushed the off button on the phone and put on the edge of the mattress. I drifted back into sleep for a short time, only to be jolted by the sound of Lydia at my bedroom door yelling at me.

"Get up and move." I was going as the disheveled other half.

We parked alongside the road on the opposite side of the church. I stared at the scattered stream of people entering the modest looking white washed building engaged in conversation, while children ran amok in the lawn. Crowds, a growing nuisance in my life; it wasn't going to be an overly pleasant experience.

The sign in front hung by rusted chains in between two white washed wooden posts reading "Unitarian Universalist Congregation of Moscow".

Nothing was impressive about the building or the people. They were dressed in casual street clothes with only the occasional few wearing suits and dresses. No one carried Bibles, and I saw no visible crosses around people's necks as we followed the mob into the building. A greeter handed Lydia and I a pamphlet, and a woman dressed in a formal robe shook our hand as we entered the foyer. "Welcome," she said quietly with a pleasant sincere smile.

We found ourselves in a chapel with pews lined up on each side of us. I directed Lydia to the back right, a natural and inconspicuous location. She followed knowing that anywhere else was deeply uncomfortable for me.

In the front of the room was a pulpit draped with a cloth hanging from the front edge with the word, "LOVE" in big felt purple letters. Lydia leaned over to my ear, pulling me towards her by my shoulder.

"What do you think?"

"I don't know. It seems nice," I said keeping my gaze up front and chin high. The pews were filling up fast. A man played flowing music on the piano in the front left of the room. The overwhelming smell of people and old wood reminded me of Christmas Eve services with my mom.

I looked down at the purple pamphlet in my hand and opened it. The first section gave contact information followed by "What we believe".

It read, "Universalism is a religious movement promoting the belief that every person will go to heaven. We believe that each person, because of her/his humanity inherently has dignity and self-worth." And further, "We uphold the free search for the truth. We will not be bound by statements of belief. We do not ask members to subscribe to a creed. Universalism is a non-creedal religion. Ours is free faith."

"Lydia," I whispered as people were sitting down all around us, "...this is different. Have you looked at the pamphlet?"

"Brad," she said in a normal voice, "you don't have to whisper." I looked around and saw that people all around us were engaged in conversation. The minister was walking up towards the front. The next thing I knew, we were standing up. Lydia pulled me towards her again.

"Let's talk about this over coffee okay?" She returned her gaze forward just when the minister started with, "Welcome. We are gathered here today out of love and a need for community to express our spiritual beliefs in openness. Turn to your neighbor and greet them today in love, welcoming them to our community being old or new." Suddenly there was a rush around me of people talking and saying hello. An older gentleman looked at me from the next pew and put out his hand.

The entire service took only about forty-five minutes. Much to my liking, Lydia and I ducked out quickly ahead of the mass of people and headed to our car.

"Thanks. It was really cool, but I needed to get away from all that."

"I figured. But what did you think?" She sounded excited. Lydia turned the key and the engine struggled to turn over, and then finally choked its way to a loud

Volkswagen purr. She took Third Street, turning left on main finding a space in The Beanery parking lot. The weather was beautiful, so we decided to sit outside with our drinks after ordering.

"I was really impressed with the church Lydia. It was strange because it screams a Christian structure, but it isn't Christian at all really. Like, it has pews, the minister is called a minister and she has a robe on, kind of like the Episcopalians. They sing songs. But looking beyond that, I saw that the songs were about peace, calling on people's individual spiritual expression and stuff. It was really weird but cool. Could take some getting used to. The people were nice. I had no idea such a thing existed. I'll bet the Christians don't accept it, say it's sacrilegious for sure!"

"Some do. Sasha was telling me that Unitarians are a mix of all kinds. Apparently, there are Christian Unitarians, Buddhist Unitarians, Muslim Unitarians, and Atheist Unitarians."

"Yeah, sure. What about Mormon ones. I'll bet they don't have Mormon Unitarians. I'm sure," I said sarcastically.

"I don't know, but I'll bet there has to be one."

"Baaaa…can't be…anyway. How did this church come about anyway? I mean, I've never heard about it until now?"

"Well, apparently, the church has its origins in Catholicism. There was this guy named Miguel Servetus who wrote against the idea of the trinity. He was put to death and then the church emerged later in Transylvania. That is where the term Unitarian came from. It meant the 'believers in one God, not three'. Then the church had some followers in Holland that sparked ideas in England, where it then came to the United State, I believe Sasha said Pennsylvania."

"Wow. You've really checked into this. I'm surprised. Do you think it is the answer?"

"I don't know. But I think it is the most accepting I've seen yet. I'm just checking it out. Don't you think these are neat ideas?" Lydia said.

"Yes, but ultimately, all religions don't accept certain things."

"Like murder?"

"No," I said back uncovering the irritation stewing within me. "How about people like Jordan."

"Actually, the Universalists are completely accepting of homosexuals. They even have homosexual ministers."

"But what if the congregation has a problem with it?" I retorted.

"It doesn't matter. The church's stance is openness and acceptance. I'm actually hoping to talk more to my sister about it. And someday maybe Jordan. I'm drawn to the idea because of him. Don't you think this could be a good place for him...if it is that open? Don't you think it is tragic that he can't get into something like this?"

"Dude, Jordan is brainwashed. He believes there is no other way. I think he would die before ever turning away from his church. It is that deep. You cannot fool yourself about the grip of that cult. Remember, we've been over that. You have to let go. He doesn't think he has an option other than what he is living. Denying himself and his identity is an acceptable sacrifice."

"Even when it means that being gay is as much who he is as being Mormon?" She questioned. "Why does dishonesty win? Where is the integrity in that?"

Lydia took my hand and I pulled her in tight. I kissed her on the cheek. We sat drinking our coffee and watched people pass by, listening to clips of conversation over springtime traffic.

Chapter Seventeen

Summer quickly turned into Autumn, bringing with her longer nights and cold mornings. The deciduous trees turned to the beauty of shorter days and slumber, and the colors painted the skyline, leaving scattered remains to the street.

Moving from October and into the ice of November, the cozy depths of long wool over coats, gloves, and scarves welcomed many intimate moments for Lydia and me. There were evenings after classes when we sat parked in front of senseless television programs, or sometimes finding ourselves walking downtown hand-in-hand. We rarely spent time with friends, only going out in public to see the occasional campus play, or small venue orchestra.

We also shared a deeper exploration of spirituality through the Unitarian Universalist Church of Moscow. After almost a year and a half of dating, we found a meaningful kinship. However, a festering conflict started to burrow its way to the surface, a conflict that was the beginning of great pain for both of us.

All great relationship journeys peak before their inevitable demise. I remember our pinnacle moment as if I were there now. It was a perfect evening, draped with romantic glitter, just before Christmas break leading into the second half of our sophomore year, the semester that would change everything.

We were dressed in our best evening clothing. She was beautiful, well over the standards of the typical college student. She had on a white evening gown with a cream hand knit shawl that at the ends hung tassels loosely covering her breasts. The perfume was light, accenting the natural sent of her skin. Anyone would be proud to be seen with her, and tonight it was me.

I, in contrast, wore the most standard black slacks and white shirt. We ate at the eclectic bistro style restaurant called the Beatnik Café. They specialized in Italian cuisine. We acted like it was our first date, with the accompaniment of anxiety as a third wheel.

The room was lit with a yellow and orange hue. Music from the 40s and 50s era played in the background. Waiting at the door only momentarily for our table, the smell of pasta and spicy meat danced around us.

"Norland and Richards?" the thin older gentleman called, holding two menus under his arm, extending out an open palm, looking at us over thin glasses down his nose.

"Yes, that is us." I took Lydia's hand. We walked down and around the corner to a row of booths in the center of the large room. He sat us at the table, pulling Lydia's chair out for her and placed two menus on the table.

"Oh, sir and madam, I am sorry."

I looked around trying to figure out what he was talking about. He then motioned towards the paper tablecloth. It had some crayon marks on it. The paper was not dirty at all, but clearly, the table had not been reset.

"I can take this away for you."

"Oh no," I said waving my hand in the air, fingers pointing down loosely, "It's not a problem."

The waiter looked relieved. A can of crayons of assorted colors sat in the middle of the table, apparently used to artistically render the table.

"Well, then, I am Morten, and I will be your server tonight. What can I start you off to drink?"

"Umm, this might be a stupid question, but what Chianti do you have this evening."

"We have several, but the one I recommend is a very nice 1987 vintage. It is a Classico that is quite popular at the Beatnik." The waiter had the slightest of accent, not Italian but quite difficult to identify.

"That sounds good. Lydia, should we get a bottle?"

"Yes, that would be nice." The waiter quickly sauntered off to the back and past a sectioned off entryway. The distinct sound of dish against dish and stove top pans worked magic on the other side.

Her arms were delicately folded on the table, one over the other. She looked at me with her typical poignant but gentle gaze. Her light red lipstick had a gloss in the candlelight. We were deeply present sharing the total experience of the evening, as if we were the only couple in the room.

The waiter quickly returned with two tall, thinly drawn crystal wine glasses, and a bottle with a distinctive white label and red-black lettering. He carefully cut the foil from the neck and put in the screw, forcefully pulling out the cork. He then took the towel over his arm and wrapped it over the shoulder of the bottle and poured the glasses about a third full.

The waiter politely interrupted a few minutes later and asked what we wanted to order. We agreed that the night's special, Fettuccini Alfredo with broiled chicken would be a perfect complement to the wine. The waiter politely put a bottle of sparkling water between us after popping off the top.

"This is a carbonated natural spring water, compliments of the house, to have with your dinner. Can I get you anything else for now?"

"No, I think we are fine," Lydia answered. He left leaving us to talk.

"Brad, this place is so nice. I'm glad you suggested it. You never like doing this kind of thing. What got into you?"

"I don't know. Just thought it would be nice. I'm not very good at it, but guys take their girlfriends out all the time, don't they? All we every do is go to church or stay home parked in front of the political debates on channel eleven." I said sarcastically. "Thought it'd be a nice send off."

"Well, I'm impressed. I was wondering if I should ask, but you beat me to the punch."

"Thank you."

"Brad, can we talk about personal stuff? I wanted to ask you about your family. You're going home, and you never really talk about them in any depth. What are you parents like, you know, besides the basics, work. I remember you talking about your gay uncle, but what is everyone else like, really like?"

"My mom is the greatest. We are closest. She has been the biggest influence on my life. It was so hard for me to come to Moscow and start school. I wanted to throw in the towel a couple of times, but she encouraged me to hang in there."

"It is so interesting to hear you say that. You hide your pain very well. I sometimes wonder if you have emotions that deep."

"I hope you don't totally believe that. I don't express them very well. But you have gotten to know me."

"Sure, but really Brad, it's strange because you hardly ever share anything of substance with me. I like the closeness and the walks and everything, but sometimes it is nice to hear how you feel, you know?"

I quickly realized what she was saying and dreaded the direction it was taking. It was familiar feedback and an area I hoped I wouldn't have to deal with between Lydia and me. Intimacy was to be avoided, the type of intimacy that leads to forever. It was reserved for the very few and only when one was certain. I was not certain, and hadn't acknowledged the point, nor wanted to. Now she was asking to go deeper, and I had to give. Physical intimacy, nights at concerts or our bodies entangled on the couch did not amount to the depth that she was looking for. I was not in love. Nor had I told her.

"I agree, that I'm not good at it. My dad is that way too. In my family it is all about our heads. We are debaters. Besides my mom, I don't feel close to anyone."

"You cared about Jordan." I didn't know what to say. I sat back and kept my eyes on the candle ahead.

"Growing up we argued over politics and social policy all the time. That is why I started to bring up my mom. We have always had a very special connection. She has been so supportive of me over the years. I want that with you too. Maybe I don't know how." I was lying.

"That is how me and my dad have been. I mean, we have such different lives, but it is so nice that we can meet middle ground. He is quite supportive, but not as radical as I am about worldviews. He doesn't understand Environmental Science at all. I don't understand the business world."

Lydia talked about her father in length. Unlike me, she referred to her parents frequently, how her mother died when she was young, how her father was a broker and brilliant businessman in Oakland.

"I want you to meet him some day." She reached and took my arm. I relaxed feeling the subject would go in safe direction.

"I would like that. Is he planning to come out for your graduation this year?" Lydia was in her senior year and already talking about other academic options. Graduation was something we hadn't really considered. It would potentially mean us not being together for long periods of time as she left for a job or graduate school.

Lydia looked down at the table. "Yes, he wouldn't miss it for the world."

"We have to face that you are going before me," I said with some caution.

"Yeah, I don't know what our relationship will look like at that point." She was direct, continuing to hold my arm.

"I don't know either," I said. "Let's cross that bridge when we get there okay?"

"Yeah. We can. But Brad, I'm going to say this, and I don't mean it to sound strange."

"Yes?" My gut took a twist with an anticipated blow.

"I'm thinking about going an extra semester to get a few more classes under my belt before I move onto a graduate program. You have to know that I'm not making this decision because of us."

"I think that is a great idea." The words were bitter sweet.

"I have to be honest Brad, our relationship does influence my decision in part. It will be so hard to be away from you. I know we can handle anything together, but it will just be hard." Her eyes were wet. The sensation of guilt floated in my chest.

Dinner arrived, after which we sat and ate in silence, except for the occasional comment about the incredible meal. The wine was a perfect addition, accenting every point, but it was hard to enjoy with all I wanted to say. I was drinking most of the bottle, and after the second glass not tasting the nuances of the wine or the meal. Lydia worked her glass down appropriately and said nothing with each refill. She sensed the uncomfortable movements in my face and comments, the dishonesty and hiding behind the blanket of alcohol.

We finished the meal, declining dessert and instead asked for an after-dinner coffee. The waiter brought the small cups with saucers and placed the black plastic folder on the table in silence. The coffee was heavy with thin dark foam around the inside rim. Both being exhausted by the hollow silence, we entered a safe conversation about next semester's classes. We quickly finished. I took the check, paid the waiter, leaving a substantial tip before leaving.

"Lydia," I said turning her towards me, "I want you to come over to my place tonight. It's been a long time."

WITHOUT A TESTIMONY

The wine was commanding me to smooth out the concerns of the evening. Evasively, the type that only an intoxicated person believes is covert, I plotted to take Lydia home, take things further than the simplest of affections. She took me by the neck and pushed her tongue into my mouth as we stood on the street in front of the restaurant. I was taken by the scent of mild roses and the taste of coffee.

Chapter Eighteen

The 747 Alaska Airlines passenger jet banked hard left, hit some mild turbulence and then banked hard left again. No sooner did we leave the ground from Wrangell Airport, did the engines quiet, beginning our decent into Petersburg. As we cruised lower, I looked out through the rain-splattered window and noticed the long flat marshy land stretching out towards the bay. The plane touched down with a hard bump and the brakes engaged with a violent jerk. My body leaned forward momentarily as we quickly slowed down.

We exited off the front of the plain, down the stairs into the rain. I had packed my jacket in my suitcase; I was covered only by my wool sweater and a pair of jeans that were instantly damp. The baggage cart waited at the bottom of the stairs. I took my small carry-on bag and went quickly towards the entrance. My mom was there to greet me. My dad stood back behind all the people with his hands in his pockets, talking with friends.

I put down my bag and held her tight. Her hair was shorter, and with a little more white than I remembered it. I didn't like the realization, noticing the signs of my parents aging. There was guilt knowing that I was establishing my life out in the world, while they remained home. No part of home is supposed to every change. It is the rock we compare our day-to-day life against. Somehow, we delude ourselves into believing that everyone's age is a stable as the place we are from.

"Hi mom," I said not letting go of her too quickly. "I like the new cut."

"Oh, it is a little short for my taste, but I'll get used to it. Glad you're home safe. How was the trip? Not too bumpy I hope?" In the small crowd of about fifteen people was a mixture of ghosts from my childhood. My high school biology teacher, the librarian that no one liked, and classmates that opted to stay island bound after graduation, waited patiently to pick up family from the flight. I desperately wanted out of room cluttered with my past, hating cordial requirements. If I had my way, there would be a special limo at the gate, whisking me to my home to avoid the social paparazzi.

"It was fine I guess. Always a little bumpy after Ketchikan. I hate that trip more and more the older I get."

"Older you get. You're still young my boy. Don't get to hating it too much, we won't be seeing much of you," she laughed. My dad broke away and pushed his way through the crowd.

"Well how are you doing Son?" He pulled me close to his rail thin body and gave me a quick hug. "You killing them down there with your brains?"

"Yeah, I guess so," I said with my gloved fisted confidence. My fingers were sweaty.

"You like your classes? I bet there are a lot of idiot academics working at that hippy hole." My dad laughed loudly. "You're going to fit right in boy."

My dad liked to give me a hard time about going the academic route. He himself was a very practical man who worked with his hands his whole life. Let alone, his son was an English major going into Journalism. That did not make much sense to a man who made his living and supported his family doing backbreaking work. Ultimately, he didn't want anything different for me. He realized early on that the academic life would lead to a lot more happiness.

After the luggage came off the plane, my dad and I loaded the bags on the flat bed of his quarter ton truck. We piled in the front seat and headed home.

I was an only child growing up in a family with parents that were active community members. My mom was in nursing, and as I indicated before, my dad was a private contractor in the area. He worked on several projects at a time, including the new high school and renovations at the hospital. Both of them were highly respected.

As I said before, my family and I were skilled at debate, especially when discussing social issues. We were also close. However, we were not absent from problems. The most tragic was a brother that died at birth, an older brother, about a year before me. My mom had a breached labor, causing the baby to die from extended anoxia. It was very hard on her and came up in conversation off and on over the years. To this day she expresses an unfathomable guilt I can't understand.

Both my parents grew up in Petersburg, with my mom's parents emigrating from England in the late 1800's and my dad's grandparents from Germany. My grandparents died when I was in grade school, so I did not have the opportunity to form strong relationships with them. However, I do have some good childhood memories.

My mom's closest confidant was her sister Morine who lived just two houses down. She taught the sixth grade at the elementary school. As kids we just called her, "Morey" for short because it sounded more natural. She seldom minded the reference unless I ran into her at school. Yes, they were very close indeed. Every morning my mother and Morine got up before dawn and walked together, and every morning after that she came home and showered up and went to coffee with Morey at the Olaf Café. I myself shared this closeness with Morey. However, in recent years I had grown distant.

And then there was my mom's other sibling Harold who used to live in Petersburg until he was twenty-five. He was about ten years younger than my mom, so I was lucky to remember the time up until he left. That was the year he came out of the closet, and it was a real drama for the small island community to handle.

WITHOUT A TESTIMONY

Harold was one of the most remarkable people I remembered growing up. Now, he is a writer living in San Francisco doing freelance screenplay writing. He is the primary reason I decided to go into English. When I was a little kid, he used to lie next to me before I went to sleep and read me a story of my choosing. Books were his life, and they quickly became mine as he always sent them as birthday and Christmas presents.

The car turned down the dirt road and into the driveway of my house. To my glee, it hadn't changed a bit. Barking and ready for the kill, ran Mickey, the golden retriever of my adolescence. He was getting old and couldn't move very fast, but still performed one hell of a welcome for new arrivals.

I got out of the car and greeted him as my dad went to the back and pulled off my two bags. We walked my stuff into the bottom entrance that entered his shop, and then a door leading to the rest of the house.

The house itself was quite simple. The outer wood was dark cream in color and in two levels. As you go inside from the shop, you pass two bedrooms that led to the bottom of a spiral staircase to the living room and kitchen. Joined at the end is the master bedroom and bath. There was also a stairway outside the house leading to the second story, one that we rarely used except to bring wood inside for the stove.

My room was downstairs, very secluded and quiet. My parents went upstairs, leaving me to get reacquainted. I took off my jacket, threw it onto the floor and took a quick look at the room. My mom left everything as it was when I left. I took in the smell, overpowered by it, remembering all the good things from the years spent there. Why do things have to change, get complicated, force responsibility? Taking off my shoes, I went up the spiral stairway and directly to the kitchen.

"A little hungry, are you?" she said as she came to me and gave me another hug. I stood at the refrigerator, pondering my first attack. "It is good to have you home. I need someone to eat up all the crap in the cupboards. With that lead gut of yours, I'm sure you can do the job."

"God yes. I'm starving." I made myself a sandwich and my mom disappeared into the back room.

"Hey, I'm headed down to get some groceries, don't suppose you want to come?"

"No, I think I'll stay and kick back a bit. Maybe unpack some things." I was already in the grips of the television watching the morning news.

"Okay. Anything you want?"

"No, I think I'm fine," I said.

She finished getting ready and before I knew it, it was just me, the TV, and my sandwich. My dad had driven back to work somewhere in town and would certainly return periodically, but for now, it was quiet.

The room was heavily arranged with Christmas decorations. In the far-left corner of the living room was the Christmas tree, covered with ornaments from my parent's childhood and mine. It was amazing how old most of the decorations were, antiques my mom kept from even her mother's belongings after she passed. In the bay window between the TV and the tree were pictures of my family laced with running Christmas lights. The holidays were a wonderful time of year. I, in particular, favored Halloween, but for my mom, Christmas was when she went all out.

The phone rang. At first I hesitated to answer it knowing it had to be someone who heard I was in town. Word spreads fast in a population just under two thousand.

"Hello, this is Brad."

"Hi there honey, how are you?" At first, I didn't recognize the voice.

"Hi, I'm fine. Who is this?"

"Brad. It's Lydia."

"Oh my God! I'm so sorry. How are you?"

"I'm fine. I was thinking about you and wanted to know if you made it home safe."

"It was a shitty flight, but I'm here safe and sound. There is a lot of snow on the mountains, but the sky is clear. I'm glad because I didn't want to deal with the flight over heading to Juneau and having to catch a fucking ferry if the weather was going to be bad." I sounded angry; I heard it in my own voice. But I wasn't.

"That would suck."

"Yeah, but I made it. It feels good to be home, but kinda strange really. I don't know why."

"It keeps getting weirder Brad. Believe me. I'm back in Oakland. It just isn't the same as it was when I was in high school. You get used to it."

"Yeah." I didn't want to talk to her. I didn't know how to get out of it, but took the route of a lie. "I'm going out with my mom to the store, so I gotta go. Can I call you in a couple of days?"

"Oh yeah, I just wanted to see that you made it home safe. Say 'hi' to your mom for me okay?" She had never met my mom.

"I will." We hung up without exchanging any endearments. This was becoming increasingly difficult for me. I relaxed in the wing-backed chair and started a fierce channel surfing session before heading down to my bedroom to unpack my belongings. I let Mickey in, so he could follow me around. He made for loyal undemanding company.

A few days went by, and after spending time at my friend Tim's house over late-night movies, my need to be around people was drawing thin. Tim was one of my best friends in high school. His dad was my band instructor, and we played the same instrument, the trombone. Our relationship was competitive in nature and most our conversation was spent over reminiscing first-chair band battles. He was the only friend I spent any amount of time with on my vacation, and that isn't saying much. And, as fate would have it, shadows in daylight were lurking about.

Tim and I were sitting on his couch watching a movie on his parents' new VCR. It had four player heads and was marketed as having a much better picture compared to what we had at our home. Tim emphatically pointed this fact out to me repeatedly.

Well, as we were sitting next to each other, I started to drift off. We watched Monty Pythons Holy Grail for what seemed the hundredth time, and this didn't seem to have any better quality than the ones before, but I wasn't about to say. My head leaned into his shoulder. He nudged me with his elbow.

"Hey faggot, don't put your head on me." I look up to find him standing away from the couch. Apparently, he did not know that I was sleeping.

"I looked at him bewildered. "I didn't. I was just..."

"Yes, you did Brad. You're gay. Everyone says you're a faggot. Don't try that shit with me."

I was honestly completely shocked. It was not unusual for Tim to fly off the handle about stupid shit. He typically called later, not to apologize, but to request my presence at his house. The only difference was that we fought over whose turn it was to pay for movies or simple inconsiderate acts. But this time, he hit me low, accusing me of coming on to him, and said that people were talking. There was no defending myself.

I got in my car and pulled out of the driveway, almost getting hit by a passing group of kids in a bronco.

"Fucking idiot," They yelled, one kid sticking his head and middle finger out of the backseat window as they drove off. It was a group of school kids, much of whom I did not recognize.

"I hate this fucking town," I said out loud as the sound of the rear drive gear made its familiar whine. I turned and pealed out onto the road.

When I got home, my mom was sitting at the kitchen table, working on bills, looking at me through her reading glasses. She immediately identified my irritation.

"You're home early. How was the movie?"

"It was fine." I plopped myself down in the wing backed chair, took the remote control from the coffee table to my right, and turned on the TV. I shifted through the channels, looking for any kind of distraction. But in reality, it was impossible for me to get away from my thoughts. What was Tim telling people? What had he heard about my sexuality? How did they know? I had a girlfriend. There was no way. What had my mom heard? I couldn't talk to her about it. It was too much too fast.

"Brad, there is a message from Lydia on the machine for you. I saved it."

"That's okay."

My mom sat out of sight inconspicuously, waiting for me to give the signal that it was time to talk, but I worked diligently at not giving in to it. I felt her watching.

"I think I'm going out for a walk." I said, needing an escape.

"Well, I was about to go out too. Can I join you?" she said as she got up and walked over to her shoes. I rolled my eyes and put on my jacket. She grabbed two sets of earmuffs and handed me the green pair, keeping the pink for herself. I put on my scarf and zipped up my jacket tight to my chin.

Walking down the outside stairs, both of us carefully made our way watching for ice hidden in the dark on the wood. I felt the hard lumps under my feet, the sound of some loosening as I stepped.

Safe at the bottom, I pulled my gloves tight to my fingers. The motion sensor light kicked on, illuminating the front yard. Crystals speckled the pavement leading to the road. My dad had thrown a layer of salt in the driveway. However, he clearly had forgotten the steps.

He was already in bed. It was customary for him to turn in before seven every evening. The life of a contractor started early. Growing up, the evening hours were between mom and me, quality time together, sitting over quite conversation, the television, or long walks.

I stuffed my hands deep inside my coat pockets and pulled my shoulders high to ward off the cold nights air. As we moved out of the shadows of the trees, the blue and orange hue of the streetlights lit the street with only intermittent darkness.

"Well, are you already thinking about your home in Moscow?"

"No," I answered defensively.

My mom bumped into me and looked up with a serious smile. "Now, don't you get prissy with me sonny bunny. You don't have to be a sour puss with me!" She turned and continued walking, waiting for my move.

"I'm fine."

"To hell you are. Now what's the problem? We don't need any of this behavior."

"I'm just sick of this place."

"Well, we can get you on a plane tomorrow if you want, since it is too unbearable to be home." The guilt tactic was her most wicked weapon.

"I don't mean it that way," I huffed.

"Well then, spit it out. What's going on? You get into one of your fights with Tim?"

Then she probed more aggressively. "You and Lydia having problems? Your dad asked me earlier because she sounded concerned that you hadn't called her back in a few days."

"Yes, it's her and everything I suppose."

"Well..."

"I..."

"I'll wait, but Brad, don't keep me from the truth too long. I may be old, but I'm not entirely dumb. I see things."

"Okaaaay." No, she couldn't. Retreat, I needed to retreat. "How have you been mom?"

We continued our walk in lighter conversation about my dad's work and drama at the hospital. She took my arm and we walked locked together side by side. Tension subsided. She didn't ask again for the rest of the walk, and we were able to put it, at least in part, to the side.

It wasn't until we got home when she confronted me head on. After taking off my outside attire, I retired to the kitchen table and perused through a maze of upright Christmas cards, ignoring the contents actually, and who they were from. One caught my eye; it was from my mother's cousin Harold in London. Every year he sent her a card inviting her to come and visit. I remembered when I was about seven he came to visit.

My mom went to the cupboard and took out two cream colored coffee cups with the familiar flower pattern from my childhood. She went down the black rod iron circular stairway to the pantry and returned with a can of cream. Pouring the cups about three fourths full, she diluted them slightly with water and placed one in the microwave. Walking over to the TV, she turned it on and shifted through channels to the evening news. The TV was white noise that constantly filled in the space, leaving you feeling naked without it.

The microwave beeped three times. She poured three teaspoons of sugar in the cup and added powdered chocolate and gave it a stiff stir. The she handed it to me and finished with hers. After everything was set in place, the atmosphere, and the sink clean once again, she took her place on the other side of the table.

"Brad, don't you think it is time? Now I know you don't want to tell me, but it is time we put some words to all this craziness." The news filled in the space; it couldn't drown out the breathless words in my head. I was cornered, no way out.

My chest felt tight. The red color in my cheeks from the cold night's air must have disappeared with the rush of anxiety. I looked directly at her wondering if we were thinking about the same thing, knowing our minds connected, but words hadn't. "Mom, I don't know what to say." A tightening pain gripped at my throat. Warmth flooded my eyes. My lips become thick.

"You're not telling me anything I don't already know."

"Mom?" Tears flowed as I tried to hide in my coffee cup, wishing for an escape.

She got up from her seat and came over, placing her hand on my back. She moved it in a circular motion. I looked up and saw tears hanging off her chin. I pulled myself into her belly. I didn't want to let go, ever.

A brief moment of fear shot through me thinking about my dad walking out, but I knew it was not probable unless he got up to use the bathroom. Even then, he rarely came out into the living room and kitchen when he did.

"How did you know?"

She pulled away and took some tissue paper from the box on the counter, gave me a delicate handful, and sat down again.

"Oh, I've known for quite some time. I think I was a little thrown off when you would call and talk about Lydia. But I knew it was inevitable. There was no way it could work out between you."

"Why didn't you say anything?"

"What could I say? It can't be any other way. I knew though. It was time. This was the year, during this trip home, I knew you were going to tell me. I'm just sad you had such a hard time telling me."

"Mom, I don't want this, but it is becoming impossible to keep to myself. I thought if I went to school, I could find a girlfriend and make it go away. It just keeps getting worse. Lydia and I have been having problems. She has been talking about us being together on a permanent basis. At first it seemed like the solution. Then it started making me feel wrong. Wrong, like a bad lie. I can't keep living this lie with her."

"She can't be that stupid. Women know these things. How do you keep it from her?"

"I don't know. She has to know something. Maybe she is as afraid as I am to bring it up."

"Brad, don't drag it out too long. I don't care how understanding she might be, but this is a world of hurt for you both if you don't tell her."

"I will, but I don't know what will happen. I really want to wait."

Black streaks marked her face. I pointed. She snickered and started crying again.

"I just want you to be happy. It is so hard. I lived through it with my brother, and the longer you hide, the worse. Is Tim aware?"

"Well, apparently everyone is because he insinuated that people were talking."

"I've overheard a few things, but nothing out of the ordinary."

"Out of the ordinary? What do you mean?"

"Oh, Tim's mom and I were at coffee with the girls the other day and she said something. I was talking about your girlfriend and they joked that they always thought you walked on the other side of the fence. God, what a thing to tell a mother. She is such an audacious bitch. They were happy you were not a waste." My mom started to laugh, and I found my jaw wide open.

"Wow."

"And Brad, let's face it. You're not as 007 as you think. You've never had that manly way about you. I think lots of people passed it off as you just being smart and an only child. You're cultured for this little Alaskan town."

My mom hadn't touched her hot chocolate. It was getting cold. She stood up and went to the microwave. She signaled to me asking if I wanted a warm up as well. I shook my head.

"I know I need to, need to tell her. It is just that I was planning on a trip over spring break, and now I'm sure she will not want to go if I first spilled the beans and then asked her. It was going to be a surprise. How would that be, "Hi honey. I'm gay and let's take a trip together." God, this gets so complicated.

"The sooner you say something the better, Brad. You're right about that."

"The second I tell the world mom, I don't know if I'm ready for everything that goes along with it."

"What about your old roommate? He handled it, at least at first, and you don't have a religion to hold you back. And whatever you do, you have our support."

I looked at her startled at the comment. "Mom, oh my Hell, does dad know?"

"We have talked about it," she said with some caution. I felt suddenly dizzy.

"What did he say?" My heart pounded heavy.

"He, like me, has not been stupid about these matters. Your dad and I share the same concern. We just want you to be happy, and when I started putting things together several years ago, I didn't feel ashamed, or angry, but sad that you would live a much more difficult life. It hasn't been easy for my brother, and I don't expect it to be easy for you."

"Mom, I didn't plan on being gay. I had no intention to tell you, but I'm so tired of hiding, exhausted with lying. After watching Jordan go through it, I was so worried."

"You have our support, that is the difference. When it is right, I want you to talk to your dad."

"Mom, I can't..." I started to cry again.

"Brad, you have to. Don't wait for him to say it. He loves you and I know he doesn't have the words any more than you do. Don't take his avoidance as a failure. I will tell him about our conversation tomorrow. Your road will be well paved."

"Okay." I went to her and we embraced each other for a moment before my mom pushed me back to look up at my face.

"And don't neglect Lydia. Do it in person. You know it is better if you tell her now. The longer you wait the worse. You're going to break her heart." She went to the kitchen and placed her cup in the sink. "Now, where were you planning on going? I hope not Palm Beach. Too many guys on the beach and you need to stay focused." We both laughed. Her lightness was a relief.

"What do you think about London? It would be my first trip to Europe, and Elaina tells me it is a must see. Wouldn't it be cool!? I'd be the first to go back, the first in our family!"

"Oh Brad, that is a fine Idea. But if you're going, don't waste it on spring break vacation. That is way too short. You have to spend a couple of weeks. If you want, I will write Harold a letter and get some ideas of dates after the semester. There is going to be two of you right?"

"If she wants to go."

"I don't think you should wait that long to tell her. That will drag this whole thing out way to long. Anyway, it goes, I will ask him to prepare for you and a friend."

"Yes, but don't you think it would be kinda weird for him if I bring a girl and then he finds out I'm gay?"

"No, Harold would not care about you being Gay. She will be considered a friend until you tell him otherwise Brad."

"I'm going to talk to Lydia before we go and give her the opportunity to decide if she wants to take the trip. That will make the trip more honest."

"Well, and if she decides that she can't deal with it, then you can go on alone."

"You mean I can go then?" I confirmed.

"Didn't I already say that. Of course! I think we can scrape up some funds. Does Lydia have the means?"

"Yes, I'm sure she does."

That night, I slept heavier than I had since the beginning of my vacation. I felt more at home knowing barriers had been taken down. I had my mother's unconditional acceptance and support. The prospect of dealing with old classmates also waned. For what did it matter what they thought anymore. They had no tools to use against me, the clearer I became with myself, through the honesty I now possessed with my family.

The next morning, I looked out to a glaring sea of white ground stretching from my house, blending into the mountains in the background. The outline of curves gave the illusion that they were much closer than before. The sky was bright blue into a white horizon, and dust cast off the mountaintops.

I heard the TV blaring upstairs. My dad's truck was gone, signaling it was safe, that he was still out with his friends over morning coffee. Footprints marked his path to tracks of his truck in the driveway. My mom's tracks went from the front steps down the street. Mickey sauntered around the front yard. His yellow distinguished markings expressed his protective rounds.

It was Christmas Eve day and I hadn't yet wrapped the presents I brought from Moscow. I stumbled to the bathroom and put on a pair of pants and t-shirt, then walked out into the shop area to go into my mother's storage closet where she kept her Christmas paper. I poked around the many shelves, pushing back old cobwebs until I found it back behind the canned cream and dog food.

Now I had to find the tape. I ran upstairs to the utility drawer. There was a role on top with not more than an inch to give. Then I remembered my desk. I ran back to the bedroom and after opening and slamming two empty draws, I finally found a large roll of clear packing tape. It was the same roll I used to pack my six boxes in preparation for college.

Sitting on my bed, I opened the small blue cardboard velvet box and took another look at the opal necklace. It was my mom's favorite birthstone, even though it was not hers. I think that was garnet. She wore it regardless. One can't choose their parents, but they can choose their birthstone. I carefully wrapped it in the paper and fastened it with strips from the oversized tape role.

My dad was a much more challenging person to buy for. He had every tool imaginable in his shop. There was no need for the labor. Instead I resorted to music. He loved 1920's Swing, and this year I decided to buy him a compilation box collection. The previous year, I got him a Big Band collection. I caught him many times playing them while working in the shop on his small low fidelity, white paint splotched radio.

I quickly ran the packages upstairs and placed them under the tree. New gifts leaned against the base. My mom was hard at work that night. Also hanging up on the wall behind the tree were three empty stockings. The lights on the tree faded in and out in a rhythmic pattern. I went over to the kitchen table to find a round of Christmas bread with a knife lying next to a bowel of butter and the cutting board. It was not my favorite, but it signaled that Christmas time was here.

It was about an hour later when the rumble of my dad's truck came down the road. He was not usually home until the afternoon. Maybe the snow was keeping him from getting any work done.

He pulled into the driveway and spent several minutes outside and then in his shop. The door from the shop opened and then slowly closed. He took quiet footsteps and stopped at about where my bedroom was. My dad was looking to talk to me. Coming up the staircase, I kept my gaze on the TV and acted tired, my knees tucked in tight. Could I ward him off? He stood at the top of the stairs, my back to him.

"Well, I know what's been going on around here."

If I could have seen my own face in that very moment, I'm sure it was a cross between terror and the look of a man about to have a psychotic break. I don't think I took a breath for well over ten minutes. I turned and watched him approach me.

"Did you hear me Son? I know what's been going on around here son. And…"

"What? What's been going on?" The words came out high pitched and dry. This is not how it was supposed to happen. I wanted to get to Moscow without having to go through the conversation. Was there any probability that he was referring to something else?

He sat down across from me on the couch next to the Christmas tree. He crossed his legs, causing his red and black-checkered work jacket to bunch up under his chin. He had on his daily work clothing consisting of patched up jeans and a flannel shirt, wool socks and boat shoes.

"Son," my father said looking at the floor far in front of him and then up at my bloodless face, "You know we are proud of ya and I don't care about gayness. You're still my son and I love ya." My anxiety was not getting better. My attention turned to worrying about him, his feelings, and disappointments.

"I'm sorry dad."

"You don't have to say nothin! You're my son. I think it is funny though. You could have any women you want. I don't understand that part. But, it doesn't matter. I'm proud of ya." With that, he got up and passed in front of me, putting his hand on my head, messing up my hair worse than it already was. Then, without any movements indicating his intention, he returned and put his arms around me. My eyes welled up with tears as he turned and started out the front door.

"Oh, I was thinking, your aunt has that snowmobile. Let's take it out tonight. Maybe we can outrun some cops!" He snickered in his characteristic way and closed the door behind him.

I sat in the chair, rocking back and forth, my knees pulled up into my chest, stunned and slightly overwhelmed by what had taken place. But I knew that I had what Jordan did not, the unconditional love from my family, and a confidence that I could fall on them in whatever situation and any time I needed.

Chapter Nineteen

There was no delay leaving Petersburg. The plane made the normal milk run of small island towns on time. Two and a half hours after departure, I was in Seattle, and then on to Moscow. I got back to the house around ten in the evening. The length of the trip was spent in waiting between each stop. I read the leaflets in the seat in front of me, repeatedly, until I couldn't take in another sight of fancy razors and chessboards or language courses.

I walked into my room and threw my suitcase to the floor in exhaustion. I sat on the bed and unlaced my damp shoes, releasing my bloodless feet. My socks were damp and my toes cold from missed landings between puddles all day getting on and off planes. I put on my gray sweats and a pair of loose fitting wool stockings and pulled down the thickest sweater from my closet. The time display on my stereo was blinking 4:13 p.m. The power must have gone out while I was away. I reached over, almost falling off my bed and reset the time with the small black buttons along the bottom.

Being back felt good, but there was a sense of impending doom hovering over me. Each time I returned from a trip home, I felt that Moscow was becoming my own. However, this time there was unfinished business that had to be addressed. Just as going back to Alaska was never going to be the same, no longer was my life in Moscow going to be the same after the truth was told. I left Petersburg in my own consciousness, self-actualized, the mask put deep tucked inside my pocket. Moscow was next on the docket.

"Hey Buddy," came the monotone, stoned cigarette smelling clothing from behind. "Did you have a good Holiday man?" It was Henri. He roomed with us starting last summer, at first taking several nights on the couch, until we invited him to stay. The financial collaboration of rent, even though he rarely paid on time, or his portion, was helpful.

I think about him the most when recalling those days, his pale skin, large bags under his eyes, and the sour body odor mixed densely with cheap cigarettes. I don't think he ever wore socks in the house, even in the winter on our cold hardwood floors. And then there were his sleeping habits. Henri didn't hold down a job due to the difficulty of getting a work visa. He went to class and slept much of the time when he wasn't at other people's apartments drinking their beer. Otherwise, he was rarely seen outside of his cage.

"Yes, it was nice to see everyone. Had an okay time." He stood in the door leaning against the frame. He pulled the cigarette pack from his shirt pocket, took one out and lit it.

Before putting the pack back, he asked, "Do you want one?"

"No thanks."

He sat at the end of my bed and I slid back putting my back against the wall. "You don't sound overly excited man."

"Oh, it was okay. I guess there are a lot of things going on, but I don't know what to do about it all." Henri could handle it. He was a confidant. That is why we loved him so dearly.

"So, did you spend time with your folks?" he probed.

"I did. I guess...there was this big issue we danced around for most of it. I don't know what I want to say about it though." I threw out a hook.

"Hey man, I can handle it. You say what you want man." He leaned forward on his knees and took a long drag off his cigarette. "Whatever you're all fucked up about, I think it's sad you didn't have the best time seeing your family."

"In some ways, you can say we broke through some big stuff. It's like the end result is great, but the issue has started something I don't know I can stop."

"Oh, well, hey man, I don't know if you'd be pissed if I said it, but..."

"What?" I put my hand on my forehead, pushing my hair up into the air.

"Man, don't take this the wrong way, but it is not as if I don't know what you're jabbering on about."

"Jabbering? You sure pick up a lot of slang for a Swiss guy."

"Man, you don't have to hide it from me. I knew you were a poof when we first met."

"A poof." I put my hand back down, resting my forearm on my elevated knee.

"Yes, a homosexual. Don't be pissed, but man, you're not completely obvious, but I knew."

"Does Elaina know?"

"Yes. Man, all over Europe, this isn't such the big fucking deal like here man. You don't have to worry about the puritan shit in most places. Did you know that prior to World War Two there was a huge homosexual movement in Germany? You don't have to worry. I think we have only talked about it once or twice. We haven't talked to anyone else. That is up to you. It is a non-issue cuz it don't matter buddy."

"I can't believe this Henri. The last thing I want is for everyone to know. Fuck! My parents know. Lydia probably does, and if she doesn't, she is going to. It is faster than I can deal with."

"You don't have to worry about the house man. You have good friends buddy." A long tube of ash fell to the carpet. He didn't notice.

"So, tell me what gave me away?"

"Brad, it wasn't what you said or your mannerisms. It was what you didn't do. It's like you have this girlfriend.

You never talk about her breasts or her beautiful ass. Brad, your girlfriend is fucking beautiful. When we watch TV, you don't talk about the hot babes. That is what tells people."

"Fuck."

"It is time you be yourself man." He put his hand on my foot and took another long drag. His eyes marbled like glass.

He quietly stood up and took a step toward the living room. I wasn't ready for him to leave.

"Henri, what should I do about Lydia?" I said quietly, almost in a whisper.

"Tell her. You're hurting that girl. And I want a date."

He laughed. I felt stuck in a dream state. Henri always appeared in the optimal moments when I needed him, and like a phantom, disappeared, leaving cigarette smoke and ashes as the only evidence of his presence.

I sat up in bed reading my mail over candlelight. The phone rang around 11:45, disturbing my calm. I wanted to be left alone. The house was quiet with only me awake to answer. I tiptoed into the living room and crossed the floor without a sound.

"Hello," I said whispering into the receiver.

"Brad! You're home! Oh my God! How was your trip?" It was Lydia. She was ecstatic.

"I'm fine, long trip, glad to be home. I'm tired though. Elaina went to bed a little while ago and I'm just catching up on some mail. How was Oakland?" I figured that if I asked about her trip first, we would not get into mine.

"It was wonderful. But hey, I don't want to talk about me. When can I come over and see you?"

"Tonight is bad. I'm no good for anything but sleep. How about tomorrow? Do you want to meet me for lunch?"

"That's fine." Her voice lowered. I knew I had to do better than that.

"Actually, let's do breakfast. Want to come pick me up? We can get something downtown."

"Good, I can't wait to see you. I got you the coolest Christmas present. You will just love it darling! So, get some sleep. I'll be there around 9:30. What do you say we catch something to eat at the University Inn?"

"Okay. So good night then."

"Okay sweetheart. Sleep good okay?" She sounded fragile almost desperate, clinging onto something that was at risk. The decisiveness and strength were missing. Or was I making it up in my head?

"Okay." I hung up. The pleasantness of the night faded into darkness. How could I tell her? When was there going to be a right time?

I flopped myself on my bed, brushing the white and brown envelopes to the floor. The candles remained lit. I lay on my side with my arm tucked underneath my head watching their orange and yellow glow. Suddenly I was back home in the company of my mom in my own home, with the scent of the Christmas tree and freshly cut Christmas bread and hot chocolate swathing around me. The voice of my mom's soothing words echoed inside of me. With detached curiosity, another voice spoke, a male voice, calling me, vaguely familiar, soothing, but distant. Not my father's. No, not my father's.

*****

The University Inn was flooded with people for a typical early Sunday morning. The afterhours church crowd must have decided to come early. We stood in line for twenty minutes waiting for a booth. People were dressed well, we, on the other hand, were about as grungy as any college student from the hill.

At first sight of Lydia I was fidgety and overly talkative about random topics ranging from the weather to the effects of the January light regime on mood. By the time we got seated, I was calm enough to stay on a topic for more than two minutes. Funny enough, Lydia was keeping up with me just fine.

We ordered our food and then she took charge.

"There are some things we should talk about," she pressed. "I don't mean to lay this big heavy on you the day you get back, but I think it is time we talked about us."

"Us? Okay," I said passively, playing the part of the unaware lamb.

"Brad, I'm not sure what is wrong with you, but something has changed."

"What do you mean?" I shifted myself in my seat and took off my jacket.

"You know what I mean. You have seriously changed. I mean, maybe I've changed too, but I just don't understand why you are treating me so bad. You're so distant."

"I'm..."

"You don't have to make up anything. I just wanted to make my point. Brad, is it because of our conversation before you left for Alaska? It seems to me that that was when it all turned around. You hardly ever wanted to talk to me on the phone. You didn't want to see me last night after being gone for over three weeks. What the hell? Am I scaring you off by talking so much about the future?"

"No." I didn't know how to respond. This was my opportunity and if I was going to be honest, I had to take it.

"No..." Lydia scowled and put her hands underneath the table as she leaned forward. "Is that all you have to say?" she yelled.

"No...I mean...I don't know what to say," I said sheepishly. "I have felt different..."

"Different...," she said indirectly.

"Yes, different. There has been something on my mind, something I've been meaning to tell you."

She didn't respond this time, except with her eyes keeping up with my face as I continue to avoid her. My heart was beating so fast I thought I was going to get sick.

"I want to take you to London to see my mother's cousin. My mom has the money for me to go, but I needed to find out if you have the funds to go to."

"What?" she said, rolling her eyes and throwing herself back in her chair. "You're kidding. You can't be serious. You're being all fucking weirded out because you want me to go on a trip with you."

"Yeah," I said with a smile. I victimized her like a jackal clever with artful deceit, less out of avoidance for hurting her, but more out of my own self-preservation. London was shelter. I was safe for now.

Lydia sat in silence with a petite smile. I wondered if she was going to call bullshit and if my face could hold the lie. Then, confirming my worst fears she said, "Oh Brad, that is such a perfect Idea. When did you want to go?"

"I was thinking May when classes get out. It is the best time because it won't be so cold, according to my mom anyway. I thought about spring break, but there isn't enough time to really enjoy it, especially when we consider jet lag." Shame filled my gut from the ease and fluidity of my antisocial act.

"My dad can help me. I'll call him right away. I've never been to London. Tell me all about it Brad. How did you decide on London?"

"Well, as I said, my mom's cousin Harold lives there. He is a really neat guy and no one from my family has been back since immigrating to the United States. If I go, I will be the first person to go back. That would be so cool."

"Sure, well, that means we have a great place to stay and get to see northern Europe." She said this with such emphasis, pursuing her excitement. "You know, I have no idea why that was such a big deal for you to ask me. We are in a good place, aren't we?"

"Yes, I think we are, but you have to understand, I felt funny about the money. If I was going to ask you to go, I thought I should somehow help pay or something." I said.

"That is silly."

We quickly finished breakfast and agreed that a drive was in order. We headed out of town towards Pullman, enjoying the rolling hills of the Palouse. It was desolate with ice but extraordinarily beautiful with the mountains in the background. I held her hand and we discussed more in-depth plans for our trip and dreamt of what we might see. London was the land of tall buildings and green countryside cottages. Lydia was particularly fascinated with the prospect.

The day's light was starting to fade when I said that I needed to spend time at home. I excused myself, telling her I needed to finish unpacking and spend time with my roomies. She gave me little protest. Lydia dropped me off on the street. I got out of the car and started up the stairs.

"Hey, aren't you going to give me a little something before taking off, Mr.?" Turning back unable to avoid her, I put on a smile and walked to the driver's side window, put my head inside the car and gave her a small kiss on her cheek. She attempted to direct it to her mouth, but I moved my head aside. I tried to cover the evasive move with a long deep hug.

Setting my keys on the arm of the sofa, I sat down in front of the twelve-inch TV screen and took in a deep breath. From the left, the red blinking light on the answering machine caught my attention. My mind was pulsating with psychological pressure. I didn't want to talk to anyone for fear of uninvited complications.

Nothing presented itself as interesting on the four channels we had. I pushed the up-channel button repeatedly, somehow wishing that on the next round a different program would be on. We needed cable.

But then the picking at my brain, like a seagull eating the first scavenged catch of the day, questioned who had left the message. The house was empty. The rest of the day was completely absent of must do events. Maybe it was my mom. Shit, I forgot to call her to let her know of my safe arrival.

I forced myself up from the sofa. The lunge caused my head to spin. I pressed the play button and walked into the kitchen. The tape made a winding sound and then its notorious loud beep.

"Hello. This message is for Brad." Initially I couldn't distinguish the voice. But then... "Found your number and wanted to catch up. I'm just calling to say hi. Thinking about you and hoped we could connect. It is Sunday, and I'm in my room. Hope to hear from you soon."

Chapter Twenty

He walked up the street, well dressed, but not in his typical Sunday attire of white button-up shirt, tie and dark slacks. Instead, he wore a pair of jeans that hung over new loafers, and his usual long campus coat. A dark blue turtleneck ribbed sweater showed from the color of his coat. It matched his straight evenly cut blond hair.

I sat on the top step watching his approach. When he saw me, he smiled, took his hands out of his pockets and ran up the stairs. I stood and met him as he quickly put his arms around me.

"Hi! It is so good to see you. What are you doing out in this crazy cold weather! It's freezing Brad. Let's get in," he said pulling his shoulders high and clenching his fists. I opened the door and followed him into the living room. The sun was starting to go down, with the west window now flooded with white-yellow light. We pulled off Jackets. He put his on the floor next to the door and kicked off his shoes as if he were in a race. I took the chair, leaving the couch to him. He quickly sat down, not without making a run against the hardwood floor with his wool socks.

"Yeah, the floor can be very slick. My mom got me some slippers because I complained so much about it."

"How is your mom?"

"She is fine. It was one of the best Christmas breaks ever! My parents were great, and..."

"Brad, you're glowing."

"Yeah, it was a bit of a transition time, you could say." I recognized the confused look on his face and continued. "I've changed a lot since high school."

"Yeah, my break was weird. My dad hardly said two words to me, and my mom just wasn't happy I was there. Oh, I, I'm sure she was, but I don't get what's going on with them. Every time I tell them about my schooling, they act only mildly interested. My mom asked me for the fifty billionth time about going on a mission, and I got a little mad about it. It pisses a guy off to have to go over it again and again you know. So needless to say, I'm happy to get back to school. The dorms leave a lot to be desired, but hey, it beats Oakley."

"Did you have to get a new roommate?"

"No, I requested a single, and since I'm a sophomore, they gave it to me. I really like it. Dude, there is no way I could have dealt with living in the same room with another guy again. You were easy. Most guys are just too damn strange. How about Lydia? How is she?"

"Fine. I had breakfast with her this morning. She is doing fine, really." I didn't know what else to say.

"Well then, how are you guys doing? You don't seem too excited about it." He sat with his legs crossed and arm over the back of the couch. I looked up at his usual sandy blond hair hanging in his face. He pushed it back, looking at me with his dark brown eyes.

"We are fine I guess."

"I guess? Mmm. That sounds convincing. Your favorite word as I remember, 'fine,'" he emphasized
"I can tell you about it later," I groaned.

"Okay, okay," he held up his hand in the air, "Sorry for pushing."

"No, you're not. Sorry, it is too complicated to get into right now." There was no way I could easily tell Jordan about my evolving self-awareness. This was the guy who couldn't be honest with himself, let alone with what I wanted to affirm to him.

"How about yourself Jordan? What are you up to lately? It was sure nice to hear from you. Shocking really?"

"Oh, getting ready for the next semester. I have a full load and hope I can keep up the good grades. Same old shit."

"Still busy with church stuff?"

"No," he said looking away from me.

"Are you still going?"

"Not been. Tired of it. They keep putting pressure on me, pressure in the wrong way. I came back determined to back off again. I'm so bloody sick of everyone asking me to the singles group. I don't need to be saved that way."

"Well, does anyone know you're gay?"

"Heck no! It would be all over for me Brad. What, do you think I'm crazy? I've got the act down perfect. My parents are buying it now. It is time to relax a little, kick back."

"If you're not interested in going anymore, then what's it matter?"

"He looked around the room. "Hey, this is a nice place."

"Yes, it is really nice I must say. We have a lot of friends that pop in and out, and Elaina is great. A little eccentric, but great. She's from Belgium."

"Where is she now. I'd love to meet her."

"I guess over at her friend Amelia's house, some friend from Paris. She wanted to see her cuz she flew in this afternoon. But man, she's a bitch. I've met her once, and Elaina thinks she is great. I can't say I understand it."

"Wow, this is the regular old international household."

"Yup!"

"You just got back yesterday yourself, didn't you?"

"Yeah, still recovering a bit. But, very glad to be back. Hey, do you want anything to drink? I have lots of bottled water and soda?"

"Sure, but you know, what sounds even better?"

"What?"

"Hot chocolate. Do you have any?"

I went to the kitchen and took a look through the cupboards. It was bear with the exception of a box of powdered Dutch Chocolate. There was canned milk in the refrigerator and plenty of sugar.

"Hey, I scored!" I yelled from the kitchen. Jordan came in and stood next to me as I took two cups and started.

"This is my mom's way of doing it. I don't know if I can get it just like hers, but hey, how bad can it turn out?" I mixed the ingredients and put the cups in the microwave and waited for the beep.

"It looks strong." He stood close. Very close, standing against the counter as the cups rotated in front of us. The smell of his cologne drew me in. The hum stopped. I reached out, opened the door and gave him his cup.

He went over to the kitchen table and sat down with his hand cupping his chin with a contemplative look on his face. "I have something I want to talk to you about."

"What?" I said as I took my seat across from him, intently trying to hide my curiosity.

"I'm...," he hesitated with a pained look forming on his face. "I am really sorry for how I treated you. I don't know what got into me...no I do...I was freaked out after Seattle."

"Jordan, I don't care. I haven't stopped thinking about you. You and I," no that's not what I meant, "you and I and Lydia had such a great friendship. It didn't stop when you left. I mean, I hurt at first. It really pissed me off that you walked away so easily, but maybe somehow I knew you would come back."

"I walked away because I didn't have a choice in my mind. My church is all I have."

"That's bullshit." I sneered, trying to catch his diverting eyes.

"Brad, it isn't. You can't understand what it is like for me. If you listen, I will explain."

Anger surfaced into the full force of my voice.

"No, there is no way, no way you can explain it. I can't understand why you walked away! You put on such the happy-go-lucky clown act, took on new friends, and didn't have anything to do with me. The fact that you can sit in that seat and say you still believe in your church says you can, and will, do it again!"

Jordan stood up, his leg hitting underneath the table, causing the hot chocolate from my cup to slosh onto the unfinished wood table already smeared with past affliction.

"Brad, if you're going to be an ass about it, I can leave. I'm trying to say I'm sorry. I just want you back. I want your forgiveness." He stood with a stern stance leaning towards me. His finger waved at me as he said, "And if you can't deal with letting go of what I did, then I was wrong about you and we never had much of a friendship to start with."

He turned and left the kitchen, walking over to his gear next to the door. I followed quickly behind, took his arm, and pulled him into me, at first holding tight as he struggled and then feeling him melt. He started to cry. His hands moved onto the middle of my back.

"I just don't know what to do Brad." I released him, wanting to hold him longer, but not wanting to give away my own secret before its time. "I'm trapped between these two things. If I say, 'fuck it' to the church and come out, it is over for me."

"That isn't true. There are other churches…"

"You don't know. You can't shake it. It is beaten into my head. It is the one true church. I'm a fag. I've known it forever. The church and being a fag can't coexist. There is a closed door on both sides, can't you see? We have Testimony meetings every month and members stand before the congregation and tell their story of faith, each professing, *'This is the one true church and I believe in its teachings,* dot-dot-dot.'"

Jordan started yelling, gesturing in the air, and started pacing back and forth in front of me, then tilting side-to-side a couple of steps at a time.

"Jordan, you can't walk away from yourself. You are who you are. Face it, they can't accept you, but I..."

"What do you know about being gay?" His finger was pointing at me, coming down just over my head. I started to step back, and he slowly put his arm down. Suddenly he went to the couch and sat on the end. I sat next to him, not too close, but at a reach. My feelings were overcoming me. I wanted to yell at his stupidity and at the same time hold him close. But he couldn't know that.

"I..."

"You don't Brad. I have two worlds and I have no choice. It is hell in the church or hell in living the truth of my sexuality. I suppose if I do choose hell with the church, I can be Mormon and celibate. But then that wouldn't work because I couldn't climb to any heaven without getting married and having children. Don't you get it? There is no place for me."

"Then leave the church!" I said with a loss of tolerance.

"If I could, I would. For now, I don't know what I'm going to do. For now, I'm going to stop attending services. I can't have a testimony being stuck in this place. My mom will find out when she calls the Bishop and he tells her that he hasn't seen me. Then the shit will fly. Who knows what then?"

"Jordan, I want to be your friend, but I can't handle you running off like that again. Can you promise me you will not leave me dry even if you start back with the church like you did last time?"

"I can't promise anything to anybody right now.

I sat back and watched him hold back his rage with glimpses of it slipping in and out of his behavior. We sat in silence, me watching him as he looked at the floor. Then, with the gentlest of touches, he reached over and took my hand from my lap. I pulled him towards me when at that moment a light knock came from the door. We both stood up quickly, caught.

Jordan pulled down his sleeve and wiped his eyes. It was hopeless as they were crimson red. He took the chair adjacent to the couch and I went to the door, slowly pulling it open. Lydia stood looking at me blankly in the shadow of the porch.

"Hi. I hope you don't mind the intrusion. I thought I would stop by and see what you were up to. Can I come in?" I opened the door the rest of the way and gave her a quick but unassuming hug.

"Hey, you won't believe who has dropped in." She gently smiled and walked into the room. Jordan ran to her and they embraced before I could take another step back.

"Oh my God. You look so good Jordan. How are you my dear old friend?" She said as she held onto his shoulders and pushed him back to get a look. "I was wondering when we were going to see you again."

"Been fine, fine." The smile made his eyes squint as he took her hand and led her to the couch, she was his princess, he her prince. I took the chair, blending into the background, allowing them to catch up. Watching them together again was like seeing an episode from a sit com, depicting two beautiful people I loved with a deep experiential connection. The three of us were united once again.

I went into the kitchen quietly and unnoticed, and fixed Lydia a hot chocolate, and reheated the two left behind on the kitchen table. Holding onto two cups and balancing one by the handle with my thumb, I slowly walked them in, placing theirs on the coffee table in front of the couch. They barely noticed my presence but simultaneously reached over and took a hold of the rounded handles, not taking eye contact off of each other for a moment.

"Hey, I think we should go take a walk. It's been forever since the three of us did that together. What do you think Brad?"

"Yeah, what do you think there 'Bradly' boy?" Jordan said laughing at me with eyes wide and intent on brightening the moment.

"Let's finish our drinks and get the fuck out of here." Lydia turned and looked at me taking in a deep breath, indicating shock at my language around Jordan.

Looking into my cup, I spied the layer of burnt milk on the surface. I carefully took a swallow, a big swallow, taking the rubbery mixture in my mouth. I kept drinking, finishing it off. It was getting cold and finding that irritating, I put the cup on the table and stood up in a start. "Okay, let's go. You guys aren't drinking anything and it's going to get really cold outside before we know it, so I suggest go now."

Their conversation stopped suddenly and without hesitation, putting on their shoes and coats. I followed and went out onto the porch to wait, while Lydia went into the bathroom. Jordan stepped out with me, quietly, trying to conceal his movements. But why? What did it matter?

He came close to me, his breath visible in the confines of the darkness. "Hey, don't be mad," he whispered. "We can talk later." He briefly cupped his hand on the back of my arm and turned to go back inside. I heard the toilet flush. Standing alone I looked out over the overgrown maple tree in the neighbor's yard, the wires running along the top hummed. I was content for a moment, holding onto the warmth of his touch, the gesture.

Starting down the street, Lydia walked between us as she did so many times before, pushing her arms through ours, and locking us together. Conversation flowed from there, all of us discussing our trips home and dreams about spring.

"And Brad invited me to London for summer break to visit his mother's cousin. That is going to be so cool." She said as she pulled me in.

"You lucky cow," he replied.

I didn't want Jordan to know. He was going to find out in time, but his knowing meant he would begin to believe thing were fine between Lydia and I, and if anything, it was going to be easier if he didn't.

The conflict brewing tortured me with every moment I breathed. The movements in my chest, the feeling in my legs, the gentle swelling of my groin every time I saw him, smelled him, touched him, and thought about him, possessed me with romantic obsession. It took me from the moment I heard his voice on the answering machine. The feelings not allowed disclosure were making me a prisoner. There was more than friendship in my heart. I could only wish the same was happening to him.

Chapter Twenty-One

The first day of the semester was always bittersweet. The Spring semester of my sophomore year was no exception. It doesn't come fast enough, lying in bed dreaming of exciting new classes and the thrill of moving farther into my major. Excitement was always followed by bursts of dread slamming me in the gut, the nature of the competition for the grade, whether or not I could perform, beat the best, especially myself.

My alarm went off at 6:30 am. Rolling over, inches from a fatal plunge to the floor, I threw my feet down and forced myself to a standing position, saluting the day. I sat back down. "What the fuck?"

Stumbling into the bathroom, I pulled off my underwear and t-shirt, and desperately reached for the water knobs in the tub. I let it run long enough to rub the dried mucous from the corner of my eyes and pulled up the shower plunger. The shower spurted then finally in full force, giving me the go ahead to venture in. It was still cold. I pulled the shower curtain behind me and created a seal against the hard water stained tile wall.

You know, showering in the summer time is never a problem. When you get out, you feel warm, enjoying the walk out into the open world. Showers in January are akin to slow miserable steps into the bowels of hell. Stepping in is torturous enough, but when the plunger is pushed back into the facet, the sudden shivering cold air moving in, shocks you into a misery that only a blanket and a warm mattress can cure.

And on that first morning of classes, I made the absolute worst mistake a morning grump never should. I forgot my towel that still slept heavy and warm in the laundry basket in the corner of my bedroom. "Fuck."

I shook off the water the best I could and pulled on my night clothes, thick with water from the shower gone AWOL. With a few choice sinful words, I danced on my toes to the bedroom, grabbed the oversized towel, peeled off my clothes again, and dried off.

I sat on my bed damp and naked, desperately wanting to lie back and drift into slumber while staring at the lights on my stereo. I hesitated for only seconds, before abruptly standing to push the play button on the CD console. The disc, part of a newly found box set for my jazz collection, played an old 40's cover. Starting with a skip on the tip of my toes, I went to my closet.

My first two classes were awesome, Shakespeare and American Literature. I contemplated adding another major in Literature & Rhetoric. The professors were inspiring; there was clear historical meaning in the writing, and even wondered if History might be a major to add.

I had a three-hour break before my next class and decided to go down to The Beanery to spend time over a cup of coffee in the quiet of my thoughts.

The usual table was taken by three hippy looking chicks that were likely high school students skipping class. I compromised, taking to a table closer to the window, choosing only the cleanest one. Even though I was only about four years ahead of them, they seemed like children, an observation I would not have made before. Is this what it meant to grow up? I was barely twenty years old.

I sat looking around the room inconspicuously wondering who others in the room were with, who they loved. Who were they thinking about? What made them excited? Was it men? Was it women? Or, were they playing my game, playing one role, a lie for years out of fear and self-confidence.

A guy looked up from his book at me from across the room. He smiled at the corner of his mouth. He knew my thoughts without my uttering a word. Secrets didn't exist in that moment. He knew why; I was infatuated with a boy.

It was a half an hour later when Lydia walked up the street and through the door. With her fast footed and direct approach to the table I sensed a confrontation about to happen.

"So, now why are you here? I thought you would be in class or home by now?" She said with her hands in the pockets of her wool jacket, looking about the room, keeping in control.

"I'm hanging out before my next class. Why?"

"Why didn't you call me?"

"I don't know. I guess I wanted to be alone. Is that a problem?"

"You want to be alone a lot lately. Like last week when you said you were going to be alone for the night, or with your roommates anyway, and the next thing I know, you're with Jordan."

"Lydia..."

"Lydia what? You're avoiding me. I haven't seen shit of you all week. If you don't like me, then fucking say it." The level of her voice attracted an audience looking for coffee room drama.

"I'm sorry. I've been busy."

"Yeah, right." She turned and walked out the door and back down the street towards campus. Embarrassed, I sat for several minutes waiting for the air to clear in the room. People appeared to go about their business without notice. I pulled out my Shakespeare text from my backpack and started to read, or actually, pretended to read as I searched for a next move. When I was sure that everyone had forgotten the encounter, I put my books away, put on my jacket and stood up. It was fort-five minutes until my next class.

It started snowing. A dark overcast sat low in the sky with its edges letting in the afternoon light through a white hallow. The wet snow underneath my feet clumped on the end of my shoes. My wool socks were getting wet around the edges, a misery I had to live with for the rest of the day until I got home after three p.m.

Then I saw her. She was standing outside the Student Union Building. I avoided eye contact in my approached, trying to hide my shame, until it was necessary to look at her face to face.

"Come over next to me," she said with a shaky voice, as she put her arm into mine, turning to walk the rest of the way onto campus. "Where is your class?"

"Life Science Building."

"I'll walk with you."

"Okay." We were arm and arm and initially pensive.

"You're not really with me anymore Brad, are you?"

"I'm sorry Lydia."

"Let's not be sorry anymore. I know what you're going through."

I acted like I didn't hear her and said, "I'll be in class until three, and then we can go and get something to eat."

"Brad, don't ignore me. It's time we got down to it."

"Lydia…"

"It never is the right time Brad. You need to start being honest with me about our trip."

"What?" Oh my God, I couldn't act my way through this now.

"You don't have to bring me. I now understand that the original reason you hesitated is because you feel an obligation because I'm your girlfriend. You haven't said anything about it since last week, and I want you to know that I can stay behind. I understand if you want to see your family on your own without me. There will be other times, and again, there is no obligation."

"I don't want you to think…"

"Brad, give me a break. You're like playing this 007 shit with me. It's exhausting. This stupid trip won't come between us. Now get over it cuz I'm getting over it now."

"Sure."

I gave her as sincere a hug as I could, before walking into the building and waved at her as I went in. Was she in such denial? Wasn't it obvious that I didn't love her? Avoidance was not going to work.

"Call me when you get home sweetheart!" She called, as I followed another student past the large oak door.

The doors on the right-hand side ran in even numbers with the left side odd. I found 130, then 132, and finally 134, the room number matching the schedule in my pocket. The door was propped open with a small worn wooden wedge. Moving around and into the full room of students, I slid along the wall to the back row towards the outside window. I took my seat and forced my coat off my back. Tugging at my sleeves and letting them fall to the side, I reached into my bag and took out a notepad, I found a pen from the inside pocket of my coat. Students were pouring in with less than two minutes to class.

"Hey! It be little Bradley. Bradley, from the Geordie Hall." It was a dark and sarcastic voice from behind me, very close, regrettable from my past. I turned. Before me, sitting back with arms crossed and a pen over his ear, sat Jake Vargas. "Oh, hi Jake," I said trying to diffuse the situation.

"How are you and your little love slave doing, my dear boy?" He said in a poorly articulated British accent.

"Just fine," I said again, pleasantly, trying to avoid a scene. I turned back to the front of the room. A jolting pinpoint jab pained the ribs under my shoulder blade. I quickly turned, deciding against cordial.

"Knock it the fuck off dick head." My jaw tightened as I pushed hot breath through my nose.

"Well, little Nelly boy is all so very tough these days now isn't she. I don't want your gay disease, so why don't you just piss off and stop looking at me bitch."

I turned back. I looked over to see the professor kick the wedge from underneath the door allowing it to close behind him. He started talking before getting to the podium.

"Your first reading for Wednesday is in Chapter One of your textbook on Utilitarianism. Simply put," he pivoted on his heels and turned to the front of the class, impatiently noting those continuing to talk, "all actions, choices you make are based in the pleasure principle."

"Jesus," I thought, "another Philosophy class."

He bore no syllabus, gave no introduction and rarely made eye contact except in contempt. He was dressed in a shabby brown cardigan and jeans. His beard was poorly trimmed, and his glasses sat low on his red and pock marked nose. His voice carried clear to the back of the room with a passionate but impatient tone.

I surveyed last year at the dorm and remembered the day that Jake and his roommate Matt walked in on Jordan and me on the bed rough housing together. The times running into them in the hall, the scowling faces, the under-the-breath comments in the shower room, all came to me in that moment joined with a flood of anxiety.

My attention moved in and out of focus on the professor's lecture. Jake whispered to someone a few times. I knew this was not over. I needed a plan. I had to either stay in my seat well after the lecture, acting as if I were going to talk to the professor, or get out a few minutes early. Needless to say, when I had the chance, I needed to drop the section.

The clock slowly made its way to the fifty-minute mark. The lecture sounded at a natural end when suddenly the professor closed his book, and without any conclusion whatsoever, left the room, allowing the door to close behind him. People looked around, one saying, "Is that it?" Chatter took over, and with it, both my plans were squashed. I quickly stuffed my notepad under my arm, and grabbed by bag and coat, and went for the door. Looking back inconspicuously Jake was still talking to the guy to his right. The shuffle of students around me was protection, making me virtually invisible among the mix of outerwear and young faces.

I headed for the door, throwing on my jacket as I quickly moved into the clear. It looked like I was safe until a violent force at my pack jerked me around.

"So, you thought you were going to get out that easy queer boy?"

"I'm not..."

"Yeah, right you aren't. You're as queer as I've ever seen. So little Bradley, are you a butt man or a dick man. I bet you love it up the ass. Do you want me to fuck you up the ass girly boy? I bet you're tight!" His friend stood behind looking on, laughing wickedly as he taunted me.

"Leave me the fuck alone asshole." My face felt hot. I wanted to throw up. As I turned to walk away, he chose not to follow this time, but yelled at the top of his lungs, "No Brad, I'm not a fag. I don't want to go to bed with you! I'm not into boys!" I put my eyes to the ground and walked as fast as I could, imagining he would just disappear. I couldn't look up, fearing the faces, the sea of onlookers.

I walked directly to the Administration Building and filled out a Drop-Add form, skipping my last class. By the time I was finished, my fear turned to anger, infecting the rest of the day. Was this going to be my life?

Chapter Twenty-Two

The weeks moved by quickly. Settling into classes came with longer days and rain. The Palouse, known for strong winds, turned light sprinkles to horizontal icy stings in-between buildings and home. Weather was not difficult for me being from the severity of Alaska. Nevertheless, the advent of dry summer evenings filled my daydreams in the boredom of drab lectures sitting in sweaty soaked clothing.

Jordan waited for me after my last class nearly every day. I looked forward to seeing him, excited to talk to him, catch the sight of his form, his handsome style, especially in the rain. His moist skin and detailed care of dress, the special way he smiled when he looked at me as I approached, showed his growing interest. But where were the words? When would I have the nerve to talk to him about the way my chest felt, my head dazed out of awareness of everything else but him?

It was true. We were crossing boundaries that male friends rarely do. We sat on the couch together, arms touching, watching television, regardless if others were home. He was at every party we threw, with Henri taking him under his wing acclimating him to the international crowd of friends. We held each other, not a cordial hug, but embraced, on every coming and going, and nobody seemed to make notice.

Lydia continued to comment about my emotional distance and avoidance. She accepted it on one level, afraid to push too hard on the other. However, every day layers of tension built up. I knew she wouldn't sit back much longer. I did not listen to the advice from my mom, or Henri. I went with a hope, the hope that she was going to figure it out, and act on it; dump me. If I pulled away enough, sooner or later she had to leave. Ignorant to her insight about my feelings for Jordan, the avoidance set up disaster.

One night, in the slumber of spring break, the time when you know you need to get projects completed before Monday when school starts up again, Lydia made another attempt. I was resting on the couch with her at my feet. She cradled them on her lap while we watched Wednesday night sitcoms. I drifted in and out of the heaviness of sleep. She put her hand on the back of my knee and shook.

"Are we going to make it?" She said in a soft voice. I turned my head from the pillow to look at her shaking voice. Tears welled to form a meniscus on the lid of her lower eyelids. Her hand rubbed from my knee to my heel and back again. The sound of my jeans against her skin drew my attention close.

"I don't know," I said, unwilling to open up the window, but set to unlatch it.

The following Tuesday night, I got a phone call from Jordan. The message was written on a jagged edged piece of paper and taped on my bedroom door. "Call your friend Jordan ASAP." It was Henri's handwriting, deciphering, requiring broad interpretations of letters and the influence of intoxication.

I immediately picked up the phone without releasing my backpack. It rang only twice before he picked up.

"Hello?" His voice sounded clear.

"Hello, this is Brad. Watch you up to?"

"Nothing, but hey, was wondering if you wanted to go to an ensemble at Bentley Theater on Friday."

"Sure."

"One of my friends is playing brass and I thought it would be fun to go."

"Yeah, sure. I think that sounds," I paused, "Oh shit, I am supposed to get together with Lydia over dinner."

"Bring her. She should like it."

"Um…well, I can ask, but I doubt it." No, it was intrusion. Lydia would dominate our time. No, I had to figure something else out.

"Who is this friend of yours, a guy?"

"Her name is Jamie. We are study partners. You will absolutely love her, the cutest thing ever. So, are you going to come? Mr. Jealous." I breathed out hard. He heard me. "What's wrong?"

"Oh nothing. What would you say if I don't ask Lydia?"

"Whatever. Is everything okay?"

"Yeah. I just need a break. Smothered. I'm being smothered," I lied.

"Whatever. I have a crazy week ahead, so I don't think I can do much until then, so why don't you pick me up at my room, okay?"

"Of course. What is the attire?"

"Better than casual. I'm wearing a turtleneck and cords. Nothing special."

"That is what you always wear."

"HA, HA, HA, funny man!"

"Yeah, well, I'm sure you have plenty of suits and ties from your Sunday wardrobe. Cords are very 50s Jordan."

That wasn't nice," he said.

"No, it wasn't, but if I was your size, I'd be over there right now taking every suit you owned for myself."

"No, I don't think so. Heathens are not allowed." We laughed and with a short goodbye, hung up. Going into my bedroom, I threw my backpack on the bed and flopped myself next to it. My heart was beating fast and happiness wrapped all around my body. Now, in a sociopathic moment, I needed to work a series of plans with Lydia for the remainder of the week and make a brilliant excuse for Friday.

All week Lydia and I did just that. Every afternoon and into the nights leading to Friday, we walked the streets of

Moscow, sat on the benches at East City Park, ate a couple of meals at the University Inn, and watched movies at her dorm. The initial drudgery passed as I enjoyed the time with her, only feeling guilt at minor points when conversation became heavy.

Then, on Thursday night it climaxed. We were sitting in the lobby of her building having a conversation about her literature class. The open setting of the lobby worked perfect for me. There was no way for us to be affectionate with each other and we were able to stick to intellectual matters, the substance of our relationship. The unidirectional sexual tension and desire sat far in the background. It was safe.

"I mean, you wouldn't believe this guy in class. He was picking his nose, totally oblivious that we were all watching him. Then he actually pulled one out and ate it! I was so fucking going to throw up right there. But no one said a word. It was crazy Brad! The professor didn't notice at all, and in that precise minute, he said, 'The character in the stanza repeats to himself that love is everlasting and unabating.' The entire class lost it. I can tell you what. If that guy has a girlfriend, I hope she never kisses him. That love is not everlasting!"

"And then, oh my God Brad, this professor is so crazy. He comes into class the other day early and sits on the table by the podium. The class trickles in. This one girl, somewhere in her thirties, who I hope knows him outside of the classroom, walks in wearing four-inch heels. They looked dreadfully uncomfortable, but he says, 'Now those are fuck me shoes.' I was in absolute awe. She just says, 'Oh Sam, just why don't you go fuck yourself, you old troll.' They laughed, and then the rest of the class laughed along. But God, isn't that sexual harassment? I would have freaked out."

It was some of the best days of our relationship, and in the late nights when I lay in my bed alone, guilt filled my heart that I was leading her on. I carried on the set up. I did it with pleasure.

Friday came, and that afternoon I talked to Lydia in the rain over steaming cups of coffee at the Student Union Building. We met to say a short 'hello' before heading up the hill for our next class.

"Hey, I think I need some time alone tonight," an easy cover since we had been together every night of the week, seen and done everything on the town. "Would you mind if I just bag on tonight?"

"Oh, I thought we could go catch a movie or something, but, hey, that's okay. You go. Do you and Elaina have something planned?"

"No, but I did want to spend some time at home. We see so little of each other, and I feel kinda bad about it."

"That's cool. I will hook up with some friends tonight on my own."

We stood as long as we could take the drizzling rain and dark afternoon clouds. I hugged her tight, spilling a slop of syrupy coffee on her shoes. I pushed my way through the rain and went up the hill, looking forward to the evening hours in my daydreams.

I raced home after my class with only an hour and a half before I had to be at Jordan's. I put on a loose fitting maroon mock turtleneck and a new pair of jeans and thin wool socks. I needed new shoes, resorting to rain stained loafers. Who would notice? A pack of cigarettes with a lighter, tucked in the plastic wrapper, was carelessly tossed on the coffee table for the taking. Not being accustomed to smoking, I dreaded being caught, but the house was quiet. I sat down and cautiously took one from the sweet-smelling paper package. Tobacco spilled onto the table. I put it to my mouth and struck the switch on the lighter.

"Hey, what's up man?" I turned suddenly, at first trying to conceal the cigarette. His hair jagged, uncombed, eyes pasty.

"Um...well, fine. You don't mind..."

"No problem, man." He sat in the chair and took the pack, lighting a cigarette and sat back, holding it loosely between his fingers, put it to his mouth and then held it off to the side, his elbow on the arm of the wing back chair.

"What are you doing tonight?" Henri inquired coming out of his daze. The odor of alcohol and smoke permeated the room. The hint of unattended body odor grabbed my attention.

"Jordan...Jordan and I are going to a concert."

"Man, you are spending a lot of time with this boy. Is there something going on man?"

"No, I don't think so," I evaded.

"I don't think so," Henri parroted.

"He was my roommate at the dorms."

"That doesn't mean much buddy. What is going on?"

"Nothing. We are just friends."

"Right man. Whatever you say." He smiled and looked at me with the joy of knowing he was catching me at deception.

"Have you told your girlfriend yet?"

"No."

"Man, you're getting yourself into a problem aren't you. Seeing a guy, or not. Whatever. And you haven't told that babe of yours that you're a poof. Man, you got a problem cooking."

I was a bird in a cage, trapped by a cat with a paw in the door, and no way out. Henri saw everything. I stood up and went into my room.

Henri continued, "Bradley, you gotta be honest man. I can tell her if you want." A malicious laugh slithered from his tongue.

I stood at my dresser drawer, trying to ignore him but couldn't, his words pounding in my head. I shut it hard and went back, taking my seat on the couch. "I know. I'm in trouble."

"It's dishonest man. It's time. The more you drag it out, the more you're both going to need a psychiatrist man." His Swiss accent rang deep, emphasizing the swirling smoke and aged odor of beer, echoing impending doom.

I turned on the TV and finished my cigarette. My lungs felt tight and I didn't care. I lit another without asking. I took harder drags, letting the ashes fall to the table. Henri laughed through his nose. Then I took my jacket that was draped on the back of Henri's chair and pulled it over my shoulders. He leaned his head forward, looking up at me with a tired penetrating smile.

"I need to go." I said calmly.

"Don't hurt her. She loves you and you love her. It doesn't have to be the same kind of love, but you do love her. That is why you can't do it. But you have to man. If you don't, you will lose her forever."

I stood over him, my forehead tight. "Thanks Henri. I know."

I walked into the darkness on the street, along the canopies of deciduous trees towards campus. An owl was hooting in the distance. The hum of streetlights in the distance sung their monotone tune. I tried to put my thoughts on Jordan, his beautiful sandy blond hair, soft round face and the smell of his skin.

But my thoughts returned to Lydia. The damage I was doing was sinking in. Imagining her standing in front of me as I told her pained me with guilt. We went to concerts together and held hands, and I loved the touch of her skin, her mind, something Jordan could not match. He was bright, but never engaged in intellectual conversation. It scared him; meant approaching the issues in his life, breaching walls he didn't want to climb.

When I reached Geordie Hall, Jake was in the waiting area just inside the door. I quickly turned down the hall before he caught me. Being back in those halls pushed back any remaining sense of well-being. I picked up pace to the room. Frantically, I looked for the singles at the center back half of the hallway. The old room was up ahead only a few doors. Two new nameplates were tacked to the side: Smith and Mathews. The nostalgia was bittersweet. I wondered if they were engaged in a secret affair among art posters in uni-frames of homoerotic art, or if the room reeked of testosterone and excessive female perfume.

His room was easy to identify, not by name, but the sound of the heavy beat of techno music. It was Trance. He had evolved. Before, he swore against secular music that didn't glorify his beliefs, a custom dictated by the culture of his church. I knocked gently, no response. Again. Then harder.

"Come in!" rang Jordan's inflected voice.

I pushed open the door to find him dressed in a red turtleneck sweater and khaki colored cords. Jordan always looked better than me and I was envious. The sweet smell of cologne scented his room against the warm air. He didn't have in his contacts, a rarity, and his thin-rimmed classes accented his face.

He was on the phone. Sitting on the book stand in its predictable place was a copy of the Book of Mormon. A narrow wood framed picture of Jesus hung on the wall above the small 3x5 window alongside another picture of his parents, one I recognized when we roomed together. Jordan sat on his bed with his elbow resting on the inside of his knee while the other reached down at the floor. He looked up at me and put a finger up in the air indicating his usual 'Just a minute' gesture.

"Well sure, but I don't think I'll be there. Don't come to pick me up, because I won't be here......Again, I am going to be in Portland for the night with some friends......They are family friends okay?"

He hung up, holding a dark look of frustration at the receiver.

"Who was that?" I closed the door behind me.

"It was an elder from the church. Some new dork just returning from his mission. Trying to take me under his wing. You know, been a couple of months since I've been going, and they think I've flown the coop. Typical. I'm sure they will be paying a visit sometime soon."

"What about your mom?" Unlike the old room, this one had a single bed on the right-hand side. Habitually I looked around for what would be mine, but was displaced; there were only Jordan's things, no marks of my personality. Keeping my distance, I sat on the floor with my legs crossed.

"What about her?"

"Are they feeding her information?"

"I think so, because my mom keeps giving me this shit that the only way I'll be happy is if I'm following the gospel, letters, phone calls, they usual bull shit. She asks me how singles group is going every time we talk. I just say 'fine'...So whatever, so hey, remember Seattle? I wish we were there now. Wouldn't that be fun?"

"Yeah, and remember that guy you danced with? He was nice."

"Hey, I actually called him last week."

A surge of jealousy ripped through my chest. If he started seeing someone, I could never let him know...

"Well, what did he say?" I hesitated.

"Nothing. Apparently, he wants to come down to see me. I'm not sure, but said I would have to get back to him because of classes and stuff."

"Oh yeah, get this! He told me that he was dating someone. A chick! Can you believe that? I don't get it, this whole bisexual thing."

I added, "It's like they have the best of both worlds." Jordan looked at me funny and went on.

"Yeah well, whatever. I wish I were fucking bisexual. Sure, would make things easier. Anyway, let's get going."

He slipped his feet into his shoes and stood up in front of me. My head was at the level of his hips and he was barely a foot away. Hesitating only for a moment, I leaned to my side, supporting myself with the floor, and stood up. His back was turned to me as he searched the narrow tall closet for the desired jacket. In my mind, my hands searched for the curves of his waist, to turn him around and pull up his sweater, kiss his stomach, push my hands up onto his chest and hold him, smelling him, taking him. I shook it off and stood to my feet.

He turned to open the door, buttoning each knob through the hooks of his pea coat. I closed the door behind me, then opened it again, reached my arm inside and turned the lock.

Passing the lobby, we were not so lucky with Jake. As Jordan walked out into the cold damp air, Jake saw me.

"Oh, hi there big boy. Here to get your boyfriend?" I kept walking, pushing Jordan through. He turned as if shot in the neck by a blow dart.

"Never mind him. He is the hall jackass who can't get any." We turned again, making a right towards Bentley Theater. We walked a distance apart and kept our voices low, synchronized, not drawing any more attention to ourselves.

"What a dick. I hate him."

"Does he give you any trouble now that you are living alone?" I asked.

"Let's just say that I play the Mormon act well enough that I am still a bit of a mystery."

"The Mormon act...I don't remember it being such an act."

"He doesn't know the difference. If anything, he sees me as a conservative weak guy who studies all the time and has no time for anything but church."

"Does he always talk to you that way?"

"No, not usually. He just leaves me alone."

We entered the auditorium with the greeter meeting us at the inside of the seating area with the program. Jordon took two and led the way down several rows.

"Let's go up front a bit okay?" Jordan said with excitement.

The room was already seated with several people, but not to the point where we couldn't be choosy. The stage was bright with overhead spotlights, and the closer we moved down, the tighter the semi-circle shape of the rows formed around the stage. A podium about a foot high stood at the apex of the arrangement with an exceptionally wide stand before it. The room was impressive compared to the high school auditorium of my childhood.

Jordan turned left down an empty row of seats. "This is perfect. If we sit too far forward, we have to turn our heads too much to see everything."

"Now who are we here to see tonight?"

"It is my study partner Jamie from Chemistry. She has a solo tonight."

"What does she play?" I said sitting down and crossing my legs at the knee. Looking around, I saw men and women dressed in the nicest of evening clothes. Suits and dresses draped over the edges of chairs, polished black shoes and glossy heels. It was another time of careful attention to standard for public appearance and respect to the performer. Being the underdressed, I was of the underclass, like the poor proletariat amongst the bourgeois.

"The trombone." People quickly closed in around us. I looked at my watch and saw that the concert had only three minutes to start. Last minute arrivals took seats wherever they could find one. The sound of chattering voices politely filled the room. They were talking about me.

"That's a funny instrument for a girl to play."

"Yeah well, I have my guesses about her," he snickered in my ear. I felt the warmth of his breath against my skin. I leaned into his ear, gently feeling the touch of his lips against my skin. He moved back and faced forward. I turned and whispered almost touching his. "Thanks for inviting me."

Jordan kept his gaze forward as the lights slowly dimmed around us. His angelic smile came to life, but only showed itself for a moment. I sat back. Our arms came together on the rest between us. The ensemble of about thirty musicians came in two parts, in unison, one from each side of the curtain behind the stage, and took their respective seats. The conductor emerged last, stood up on his podium and bowed to the audience. Polite aristocratic claps filled the air and died when he turned. After two short tuning sessions with the players, the baton went into the air, stopped, and came down fast with a pounding jolt of his fist.

The opening notes hit me with a force, moving my chest cavity, vibrating with the energy of the forward instruments. Dynamic explosive measures came at me causing me to shield my soul like eyes in a dust storm. Never before had I experienced such perfection and clarity of sensations in my body through the simple power of air blown through metal tubing. The energy joined us. The movements between us, the warmth of having him near, our souls had touched months before and now I had him next to me in the explosive air. He gazed wide, experiencing every measure with thrusting and pulling, breathless, connected with mine, and mixed with the waves of sound piercing him, piercing me. We were one in the mutual experience.

My hand dangled off the end of the armrest. As my mind breathed in every wave of sensation, suddenly, with but a breath of hesitation, the melody came through, slowing to a beautiful legato, then allegro. Like the mist forming over a secluded pond in the moonlight, I gently moved my fingers over his. His soft skin took mine as I turned my hand over. In the safety of darkness, we stared forward, not paying attention to anything but the union and the sound.

During intermission, I got up to use the bathroom. He followed. Our jackets marked our place. We walked up the aisle way and through the small concession stand in the foyer. I went into the bathroom, noticing that no one else was there. Walking into the last stall on the end, Jordan followed. With the quick force of his body, he pushed up against me, my back hitting the flimsy metal, and we embraced in a deep long kiss. I was rum toxic, feeling his hardness against mine. He pushed against me like a magnet, both of us unable to pull away.

The door opened and the sound of footsteps walked up to the urinal along the wall. Our breathing was heavy, impossible to control, as we looked in the direction of the man, not visible. The sound of the zipper pulled, the pissing, lasted an eternity, wouldn't cease. He finished and walked out of the room.

Jordan whispered, "God, he didn't even flush or wash his hands." I giggled, feeling the sweat on my forehead, then leaned over and kissed his neck. His sexual energy still vibrated in my chest. I was shocked at his sudden movements, a reflection of the many years of pent up emotions and sexuality.

"Do you want to come over to my place?" I asked without inhibition or concern about his answer. He smiled and took my hand. For a brief moment we stopped to listen before opening the stall door. When we were sure no one was going to come in, he pulled me into the open, turned to smile and released me.

Jordan went to our chairs and took our coats. His was already on when he got to me standing in the foyer.

Entering the late evening air, I noticed the sweet smell of old rain. A fog covered campus, and the street lamps cast an orange glow about the grounds.

"Jordan," I whispered.

"What?" He turned to me, casting a look with his deep brown eyes.

"Are you, are you, okay...?"

"Of course I am, silly." He started to run ahead of me and yelled, "And stop whispering!"

His arms went into the air and down again. He stopped, turned to me, waiting patiently as I came closer. "I knew it. I so knew it and wanted to know it," He said emphatically. He hugged me for but a second and we turned and walked, continuing.

"You're the only person, besides Henri and my mom, that know."

"Yeah, hard to hide the fact that you kissed me. I have the perfect evidence that no one else has. Now you haven't been kissing anyone else, have you?" Jordan's forwardness felt foreign.

"No, you're the first."

"And the last?"

"I hope so. But, I don't want you to freak out on me. You always freak out Jordan."

He glanced over, then turning his face directly in front of mine. "I won't freak out. Get past that one Brad." He slowed his pace. "Why did it take you so long to do that?"

"Do what? You're the one who jumped me."

"Oh, come on. You held my hand Brad. That's when I knew for sure."

"I thought if I made any move, you might run. I don't want you to run."

"Come on silly. I'm right here, aren't I? Anyway, you don't have to worry anymore. Like I said, I'm past running away. Those days are gone."

We got to the dark canopy of trees a couple of blocks from the apartment. This is the place where the streetlights are far apart, and the long shadows begin. We slowed our approach wondering if anyone was home. The living room was well lit. I stopped, pulled him to me, my lips starting to tremble. I pressed mine against his, opening my mouth to invite him. He pushed his way into me, taking the back of my head in his gloved hand and holding my neck gently. Then he pushed me back, his hands moved to my chest. I looked at him, my lips still wet, and said, "Jordan, I have waited for this moment for so long. Please don't run away."

"I'm here with you Brad. I can't believe I'm here with you either, and I'm here with you to stay." His voice trembled.

As we approached the unlit stairs, careful to be quiet in our approach, the familiar female voice shook me from above. I stood dead in my shoes. I quickly turned to look along the streets. Her car wasn't there. We weren't the only ones out on a foggy night walk.

"Hey boys. What are you up to?"

"Umm…nothing…"

"Thought I would come by to say 'hi,' and look who else I found. It's the threesome back together again. Glad I could make it! Brad, your roomy is great. Henri! He has been just talking my ear off." Her voice wobbled.

She had a bottle in her hand and was hanging onto the upper half with the tips of her fingers. The odor of beer wafted between us. Jordan fell into character, compensating for the pale shocked look on my face.

"Hey friend. Looks like you're having fun! I want one!" He ran up the steps and went inside. She followed, and I behind her, after a brief moment to catch my thoughts.

Henri was sitting on the couch, smoking a cigarette, and recklessly holding a drink at the end of his fingers. Three bottles sat on the coffee table and music played on the radio. Jordan and I took opposite sides of the room on the floor, looking at Lydia and Henri on the couch. Shot glasses and a half full bottle of hard liquor were under the table. I took the bottle and tipped it back. Jordan moved over and took it from me. His lips were wet with the rim of the bottle.

"So where were you guys? I thought you and Elaina were going to be hanging out."

"She went out with friends."

"That's too bad. How did you two hook-up?"

"Oh...I...,"

"Wait, let me guess," she said with an intoxicated slur. "You were out on a walk and ran into Jordan on campus. Sure, dressed up nice for a walk out on the town."

My head found the wall behind me.

"Jeesh Jordan. You are sure getting comfortable these days. Drinking? Hanging out with our heathen kind." Her words bit, looking for weakness. "But hey, I'm happy for you man. You got out of that crazy fucken religious shit. About time, CHAP!" She slipped a hiccup, putting the back of her hand to her mouth.

Jordan looked at her carefully. "I missed you guys."

With that, Lydia got up, bracing herself against the coffee table and gave him a hug while he remained sitting.

Meanwhile Henri went to the kitchen to get beer. Returning, he handed out the open bottles, Jordan taking a quick sip, looking over at me, trying to track how I was doing. I gave him a confirming, "Oh my fucking hell."

The next hour went by, but not quickly enough. We drank more beer and took a few more swigs from the bottle, but in measure. Lydia continued to drink heavily and was increasingly apologetic. The beer kept coming, not for Jordan or me, but Lydia. After the first, we refused Henri's generous offer. He wasn't drinking either.

When it was safe, I followed Henri into the kitchen. "Hey!" I whispered, "What the fuck are you trying to do? She is way gone. She gets water now, don't you think?"

Henri kept his back to me. "Man! What is your problem? The girl is in pain. Can't you see that?"

"No, she isn't. I don't think she feels anything right now. What did you tell her? God, please don't tell me…"

"Nothing…well, I just said you were out with Jordan."

"Fuck! What now?"

Henri didn't answer, only turned and headed back into the living room with another beer. She took it warily in her hand and held it to her face, looking through the glass.

"Oh man. I don't think I can have another."

"Yeah. You should stop," Jordan added. The skin on his forehead was tight around his eyebrows.

She put the bottle down and it toppled over, beer pouring out onto the table and to the hardwood floor, dust collecting on the foamy surface. Jordan jumped up, ran to the bathroom and returned with a towel.

"Thanks sweetheart," she mumbled.

"No problem dear."

"Henri, let's go out onto the porch. I want a smoke."

"No, let me walk you home darling. I think you need air. It's a beautiful night." Henri already had on a light jacket and carried hers, ready to push her arms through. I helped her up. She turned and held my neck, drawing herself up to me and gave me a kiss, before slowly backing away with a saddened face, realizing her mistake.

I followed them out the door and watched them step carefully down the stairs, slowly disappearing under the canopy of trees. Before slipping into the darkness, Henri put his arm over her shoulder and looked back with a smile.

Jordan remained in his place. I went to him, sat down, crossing my legs across from him. The music from the radio was distracting. I reached over and turned it off. Jordan was looking down at his knees. Brushing his hair gently up into place, I whispered, "Are we still here together?" He looked up slowly, his hands trembling coming up to my face. He held my head gently and kissed me. His mouth opened and we kissed long and deep, the air drawing in and back out of our noses. He pushed me back, at the same time pulling himself on top of me, straddling my body. He moved to my neck, gently caressing his lips against my skin, sending warm chilling waves down the length of my body.

I wanted to say something but didn't know what. We had gone so quickly from being together to this. Then, overwhelmingly I took his face in my hands and pushed him into focus.

"Hey, what would you think about going for a walk."

He smiled back, kissed me again and sat on my hips. I could see his erection through his cords. He pushed mine flat into my groin. "I think that is a great idea."

"Lydia…"

"Yes," he took over, "Lydia, you have to do something about Lydia. You can't have both of us."

"No…"

"No, no you can't."

"No, I can't."

He leaned over, his lips touching the hairs on my earlobe and breathed, "I love you."

Chapter Twenty-Three

It was hanging on the door when I arrived home after class, attached with a safety pin to the screen. The note was folded once and then again, with tape sealing it shut, concealing the contents. I pulled it down, throwing the pin off to the side of the porch into the mulch. Placing it in my mouth, I franticly searched my pockets for my keys while keeping control of my book bag and holding onto the mail. Frustrated, I put everything down and hastily went through my pack, looking in every side pocket and hidden crevasse. At last, I found them crammed between the pages of my class notes.

The house was empty except the remaining essence of cigarette smoke and candle wax, indicating someone recently left. The house was comfortably quiet. I looked around to make sure I was alone and then threw myself into the couch and forced out a heavy breath. Tea, I needed a cup of tea.

I stood at the kitchen sink looking for the kettle and remembered the note. Reaching in my front shirt pocket I pulled it out and released the tape. It wasn't Jordan's penmanship.

It was from Lydia.

"Dear Brad...stopped by to talk. I will be at the Student Union Building until 6:00 p.m. Meet me and be alone. It is urgent. Don't forget! Lydia".

Before I gave myself time to think, I put my feet to the road and quickly went to meet her. It took less than fifteen minutes to get to the front door of the lobby. I pulled the door back intently stepping in, looked around the open room, searching for her familiar shoulder length hair. There she sat, with her back to me. I approached carefully on my feet, trying to catch my breath. Her feet were propped up on the low coffee table before her, and she read what looked to be a term paper on her legs. She held a red pen, drawing lines under words and crossing out others.

"Hi." I walked around and sat next to her. She put the paper on the table and turned to me, gave me a hug and sat close, her knee turned between us. I sat facing out from the couch with my head turned to see her.

"Thank you for coming." Her eyes were red and her face puffy.

"What is going on?" I asked, prepared.

She pushed her hand to the side of her forehead leaning into it with her elbow on the back of the chair for support. "It is time we talked. It's about the other night."

"Are you mad I didn't call and invite you out? I'm really sorry. It was just..." I said, trying to cut her off.

"Brad stop," her voice taking on frustration and her eyes digging into me. I didn't say anything more and became acutely aware of the many people sitting around us, each studying alone and in groups.

"I saw you Brad, you and Jordan together." She began to cry holding her hands together. "I am so hurt and mad and can't understand why, how you can do this to me."

"Lydia..."

"Shut the fuck up Brad," she said with her jaw clamping tight. "You need to shut the fuck up and listen. Don't say one fucking word, because there's nothing you can say. You and Jordan. I am so fucking pissed. You and Jordan. You stood there thinking you were so fucking safe and I saw you kiss in the dark. The shadows gave you away. You can't escape that Brad. You have been lying to me all this time. I thought our little platonic relationship was so gentleman like and now I realize it was a cover up. You're gay. And, and you used me!"

"No, I didn't. Lydia..."

"No, I'm not finished..."

"No, you listen. I wasn't sure. I wanted to love you Lydia."

"You're telling me you didn't know you were gay? That is a bunch of fucking bullshit."

"No, I did. I have all along. I couldn't admit it. Then I met you, and I wanted, I thought, I wanted to be with you. You were so perfect. It seemed so possible until Jordan…

"Jordan what?"

"I fell in love with Jordan."

"You didn't even have the decency to tell me. I had to fucking catch you in the act Brad? I don't remember the last time you kissed me like that. God!" Tears streamed down her face, "I stepped out to get some fresh air, sick from all of Henri's cigarette smoke. I stood in the dark and heard you coming up the street. You laughed. You haven't laughed with me like that ever. You stopped and…" She grabbed my hand and became quiet again. "And you know the funny part of all of it? I wasn't even that surprised."

"I am a chicken shit. I didn't want to face you. When I went back home for Christmas I told my mom. She told me not to let it drag out. I just wanted to escape. It is my way, has always been. I wanted you to break up with me. I hoped that if I got distant enough from you, you would break it off. It is chicken shit, and I have always handled things this way. I am so sorry…"

She sobbed holding her head in her hands. "Don't, I don't want sorry anymore. I want to get away from you and never ever see you again. You used me, you fucking used me. It was me you hid behind, so you didn't have to come out to the world. I don't care how hard being gay is. You lied to me every time we kissed, every time we slept together. You tried to lie even tonight."

She reached out and took her paper from the table, stood up, putting on her light brown cardigan. Looking down she put out her hand and pushed my head to the side with an overpowering force. "Don't ever try to contact me again." She turned and left, leaving me sitting with curious onlookers, wondering my next move. I was embarrassed, and more importantly caught in serious malfeasance.

I went back outside and found the payphone to the left of the entrance. My phone card was in my wallet partially bent from hours of sitting. I dialed the number, decisive and calm.

"Hello?"

"Hello?"

"Mom."

"Hello Son. What are you doing? Haven't heard from you in a while."

"I did it."

We talked for over an hour as I gave her details and processed my feelings, where things had gone wrong. "I'm glad things finally broke loose," she said.

"But mom, I didn't say anything. She did." My mom remarked on my avoidant pattern through the years. Nevertheless, she remained supportive. As I told her about Jordan, she expressed happiness. However, I sensed the sadness that I predicted she would have, knowing my life was never going to be the same.

*****

I didn't want to go home. Nor did it feel that it was the right time to talk to Jordan. I walked off campus turned up Sixth Street, past The Beanery, onto Main, and sat on the bench in front of the "Book People Bookstore".

It was closed, but the showcase had a brightly lit display of fairy and folklore books, just the escape I needed. As much as I tried to imagine myself on the covers of the display, I couldn't get my mind off her face, the tears spilling onto her blouse, the times we would never share again. I had lost a partner, a friend.

It started to rain, and like an ominous phantom it set forth the darkness churning in my soul, the chilled dampness of the late evening. I got up and walked up to Third Street, turning up past my house on the other side of the street, unnoticed, and went into East City Park.

I was alone there in the black of the night, without peace, with a hateful need to be with myself, drenched in my inadequate wool jacket. It soaked up every drop, my feet wet and pants wet. The stage at the center of the park rested flat, the partially rotten planks flaked and weathered gave no protest. It stood like an altar against the black.

I jumped and sat on the front of the stage and lay back, the rain hitting my face. A steady wind pushed over my body. My face took the cold moisture biting at my skin, and I didn't care. I closed my eyes, seeing everything from the past few months playing on the screen of my mind: Lydia's sad angry eyes, Jordan's angelic face, mom's hot chocolate, dad's Lucky Lager cans of beer in front of the fire place, my high school classmate Tim, quiet nights over tea with Elaina, and Henri's wealth of Swiss hippy wisdom. They ran through my mind in a continuous loop while my eyes remained shut.

Chapter Twenty-Four

From there, I sunk into a deep melancholy that can only be described as a pit of tar. The darkness clung to me, unshakable by all means. Going for walks, talking to Jordan on the phone, or conversations with my housemates, only left me feeling more exhausted. I became increasingly self-absorbed with guilt thinking about Lydia. A kind of self-deprecating obsession took over my body as I slept into the day and missed classes.

Trying to describe depression is a daunting task. If you haven't felt it yourself, it is difficult to understand. First there is the emotional aspect. Feelings don't exist, only numb and incessant awareness of a lingering doom. Bouts of crying come and go brought about by watching sad commercials or replaying events in the mind. Similarly, negative thinking takes over as you slowly discount everything positive around you, and over generalizing any negative action in your day as a reflection of your entire life.

Finding the television a comfort from reality, I spent waking hours laying on the couch ignoring everyone that passed by and their inquiries. I didn't want to see or talk to anyone, not even the man that changed my heart forever; the man that I kissed, held against my cheek, the man that changed my spirit forever. In essence, I didn't care about anything, anyone, not even myself.

It wasn't until the following Tuesday night when Jordan came to see me. His usual quiet knocking gave his identity away. I desperately wanted to ignore it, wishing it were a dream. I was in bed, listening to talk radio. I had on pajama bottoms and a loose flannel shirt.

"Hi Jordan," I said wearily, withholding the usual warm embrace. He pushed the door. Unable to give resistance, I stepped back. He stood before me. The concerned look on his face frustrated me. It was the last thing I wanted from anyone.

"Why haven't you called me?" he started at me, hostile with pent up frustration. "What in the hell is going on with you?"

"Nothing. Everything is just fine."

"Bullshit. It's like you don't want to see me anymore. Are you dumping me too?"

"No. That isn't it. I'm just kind of out of it." I went to the kitchen table and flopped myself in the chair, pushing my hair back with my palm. He followed, taking a seat across from me.

"I saw Henri on campus. He told me about your fight with Lydia. I'm very sorry it had to happen that way. I'm surprised she isn't upset with me."

"Who can be upset with you?" I reached over and put my hand in his and rested my head on the top of his arm that lay in front of him. He stroked my hair then bent down and kissed my temple. That was what pulled me through, feeling his warmth again. I started to cry, only gently, but then he kissed me.

"I think you need to get out of this house. How about we go downtown and rent a video."

I went to my room, closing my door and got dressed. Jordan remained at the table. Going into the bathroom, I brushed my teeth and ran my head under the faucet to make my hair pliable. I combed it, washed my face and put on some cologne.

When I came out, Jordan wasn't in the kitchen. The lights were turned off. What was going on? Did he leave? I had really done it this time. I tried to feel my way around. The darkness was set off with the incoming glow from a distant streetlight. The room was still.

"Jordan, are you there?" The song started on the CD player. I turned.

"Jordan?"

Then his hand touched my shoulder, turned me around, pulling me in with his head at my shoulder just under my neck.

"What?"

"Shhhh…"

His hands came around and held the small of my back and we began to sway side to side ever so gently with the romantic melody. I put my arms around him, resting my head on his. The sound of our socks rasped on the hardwood floor.

An overpowering urge took me over. Taking his head in my hands, I tilted his head up and pushed my tongue into his already open mouth. Jordan pulled me closer, and in that moment, I thought my heart was going to explode. We stopped swaying, our hands gently moving up and down each other's sides. Then his hands reached up under the front of my shirt, pushing it up and over my head. All inhibition was left behind in that very moment.

I pulled his shirt off, only briefly getting his sleeve caught on his watch. His chest against mine, made me hard. I reached down the back of his pants, loose enough to allow my fingers, but tight enough to prevent my hand. I bent down, twisting my neck, taking his nipple into my mouth. He was shaking, moving his mouth along my neck, his fingers through my hair. I bore down and then let go.

"Ouch," he whispered.

I pushed him back, took his hand, leading him into the safety of my bed. I closed the door and felt a pulling at my jeans. He sat on my bed pulling me to him. His hand slid up my back as I stood moving his hair in spirals with my hand. My pants were unbuttoned and then quickly pushed down. The pain and pulsating were agonizing. He took me into his mouth, the warm wet sensation nearly finishing it all.

I pulled out and pushed him back. He unbuttoned his pants, and in the darkness, lay naked in front of me. I kicked off my pants, startling him as I leaned over, kissing his body from his head, and then down, taking him into my mouth as he moaned. He quickly pulled me upwards meeting my lips with his.

"Brad, I..." he whispered into my ear. I felt his penis touch the skin of my upper leg. "Yes?" I replied.

"I love you." The words sounded so natural and were met with a soaring inside of me. I wanted him.

"I love you Jordan." Sweat beaded on his forehead, and in that quiet moment our breathing almost seemed to stop. Taking his hands in mine while holding them down above his head, I gently pressed him into me. At first, just a little.

His head turned with pleasure. It pained me. I sat up.

"We don't have to," he said.

"I want you," I whispered. My lips touched his forehead and again I pressed him barely into me, and then out again, feeling the stretching pain. I bit my lip, waiting for the pain to subside. Then, I took him all the way. His breathing became heavy. I felt a pleasure I had never experienced before.

It was a combination of giving myself to him, along with the overwhelming pleasure moving inside me. His skin felt hot. I moved up and back down again, forcing him in and out. He pushed inside of me, with a gentle moan. "God, I love you, Jordan."

My lips felt swollen against his as I leaned down and kissed him again, still moving him in and out of me. His breathing came faster. He pushed again...I wanted to cum.

Taking his hand, I put it on my cock. He held it tight and I pushed myself into his hand, at the same time while rising off him and back again. He licked his hand, then moisturized me. He started to breath loudly.

I felt him swelling inside of me as he moaned, his hips pushing into me deeper, faster, and harder, and finally ending a gush of warmth. Uncontrollably, my belly rushed with heat and I came on his chest. I collapsed onto him.

He remained in me, still pulsating, our bodies sharing the moments of oneness together.

"You're never alone," he said, stroking my hair, kissing my forehead. "You're never alone."

Chapter Twenty-Five

Running into Lydia on campus was inevitable. Fooling myself or living the romantic fantasy that she was a chapter put far behind, hinted at the ridiculous. On the first nice day of spring, following a stretch of hard April rains, I saw her from afar standing with her back to me in front of her dormitory. I was headed to my French class in the Administration Building. She was in the middle of a group of housemates engaged in a rather animated conversation. Like a battle fought by Faustus the devilish voice on my left shoulder told me to take leave, find an alternate route. However, a deeper consciousness stepped forth urging me to face her.

They were talking about an upcoming campus election. Lydia was in the middle of arguing against one of the candidates when I stepped into the circle. A breathless silence broke their flow.

"Hi." I said stiffly. At first, she looked at me without a reply, shocked by my directness.

"Hi Brad."

"Well, we should get to class. I hope you have fun tonight Lydia. See ya!" They left giving a polite wave, leaving Lydia and I standing awkward and defensive. I protected my chest with my books.

"What do you want Brad?"

"I saw you with your friends and wanted to say hi. That's all." I rocked back on my heels, my back slightly over arched.

"How are things with…"

"Things are great! Couldn't be better."

"Better… I don't know if I should thank you for that or walk away," she continued in her tense dull tone.

"No, I meant…"

"Umm, you know what? This is too weird. I don't know if I can do the small talk thing with you just yet Brad."

"I'm sorry…"

"Would you stop with that? You're a broken record man. Fuck, you are so damn unassertive! Saying you're sorry doesn't cut it. There is nothing you can do or say Brad to change what you did. In the last month, I've gone through every emotion possible and right now I don't have it to give. So, if you've come to relieve your guilt, then fine, I don't hate you. Be gone okay?" She waved the back of her hand high in the air shooing me back.

"What are you doing tonight?"

She pulled her head back squinting. "I'm going on a date."

The words burned. I shifted side to side on the edges of my feet. "Where are you going?"

"To a movie."

"I'm glad. I just hope you don't…"

"God get over yourself. I don't hate you. I need some time. I need to date guys that like women." Her body relaxed.

Casting my eyes wide, I said, "Thanks."

"How is Jordan?" she asked, putting the emphasis on is.

"Fine. He misses you. Feels bad."

"Tell him hi. You take care of that boy. He has always been interested in you, and you could crush him."

"Interested in me?"

"Look, I don't want to get into all the high school shit of who likes who, but you can't be so ignorant. I saw it coming. But all that doesn't matter now. What I need from you Brad is time away from you."

"I miss our relationship."

"You miss the idea of our relationship. We had a great platonic thing going on, that's all. Don't worry, we will be friends one day, but give me time. How about I call you when I'm ready."

"Okay."

"I just have one thing to ask of you Brad."

"What is that?"

"When I do find you again, don't jump into expletives of how wonderful you and Jordan are doing, okay? I don't want to hear about how perfect your life is with him and see how inadequate it was between us."

"I can do that."

She reached out and took my arm in her hand, squeezed gently, and walked away without turning back.

"Bye," I said in a whisper.

Chapter Twenty-Six

It wasn't long before I started to attend the GALA meetings with Jordan. Spending time in a group setting wasn't my preference. Jordan, since breaking the ice over a year ago, felt it was the next step in our relationship and our coming out in Moscow. I personally didn't feel the need as I was becoming more private and absorbed in school, but it was an important move for him, and not to mention that the exhilaration to be known in a larger group as a couple, to be seen with him.

I will never forget the meeting. Now, you have to understand, I was the more closeted of the two of us, regardless of his serious dissonance over identity and religion. What a mystery right? Why would a guy who has no opposing factors such as a fundamentalist upbringing, struggle with being open about his sexuality? Well, the only true explanation I have sorted out is my strong tendency, and uncontrollable movement towards, introversion.

There is one other factor that I should mention in this story. Rarely did I ever have to fight for acceptance. I always had support with my family. It built in me a kind of weakness, I suppose, when it came down to it. It is quite the paradox. I hid my sexuality so well. Kids never teased me. I never acted overly effeminate. Simply lucky I guess.

There must be something about having to fight for your psyche that makes you hunger for survival, a quality that drives you to work on through to the end, at least to the point when you can barely stand it. Jordan possessed that kind of strength, a heavy sword I couldn't pick up to swing. I went along with life, rarely taking up any fight.

But even he lost momentum, eventually leading to his demise; a tragedy that I am building up to. But, for now, it is important to tell you about the gay community and what we faced together as a couple.

The meeting was held once a week in an undisclosed location on campus that could only be located by contacting the GALA number. Jordan called early in the week and was received with excitement. It was as if he had found long lost friends. He was very excited. I didn't share his enthusiasm.

The only time I ever went to the group was with Jordan. My difficulty with groups of people in social settings, along with the challenges I had with the gay community as a whole has kept me from wanting to participate.

The meeting was on Monday night. Jordan arrived at the house early. He dressed nicer than usual, but not overdone. I wore the standard jeans put on a nice cashmere sweater. Jordan, although more sophisticated in fashion, especially since getting together, looked more beautiful than I on any given day.

We walked up the stairs onto a wide landing and opened the old wooden door held shut with an exhausted squeaky spring, and entered the room packed with several guys and a few women. The atmosphere was open and uninhibited and therefore less mature than I expected.

Me, being reserved and slightly pretentious, feedback I get even to this day, stood back and let Jordan take the reins. It amazed me, even to this day, how animated he became, not overly assuming, but cordial and very friendly without any pretense. Nor did he match the general immature sexual jokes in the room. There is something about a repressed group that brings out the worst in people, when let loose without defined social boundaries.

Jordan introduced me, not as myself, but his boyfriend. I can't tell you how good it felt for him to publicly acknowledge me. We were living behind closed door as a couple and now we were public. I felt slightly dizzy.

My initial judgments found displacement with curious acceptance. Everyone received Jordan and me, an indication that I needed to lighten up. They were quick to introduce themselves, seeing my discomfort. People were respectful but very intimate. Boundaries were fuzzy, rather difficult at first, but I adjusted. The norm among the men was to hug, even upon first meeting, and sometimes even a kiss on the cheek. Women were less affectionate, but close relationships were clear.

For all practical purposes, we had come to a meeting where people communed in a collective consciousness driven by the need for belonging, and to step out of hiding in a world that denied them acceptance.

The room naturally died down to a lull and everyone took a place forming a circle on the floor. An agenda went around the room. A bullet list of items included: Making Ourselves Visible on Campus, National and Local Politics, and Planning the End of the Year Dance.

The meeting started with a customary sharing of member names. The president, a short but thin, well dressed woman named Becca, broke the ice. She introduced herself, then told the group how long she had been a part of the community, and a quick synopsis of her coming out.

There were approximately eighteen of us, making this the longest, but most informative part of the evening. People shared their success stories of family acceptance and friends who embraced their open lifestyle. There were others that shared very tragic stories. As we went around the room, members listened compassionately, but also asked provocative questions. It became clear that this was not simply a political group driven by the desire to educate the world about alternative sexuality, but also a support system. The agenda was quite secondary.

The saddest story was from a lady who was about three years older than Jordan and I attended the group off and on since moving to the community two years prior. Her name was Mary. She was born in the Basque country and immigrated with her parents when she was barely four years old.

The story started with her explaining that she was going to Stanford when her parents discovered she was seeing a woman during her freshman year. She played Basketball on a full ride to the Ivy League college and was active in the gay community.

Her parents pulled her from the college and sent her to Moscow where they thought she would be better off in a more conservative community. They couldn't have been farther from the truth. Sadly, they recently found out that she had not stopped being a lesbian. Her parents stopped paying for school. With no financial or emotional support, she eventually dropped out after three semesters of failing grades and gave up any hope of playing professional basketball. She further shared that her mother hadn't talked to her in almost two years.

When it came around to me, I found no words to describe my story. I had received acceptance from everyone around me, with the exception of high school friends and the occasional jerk on campus. The only hatred I suffered was from me. I was ashamed about dating a girl and certainly didn't want to share how I had victimized someone out of my own sexuality.

"So, Brad," Mary probed, "You're saying your life has been virtually great since coming out to your parents? I don't believe you."

She shook me in my seat. Maybe it was my fake self-confidence or insistence that everything was fine that made her push. I pushed my wall up higher. "It wasn't bad for me."

"What is that shit. It is difficult for everyone," Mary insisted.

The room stood silent. All eyes, including Jordan's were on me. Why wasn't anyone else getting this treatment?

"It wasn't bad for me." I repeated, keeping my demeanor.

"Do you accept yourself?"

"I guess not."

Her words hit me like a massive brick dropped from the top of a building.

"So, why are you talking to me, really?"

"Because I want to. I'm here with my boyfriend. I...I want to know more about all this. It's not like I haven't been around gay people. I accept them, but their struggle wasn't mine until I fell in love with Jordan."

I looked over at him. Tears dampened his cheeks. The whites of his eyes were streaked crimson.

"Them... Interesting choice of words," she added.

Then she moved to Jordan. "Tell us about you. Why are you here?"

"I think for the same reason. The only difference is that most of you have told your families. That is something I can't do."

"Why not? Wait, I need to back off. Sorry. Coming out to your family is hell. It's like you have everything to lose."

Then, another person from the group added, a rather effeminate guy with pink tipped hair, "I thought I was going to die telling my father. But, he found out from my mom, and it was fine. Your whole life teeters on how people accept you. That is what pisses me off more than anything. We never treat the heterosexual world that way."

"For me," Jordan continued, "I'm Mormon. I will be excommunicated from the church if I tell. That means the end of my family life, and the eternal one from their perspective."

Mary added, "You mean from your perspective."

Jordan was quite for a moment. "Yes, but I believe that too."

"Religion is not kind to gay people. I don't know one that is."

Another member, a masculine looking woman next to Jordan, rested her hand on his leg and looked at him.

228

"There are a few. You must look around for alternatives. It's a gift being spiritual."

"No, I can't walk away from Mormonism. Like I said, I will have no acceptance. They think being gay is a lifestyle choice."

Mary jumps in, nearly to a standing position, "Yeah, like what is that? Do they think we are a bunch of dumb fucks? We just choose to risk losing our friends, families, jobs, and even getting the shit kicked out of us just to live a gay lifestyle? That doesn't make any fucking sense."

"We see it as a perversion."

"Do you believe that Jordan?"

He didn't answer. I wanted them to back off, but also wanted to hear what he had to say. When Jordan disappeared from my life last year I was shocked by the sheer power in his ability to become completely someone else, to change his personality and take on an entirely different life. Then he came back, completely out of the blue. I was afraid to bring it up; he was too, an unspoken taboo topic that we both wouldn't breach. Who was the real Jordan? I wasn't sure.

"Guys," she said singling us out. "I realize this is your first night here together. We want you to know that we accept you and hope you will continue to be a part of this group. I hope I didn't drill you too hard, so please forgive me. You seem like great guys. Let's move on. Welcome Jordan and Brad."

The rest of the group, one by one finished with their introductions, ending with the woman next to the president. She then shifted position, pulling one leg behind her and leaned over to read the sheet of paper on the floor.

"Okay, I think we need to talk about the dance next week. Do we have all the logistics worked out Thomas?"

Thomas was a short Hispanic guy, quite overweight and sweating profusely from his face. "Yes. Jackie said that the farmhouse is ours as long as we clean up before we leave. Rick will bring beer, and there will be a small cover at the door. We calculated it out to be three dollars per person provided we get enough people. We can fit about seventy-five. Oh, yes, there is also a backyard and we thought about having a barrel fire."

"Okay, of course, everyone is invited, gay and straight alike, so tell your friends everybody. But, we strictly want to keep the location secret, so don't over advertise."

I leaned into Jordan. "We're going."

*****

The dance was on Saturday night. We frantically tried on different clothes, hopelessly searching for the right outfits, not sure what people would be wearing. The first problem was that it was a barn dance. Would everyone be in cowboy attire? That was a NO WAY for me. Second, did we want to dress alike? That might look simply too weird. We couldn't decide. It was fun at first but nevertheless frustrating.

Henri sat in his customary chair and watched as he held his cigarette high in the air, while he braced a bottle of beer between his knees. He was on the third day of a drinking binge with another Swiss guy who was sleeping in his bed. Henri smirked.

"Hey girls, there is a man in my bed." We stood in place, holding our toothbrushes in our mouths for a second and then blew him off. He smelled terrible, the odor of bad feet and alcohol. But I didn't mind. He was the one true friend I had.

The franticness slowed to a dull roar. Jordan stepped into the living room and put his arms high overhead in a feminine arch. "Is this fabulous or what?" For whatever reason, we both became more feminine in our gestures and

words since attending GALA. I'm not sure if it was
liberation of the soul, or just young gay antics, but everyone
noticed. Henri looked on with amusement and commented
little, enjoying his beer, warding off detox.

"No silly," I exaggerated with a limp wrested slap on his
ass, "this is a farm house. We cannot be seen overly dressed.
I'm thinking jeans, flannel, and maybe a designer watch." I
swished back to my room on the toes of my socks, pulling
him behind me and closed the door. We kissed. "I love
you."

"I love you my Alaskan fashion queen. Isn't that how
all Alaskans dress, in jeans and flannel, minus the watch?"

Mary picked us up at the house. We asked her if she
was willing to drive since neither of us had a car.

"I can't figure out this fucking map," I said with a scowl.
Jordan was in the backseat singing to the radio.

"Haven't you been there before Mary?"

"No, not his one. The chick that owns the house is
someone's aunt. I've never met the chick."

The map was a photocopy of a pencil drawing, faded
and rough around the edges. It was most frustrating
because I didn't know my way around the county roads
anyway. Jordan was oblivious to our halting jolts in the
dark, quick reverses, and shove offs down dirt roads. I
imagined horrifyingly the scene of a truck and two redneck
cowboys racing alongside, pulling us from the small light
blue Volvo and beating our obvious faggot asses to a pulp.
It was a morbid jogging of the brain. But the dark unlit dirt
roads certainly had a foreboding persona.

Then, up ahead I saw the lights to a house. A fire
burned out back with shadows of people standing about.
"There it is girls." I pointed and suddenly felt a pop on the
back of my skull.

"Who you callin a girl, you girl." He pulled himself up and kissed my cheek. I reached my hand back and he gave me his. I looked back with affection.

We walked through a wall of people who stood outside the door smoking cigarettes. I desperately wanted one. Mary nodded her head at a few that she knew, but keeping her attention to Jordan and me, having the innate understanding we were both suddenly petrified. Jordan kept looking back at me with eyes wide and a pale expression. I had no energy to console him except hold his hand pulled in close to my stomach.

It was a large room with dozens of people socializing in a variety of groups. As we entered, mesmerized by what we saw, a tall lanky guy held a rubber stamp in his hands, and took Mary's money.

"I got it," she said firmly.

"But...," I protested.

"No, I got it."

He reached forward with his stamp. "I need your hand honey," he said pointing to Mary first, followed by Jordan, and the me.

Mary walked past the admission table and disappeared into a small group of people, leaving us standing like a couple of great blue herons hunting for a meal. I desperately looked around the room, trying to find people we knew. Mary turned and signaled.

"Brad, Jordan, this is Mark, Magne, and Tom." We reached out to shake hands but were met with light hugs. "Brad and Jordan are new to the community. Isn't this your first dance guys?"

"Yes," Jordan said with confidence, trying to hide his shaking voice.

Mark asked, "How long have you guys been out?"

"I didn't know how to answer the question. Did he mean since we started telling everyone, or our families? I sported the answer.

"Oh, about a year or so." Jordan looked at me with disapproval.

"Actually, he barely came out this month. I told him about me over a year ago," he corrected. My face flushing warm.

"How long have you two been together?" Mark continued, assuming correctly.

"A month," I said, trying to collect myself.

"Oh wow, so you came out a month ago and have been together ever since. I love a story of two friends falling in love," Magne added.

"Magne. That name. I recognized it from conversations with my mother. That is a Norwegian name, right?"

"Well yes, yes it is. How do you know that?" He brightened up, shifting his weight back in surprise.

"My mother had a roommate in college, her best friend actually, who was from Norway. She talks about him all the time. His name is Magne. Doesn't it come from Magnus?"

"Yes. Wow, impressive. Nobody's been able to do that before. You're a regular linguist Brad. Did I get that right?"

"Yes, my name is Brad."

"Cool. Do you know a lot about Norway?"

"Not much actually. But, I am thinking about going to London this summer for a couple of weeks. Not that it is all that close or anything. I've never been off this continent."

"I've been to Europe several times. My family is from Kristiansund. I love it there, my second home you might say."

We discussed Norway, London, sights to see during my vacation and world politics. Magne was a step above anyone I met in the gay community thus far, a combination of Henri and Lydia, not intimidated by intellectual conversation.

Jordan and I became more comfortable and separated from the group. We walked around the room hand-in-hand trying to absorb the scene. After getting drinks we stood against the far wall opposite the entrance and watched the crowd.

I hadn't noticed it before, but, it struck me that there were people of the same sex dancing together. Of course, we were at a gay dance, but you only realize the dramatic when it is right in your face. Subconsciously, I assumed that we were the only gay couple on the planet. It was shocking to say the least. Not only were they dancing together, but also there was the occasional deep embrace and kiss. The realization hit me, "Oh my fucking hell. I'm actually gay."

A slow song quietly started over the speaker system and built to full sound. The base was rich, giving the music a mellow quality. I wanted desperately to dance with Jordan, our first dance together in a group of people. Ignoring the anxious self-conscious voices in my head, I took Jordan's hand, placed my drink on the floor, and led him out into the middle of the room.

He turned into me, my hand around the small of his back, the other high and holding his. We kissed, looking into each other's eyes with tender smiles and passion. I was in the moment, the best moment of my life, at my first gay dance with the man I loved. He turned his head away and rested it on my shoulder, his hair warming my neck. "I love you Brad," he said quietly. I kissed the top of his head and we continued to sway together. Mary danced with a woman on the other side of the room. I caught her eye. She looked on at us, approving and clearly happy with her newfound friends.

When we finished after two songs, the second much faster, but slow enough to continue enjoying our embrace, we went back to find our drinks.

"Hey," Jordan started. "You started to say something about your London trip. Are you still going after the situation with Lydia?"

"I was supposed to take her. But... I mean, if we had remained friends... I don't think she would go now anyway, even if I wanted her to."

"Are you going alone then?"

"Actually, I hadn't really given it a thought."

"Brad, I'm not going home this summer."

"What?"

"What are you going to do?"

"I want to stay and get a job. Maybe at that bookstore downtown. Wouldn't that be a cool place to work? That way I can stay and be here with you."

"What are you going to tell your parents?"

"That I need to stay and make some money. They're going to find out anyway. I know it. I can't keep this...you...a secret forever."

"It's a really big step. Is it one you're ready to make?"

"I can't live the rest of my life in the closet."

"Jordan, you know I don't want you to leave. Three months is a long time. I don't want to be away from you that long." I took his hand, meshing his fingers in mine.

"I don't want to leave you Brad."

"Hey, what do you think about holding off on getting your job until we get back."

"We...?"

"Yeah. I want you to come with me to London. My mom is going to set it up for us. We can stay with her cousin. I have some money saved up and wouldn't mind helping you with a ticket."

"If it isn't outrageous, I think I can do it. I made a bunch working last summer at home. But, what about us? What will your cousin..."

"My mom said he wouldn't care at all. We will be there, not as friends, but as a couple."

He hugged me and took a drink of his beer from the opaque cup. "A gay couple in London. Fuck, now THAT is crazy. It's all too crazy!" His eyes glassed over. I kissed him, tasting the hint of beer against his lips.

Chapter Twenty-Seven

The gay community was our solace. It defined us, especially early on after becoming a part of GALA. It was not just any community, it was ours. For the first time in my life, I found a connection with people. I got used to being different in a straight world, seen by most as aloof and eccentric. The safety and companionship I experienced, acceptance and validation, outweighed my pretension in those days.

That isn't to say I completely embraced every aspect of the gay community. Along with the overwhelming good in most everyone I met, there was also a very maladaptive side. Everyone at one time or another has learned of the difficulty gay men have with relationships, particularly, young gay men. Older gay men are outcasts, and older is qualified as twenty-five and over. The obsession with age, and challenges with substance abuse destroy sectors of the gay community and remain the most visible parts to the world. Unfortunately, it is this side that fundamentalism exploits in small town rural media and after church conversation, only fostering the deepest of homophobia.

As I remember dealing with the coming out process, I can identify two primary issues: that from heterosexual society, and that which is directed at the self. Homophobia's original meaning is, one who 'fears' the homosexual. The definition is a bit of an overstatement, because I don't believe that bigotry is about the person's fear of the object, such as arachnophobia, the fear of spiders. There is a deeper meaning of homophobia; it is a disliking, a deep form of loathing of gay persons, simple indoctrinated hate.

Then, there is the gay person's feelings about themselves; self-loathing, a deeply rooted shame, also a form of homophobia, a fear of being gay, not wanting to be gay in a heterosexual world.

It is this complicated dynamic that speaks to the challenges of living within the gay community. The combination of both societal hate and self-directed homophobia mixes into a froth of challenges in the everyday life of a homosexual. The solutions are multi-factorial with no easy answers.

At base, society gives off repeated messages that gay people are perverts and deviations from what is biologically natural. Now, I can say, that the 90's was the gay era. Homosexuals experienced more acceptance than ever before, evidenced by gay characters in television and movies, and a President of the United States that made his first action in the White House supportive of the homosexuals in the military. Nevertheless, the covert message in most every circle you hang in, however liberal and accepting, is wrought with the subliminal subtleties of the abnormalities homosexuals bear.

My own shame, the result of homophobia directed inward, pushed me to absolute insanity. My psyche is embossed with the story even now, now as I tell you the tale, the incident that launched the chain of events leading to a terrible darkness.

It was an exceptionally beautiful day in May with only a few scattered clouds. The sun dodged in between the cotton puffs above, teasing on the advent of summer. Jordan and I were walking past the University Classroom Center, headed to my house to see what everyone was up to. As we came around the corner past Memorial Gym leading down the short cement stairs, about thirty people stood in the large arena, huddled together. They chanted holding signs high. It was a demonstration. Initially I found it exciting, not realizing the event. Jordan and I looked on, getting closer to see what the fuss was all about. My excitement turned to utter horror.

The signs were painted in large red marker, "God Hates Fags", "Stop Fags—Stop AIDS", with a banner stretched high between two middle aged women, "Keep Fags Away From Our Children". The crowd chanted, "Keep American Family Values. God Will Reign!" Mixed in the crowed were children not older than ten, the most desperate tool any adult with an agenda could use. It was simply horrific.

I stopped, pulling Jordan back who was in a zombie trance. We stood too long, for over ten minutes, mixed in with a sparse group of awestruck onlookers.

The University of Idaho supports free speech rights. It is the nature of the university environment, and should be. Open debate on philosophical and ethical issues is the breeding ground for knowledge as long as there is no open display of violence. I understand the importance of free speech, but back then, free speech to me meant that the only valid argument was my own. Nevertheless, it was impossible for me to understand how people believed such hateful things.

In 1992, Idaho suffered a movement to put into law anti-gay rhetoric. Enough votes were gathered by the states Christian Coalition to make the ballot. In the end, it didn't pass. But, if it had, it would have made it legal to fire gay people from jobs, deny employment, and even allow eviction from rental housing, simply for a person's sexual orientation. The atmosphere was tense around campus as the vote came and went. A similar bill came up in Colorado and surprisingly passed. However, the Supreme Court turned it down the following July.

On that beautiful Spring day in Moscow Idaho, standing with my partner who I loved with every cell in my body, the impact was more powerful than any storm I weathered before. Such hatred was never spoken in my home, or in my community.

Jordan stood in silence. I attempted to get his attention, but he couldn't take his eyes off of them. His face grew pale, and he looked like he was going to be sick.

"Hey, are you okay?"

"Um...I...Yeah...I'm fine"

"Let's go. This is fucked. We don't have to stay. Fuck this bunch of fundamentalist freaks!"

"I...I want to watch...just for a little bit." He glanced over at me, relieving my fear.

I looked at the people standing with us looking like the audience of a spectator sport. Whispers floated on the air, most in shock and appall.

He pulled at my arm, signaling that he had enough. We wove our way through the developing crowd of onlookers, trying to get out of the circle, having to walk far too close to the protesters. They were getting louder as their audience grew bigger. Jordan saw an opening, and we pushed our way through, when suddenly a familiar voice shouted my name from behind, sounding like it came from within the crowd amongst the signs and redundant chant.

"Yom, Brad. Faggot!" I resisted the urge to turn but couldn't. I knew that voice. I saw him out of the corner of my eye, and kept walking through the onlookers, Jordan hanging onto my arm, pulling me along. Then, a sharp pain jabbed into my back. My head flew up. I shook it off, oriented myself and turned around. Facing me was Jake, holding a sign, the end pointed directly at my face.

"Here, ...here, this is one! And look, he is with his boyfriend."

I was petrified, breathless, plotting an evasive move. People started forming a circle around us. I started to back up, Jordan continuing to pull at my shirt.

"Now, look, how cute. You think you're so clever little faggot boy. Where you going? Don't you want to stay and support our little gathering?" His voice turned low and direct, looking at me with his head low like a dog ready to attack. The chanting droned on in the background.

"Fuck off Jake."

"Jake turned and spoke to the people around us. "So, he is a scared little homo who can't take the fire."

"I'm not a faggot, and you have no right to…"

"Not a faggot? Then who is that hiding behind you? Your brother I suppose…mmm…"

"Leave us alone."

I turned to leave, and this time the pain came to my shoulder blade, the flap of the sign pocking at my neck. I kept walking, using the onlookers as a shield for further attack.

"You run little butt fuck boy. I'll see you another time."

We walked as fast as we could out of the arena down the hill to Sixth Street, saying nothing to each other. Jordan walked ahead of me, not letting go of my shirt, making sure we were in the clear before letting go.

"I hate them. Bigots. I can't fucking believe this shit. Who the hell gives them the right," I started? My throat was tight, but I couldn't release it.

"I have never been so scared. Why are they doing this?" he said bewildered.

He continued to walk, looking down at the ground, trying to hide the tears flowing from his face. I wanted to hold him. He was in pain. But we were out in public. Cars passed by, some noticing the pain in his face. I continued to stay behind, fooling myself that I was giving him his space, when in reality I was afraid, horrified. Not of what others would think as they drove by seeing two guys walking down the street arm and arm. It was shame, pure shame. Shame drove my actions to keep my distance; shame that I would be doing something wrong; shame that I was in love with this man and someone would see.

When we got to the house, the TV was on at low volume, but no one was around. Jordan went directly to my bedroom, throwing himself on his stomach between the clumps of piled blankets. I did the same, turning my head to look at him.

"It is all so strange," Jordan said.

"What do you mean, strange?"

"Never thought, or even imagined that I would have to see that."

"A lot is done in the name of fundamentalism." A short silence followed. I reached over to kiss him. He turned his head away and sat up. I followed.

"The church is right. Being gay is dangerous. It is an unhappy life."

I tried to hide the shock surfacing on my face. "Well, it is dangerous, but it's not like we can do anything about it."

"I don't know…," he passively looked away from me.

"Jordan, what is wrong?"

"What is wrong? I'm just kinda freaked out right now, okay?! Can you handle that? You can't gloss over this one Brad! You almost got the shit kicked out of you!"

"Jordan…" I glared with anger.

He pulled himself to the end of the bed and stood up, leaving me sitting and watching as he left. When I went into the living room, he was sitting on the couch, staring at the TV and going through the channels quickly, ignoring me.

"Jordan, don't ignore me. I want to talk about this."

"There is nothing to talk about. I'm just freaked out and don't know what to say," he said, not taking his eyes off the screen.

I sat next to him. He didn't move. I reached over and put my fingers into his hair.

"Don't!" he said as he pulled away. "Go change your shirt. There is blood on your back."

I sat in the corner of the couch.

I surveyed the events of the past hour. Where did it go wrong between us? It had all gone wrong, and neither of us was in control of the situation, the ignorance. As much as we loved each other, the hate was able to drive a wedge.

I sat looking at him and started to cry. Shifting his position, he leaned forward towards the TV. His face hardened.

"Go change your shirt Brad, there is blood on it! It's disgusting!"

Chapter Twenty-Eight

We never talked again about the incident at the University Classroom Center. It was the first time since being together when communication broke down into unspoken words leading to hidden resentment. It was not a growth experience, like the fights that lead to a discussion and relationship building.

Talk of our trip to London started to intensify as the last week in June approached. The semester drew near to an end with only three weeks to finals, and another three before our departure in June. My mom sent my ticket in the mail through a reservation agent she knew back home. In the envelope she attached a four-hundred-dollar check with a paper clip for spending money. She never gave spending money; she abhorred it out of principle, some work ethic bullshit. Maybe she started taking some form of mood altering medication. "It's about time." I said punching my elbow into Jordan's ribs.

The next hurdle was getting Jordan's finances taken care of. We could not rely on help from his parents. I used part of the money my mom sent, plus part of a small savings I had from summer work. We met with a local travel agent and were lucky enough to book him a seat on the same flight, but not sitting together. After the transaction was complete, things clicked along for us, at least initially.

Shadows started to appear, creeping in from the corners at night, then in the day light, looming back from the past, and taking the all too familiar form.

"It's my parents. You know that by now. How in the hell are we going to deal with that? They will find out Brad."

We were at the kitchen table drinking coffee, still in our pajamas.

That night we were out at Mary's house for what started out as a small get-together, quickly turning into a very large party. We got in around 2:00 a.m. We had way too much to drink, and then we stayed up another hour wrapped in the embrace of alcohol and physical intimacy. But the shadow, it watched.

"They don't know I'm still hanging out with you Brad. That's the first problem. I'm sure they know that I'm not right with the church. And, I haven't even told them that I'm not going to go home for the summer. All around, I'm basically fucked."

"I assumed this was all worked out. So, when is the last time you talked to them?"

"Just after Spring break. It was a stupid conversation about my classes."

"Your classes..."

"Yeah, my classes. And classes I took last semester. She actually asked me how I was doing in them. God."

"Hmmm. What if you just tell her you're not going to come home and leave it at that, okay? Then we just go, and your parents don't have to know."

"When they find out about the money missing from my account, they'll be checking Brad. God! It completely pisses me off how you act like everything just works out all the time!" He started to walk away.

"I don't want to go without you."

He stopped, and then turned with a reassuring gesture, his pajama bottoms hanging loose off his hips.

"I'm going Brad. It's just not as simple for me. I've got Nazis for parents. I'm exhausted running around lying all the time and about you. It's hard to live with that on my back every day. You can talk to your mom about us. I don't have that privilege."

"It's not like they have been overly involved in your life anyway."

"I might not get or make very many phone calls, but believe me, I will always be the target of their conversations, especially when they find out about you."

"You wouldn't tell them, would you?"

"No, not for a long time, but I can't hide forever. I wanted to at first, but it isn't a good idea. I see that now." He looked at me, intent on sorting through his anxiety. His voice was shaky. He stood on his feet strong. He reached out and touched my arm.

"I'm not going to tell them," Jordan went on, "...about the trip. We can deal with it when we get back. What can they do? They can very well fly to London and find us if they want."

"Like you said, my mom, on the other hand, was very supportive Jordan," I said, pulling his arm down, sitting us to the couch. "She asked me about you, us. I told her that I wanted to take you to London. She was enthralled in the details about our relationship. She knows I'm in love. You see, she has been worried that my life was going to be far more difficult, that I was going to be alone. Then I met you."

"It would be so nice to be able to do that, talk to my parents like that."

"That is what was strange. I told her that. She couldn't fathom how difficult and isolating it must be to not have a relationship with them, that it's unnatural. She couldn't understand why your parents were that brainwashed, to reject their own kid because of a religious belief?"

"You told her that?" A twist of irritation hung in his voice.

"I didn't quite put..."

"I don't want to go there..."

"I'm sor..."

And then he put on a calm demeanor and shifted yet again. "This isn't the first time you have talked about us, is it?"

"Oh no, I've talked about you since I've known you. I told her when we first got together. Remember? She has asked periodically, but I think she saw how serious things were when I said I'd be taking you to London with me. Maybe in some way she needed some time to let it sink in."

"What did she say?"

"She wants me to be happy. She even said that she wants to meet you some day."

"I don't know if I'm ready for that."

"I think you are."

"How do you know?" his spine rigid again with defense.

"You..."

"You Brad are very assuming," he defended with his voice tight.

"Okay, okay, you're right," I said, trying to smooth it out.

"I don't get it! How does your family just say, 'Not a problem' just like that?"

"It's not like they jumped up and down and had a party over it. My parents don't love the fact that I'm gay. They will never have grandchildren, or a wedding to prepare for, and all the white picket fence aspirations for their son. Every dream they have, every expectation since I was a little kid has had to change. They had their suspicions way before I told them. When I did tell them, they had already prepared themselves for the conversation well in advance. What's most important is that they love me!"

"That would never happen with my family. They just dance around and around, trying to figure a way out of it, trying to save me from this self-imposed hell that they refuse to acknowledge. One day, they will hear the words from my mouth, and I will blurt it, and they will fall on their asses, and then it will all be over with, and I can live my life without them if they so choose it."

The soft skin of his face struggled with pain, darkening to pale red-blue wrinkles. Teeth and fist clinched in force. Jealousy of what he could not have, brought out charcoal hate. I leaned back, unprepared, shaken.

Then, abruptly, he changed the subject, his familiar figure returning.

"Tell me, what are we going to do in London. Have you ever seen pictures? What is it like?"

"I don't really know very much, but it is quite a wonderful place according to what my mom has told me. She herself hasn't even been there, but she is in good contact with her cousins," I said, experiencing relieve in a needed shift.

"My mom explained that her parents, Robert and Martha, immigrated to Petersburg Alaska because Robert had a cousin that first went there to check things out. My grandfather wanted a new life in America and thought that he could do it in the fishing and logging industry. And that is what he did. There were some tensions in England after he left, resentments for leaving and not having the best of contact, but I guess that all got worked out. Frankly I don't care about that stuff. I don't suspect we will hear anything about it when we are there."

"What do you mean?" he asked, pulling for more of the hidden family drama.

"Well, apparently, he had a sister, Anna, that was very sad he left. They were very close. This sister is the mother of the cousin we are going to stay with. Anyway, she wrote many letters to him, begging his return visit. There was a great deal of sadness in the family that it took him over fifteen years to come back and visit."

"Then there was the issue that he held quite secret until that trip. That is, the relationship troubles that had eaten at him for so many years. His wife Martha was an evil vile woman who didn't keep the honor in the relationship. Sometimes when Robert went out on fishing trips, she had male companions stay over. On top of that, she had a drinking problem and was a drunk until the day she died. He went to his deathbed speaking very little about it, except one statement to my mother in the last days of his life. He said, 'don't ever marry anyone you don't love.' It was spoken simply and without elaboration. My mother immediately understood him and has rarely repeated it to this day."

"After the family found out the hardship he was experiencing in his American life, they urged him to get his children and move back to London. He felt a disgrace and didn't reply for many years."

"His sister continued to write letters, but he rarely answered them after that, clearly avoiding his own pain. I think that now, the family understands his situation and what it was like for him."

"You know a lot more than you let on Brad. I'm impressed. Did you know that family history and genealogy is a very big part of Mormonism?"

"No, I didn't. Do you know a lot about yours?"

"Research is a valued part of the church. We are called to it." He sat closer to me. "Let's leave that for another time." He put his head on my shoulder. I pulled him in and drew his scent into me. His shirt felt soft. "I think you should write all this down some day," he added.

I kissed him. As I pulled away, we both smiled. I tried to hide the swelling under my pajama bottoms.

We used the rest of the month to prepare for our trip with intermittent studying to get through the semester. Keeping our focus on school and targeting finals was difficult underneath dreams of London towers and bridges. Nevertheless, we were able to discipline ourselves with only minor squabbles.

And before we knew it, the summer drew rapidly upon us. Jordan hadn't told his parents about staying in Moscow for the summer. I didn't press the issue, trying to have faith the old passive persona was left behind with his closeted self of almost six months ago.

Since Jordan and I ran into Jake at the anti-gay rally, Jordan spent the majority of his time at my place. He was living with me in my bedroom amongst all our other roommates that found their way in and out of our apartment. We formalized it when finals week ended, and the first boxes started to find a place in the corner of my closet.

It was Thursday, and just one more day until the close of the semester. Jordan finished his last final early that day, I on the day before. We spent absolutely no time talking about our grades. For the first time, I don't think we cared one bit.

The evening sped into the late hours of the night. We went to his room to start getting the final belongings organized for transportation in Henri's car. Needless to say, we didn't get much done. I strictly avoided any kind of heavy exertion, only wrapping myself around Jordan while he sat looking at a picture book on London he got from the library. He was entrenched and horizontal on his sheet-less bed, periodically showing me pictures of stone castles and green countryside.

The phone rang. Playfully, I quickly reached and took the receiver.

"Hello," I blurted, Jordan laughing, trying to get the receiver from my hand.

"Is this Jordan?" Her meek monotone voice searched. It was his mother. I handed over the phone, not having to tell him.

He took the receiver, not taking a breath, putting his hand on my chest. His eyes became narrow, and said, "Hello?" He sat up and nodded his head.

"Yes, hi mom, how are you?"

"No, that was my old roommate. You remember Brad."

"Well, no. There is something I need to tell…"

"No…"

"Mom, I'm not coming home…No, I'm going to stay and work…Yes, that is what I'm going to do…I don't know, I am trying to get a job at the bookstore. Church is fine…The Bishop?...No mom, I've not been going very much…Yes, I know I need to, just been busy. OKAY mom…I'll be here."

He hung up and moved to a standing position. "She didn't like that very much." His voice was flat, but not anxious.

"Did she freak out?"

"Less about summer, and more about church, and…and you. Wow, I can't believe I actually admitted I wasn't going! Fuck, am I crazy? She asked me where I was going to work but just kind of skipped over most of that and told me that I needed to be going to church and that I needed to keep up the deal they made me."

"Deal?"

"Remember? Last year they said that I had to go to church or they would not continue to pay for school. I'm almost ready to tell them to keep their fucking money. I'm tired of their manipulative shit."

"They would never deal with you being gay. I don't think you should tell them anytime soon. Or you can kiss your money and school goodbye."

"I'll tell them when I'm ready. That's my decision. They will have to accept it, or I'm out of there. I'll find a way."

His words were tough, but I knew it wasn't all that simple with him. Internally a battle was stirring. Time told me it was the biggest battle he would fight yet. Old behaviors started showing themselves. After that evening, Jordan tried to hide his conflict from me. He lived like an alcoholic trying to hide his disease. The symptoms were only subtle at first. His language changed. He started saying 'Heck' instead of 'Hell', and even 'Darn' instead of 'Damn'. Slowly the internal conflict was rebirthing itself.

Chapter Twenty-Nine

Two days to London. The house buzzed with insanity. Our passports had arrived on time. I checked over the flight numbers, comparing them against the arrival and departure times several times over, making sure everything was in order. With luck, we hoped we could maneuver sitting next to each other provided there was extra room on the Atlantic connection. With little time remaining we worked on the detailed packing, matching pants to shirts, and shoes to socks. The bathroom attire alone took up a fourth of one suitcase.

I was pleasantly surprised to find out that Mary, and her newfound girlfriend that she met at the barn dance, wanted to throw a sendoff party. However, the overwhelming feelings of the travel made it seem bigger to deal with than I wanted.

Jordan said he was also overwhelmed, bordering on despondency. There were passing comments about lying to his parents, withholding his whereabouts, and stealing money. Up until planning for London, we rarely talked about them since being together. Avoidance. Now, and in the most difficult moments before our trip, his mood was unpredictable and physically withdrawn.

The night before our flight, we pulled a set of clothes from the stuffed suitcases next to the bed, quietly got ready, and then walked into the warm June air to Mary's campus side apartment.

Everyone we knew was there, our friends from GALA, and countless other acquaintances. The wildest group of jean loving lesbians took over the living room floor dancing to heavy beat gay generation music. Everyone went completely out of their way to give us the warmest send off.

There was a wall of food and alcohol, enough to keep us going all night.

Jordan didn't say much to me that night. He looked at me periodically from across the room, worried, questioning, displaced, and then would turn away, re-involving himself in the circle he mingled with. He also wasn't drinking, uncharacteristic for him since we got together. I put it away in the back of my mind, choosing to forget.

Mary sat with me at the kitchen table sharing her experiences of Europe. She had been back several times seeing her family. She told me that her next adventure was Nepal. She had another rock climbing friend who wanted to take her, apparently to Katmandu and mountain trekking from there. She heard stories of the poverty of the people, the dogs that ran the street with mange. This was Mary, adventure to the core.

The next morning, Mary arrived early, honking her horn, the engine puttering at the bottom of the stairs while she waited. Jordan had hardly said a word but was dressed and ready to go. I put the suitcases next to the door after getting up. There were two suitcases with two small carry-on bags sitting next to them. I took them outside, Mary also acting rather distant, took them from me and loaded them into her car. She gave me a soft short hug and handed me a small package wrapped in cloth. I sat in the front seat and opened it.

Jordan sat in the back seat without saying a word. My attention was on Mary. Behind her gruff exterior was a giving heart and a feminine side rarely seen by people. Pulling the cloth corners out to the side I saw the small narrow box, an old box that had been well used. I wiggled the top back. Inside was an old slightly tarnished pin in the shape of a feather. I put it through my shirt and pushed the back on.

"An old girlfriend gave it to me before a trip I took back to the Basque Country years ago. I want you to have it. It means nothing really special, except to get your ass home safe."

"Thank you," I said laughing under my breath. She messed up my hair and pushed me to the side before looking back at Jordan. I undid my seatbelt and hugged her. She briefly squirmed and then relaxed. I kissed her on the cheek. "Thank you very much. It is beautiful."

"Get home safe you," she finished and then pulled out into the traffic headed out to the Moscow-Pullman airport.

It wasn't until we reached the airport when the shadow showed its face. Mary pulled into short term parking, turned off her car, the sound of her keys hitting the dashboard as she pulled the oversized cluster out. "Okay, here we are." She opened her door and got out, going to the back and opened the trunk. I followed. But Jordan remained in the car.

I looked through the rear window. Going into a trance, I immediately knew. I went around to his door. He kept his eyes fixated in the distance, his lips slightly parted. He was motionless. I opened the door. Mary stayed behind the car, her hands in the back pockets of her tight-fitting jeans. She looked away, giving us privacy, but remaining close.

"Jordan! We have to get checked in." He didn't move or appear to take in air. I closed the door, walked in front of the car and around to the other side. I got in next to him. "Jordan, what is wrong? Is everything okay?" I turned to face him, but his stare remained fixed in the infinite space in front of him.

"She asked," he said slowly.

"What?"

"She asked about you."

"Who?"

"My mom." Tears started down his face.

"What the fuck are you talking about?" I wasn't able to keep my composure any longer.

"She asked Brad." He looked at me. "She asked if we were more than friends. She knows Brad, and she is coming tomorrow to get me."

"When did you talk to her? We haven't been alone for days."

"I called. You were in bed. I had to tell her Brad. I had to tell her where we were going. Then she asked about us, and I told her. She sounded happy for me at first when she asked. Then it changed. It all changed. She told me in her calm sullen way that I would never be happy. She said that being with a man meant I would never find true happiness in this world, and homosexuality was not in Father God's plan for me, and that I had to come home immediately. If not, I would be dishonoring them and the mission that Father God had given them to raise me. Then she reminded me of how much they have done, and all their sacrifices. Yes, she said that, after all they had done for me, I had to tell her that I was gay. She said I could have it changed."

"Oh my God. Jordan, we need to go. She can't get you if you're not here." I took his arm. "Come on, let's go." He pulled it back and said, "I can't. I can't go. Brad, it's over," he said looking at me. I put my hand on his. He pulled away.

"This is fucked. I can't believe that you're going back to that psycho bunch of shit," I screamed. "My God. Please, don't do this."

"It's over. I can't run anymore." His crying intensified, but he tried to force it back, his face contracting in painful motions, leaning forward, his head going to his knees. I cried, not knowing what to say. In desperation I held on. He couldn't leave me like this. He couldn't leave me for his family, for his church.

"You are going, and there is nothing more to it than that? Get out of the car now and we are going to London and you are never going back home again."

"No, I'm not going. Mary will take me to her place until my mom gets here."

"Mary? What does she have anything to do with it?" I felt the horrors of panic and betrayal.

"I told her."

I absolutely couldn't understand how all this came about. Jordan had a secret conversation with his mother. Then he talked with Mary. All without telling me. Jordan, my partner, and Mary, my friend. And, neither was willing to say a fucking word until this point?

Just then, Mary came to my side of the car and opened the door. The windows were fogged. "Come on Brad." She put out her hand. She was crying.

I got out of the car. I went back to the trunk and put all four bags back in and closed the lid. "What are you doing?" she asked calmly. I ran to the front door in a manic state.

"I'm going home. Take me home."

She got in the driver's side, holding her keys in her lap. "Brad, you can go. I think you should still go."

"No, I want you to take me home."

"I think you're making a big mistake," she said calmly and disappointed.

"Well, that is my mistake now isn't it," I retorted.

I barely remember the drive home that day, or what I thought about. It is moments such as these when egos are protected by psychic numbing, a space of being physically awake but emotionally asleep.

I remember getting out of the car and Mary meeting me with her key at the trunk. I took out my two bags in silence and walked up the stairs, only briefly looking back as I heard Mary's car door shut and the engine start. For that short moment I saw Jordan with his head leaning into his laced fingers against the window. They were gone.

Part Three

"Grasping with Knotted Fingers"

Chapter Thirty

Elaina sat up in the chair, pulling herself off the warm leather. She felt sore sitting in the same position for so long. She looked at her watch. It was three hours since they first met at The Beanery. Her teacup was empty again, but the anticipation of the story and where it was leading made her crave something stronger.

"You didn't go to England at all," she groaned. "Tragic. That is really way too bad in my mind! It could have saved you...saved Jordan." Elaina shifted her weight again, looking for a cooler spot on the couch to rest her arm.

Brad slouched deep in his chair, his mind exhausted. The story had an ending to tell, and he now couldn't avoid telling it. The temptation to cut it short passed over his consciousness and lingered for consideration. But no, he needed to get it out of him, like a satanic verse running through his head, needing exorcism; he needed to purge the poison.

"I stayed. If I had left that day without him, I would have tortured myself the entire vacation. I hung onto the hope that it was a passing phase. He had to come back to me, right? We were so in love Elaina, and I was desperate. My mom, on the other hand, was pissed."

Elaina pondered the story. Her experience of Brad was not deep, their friendship underdeveloped, mostly knowing each other as party buddies. Thinking now, she felt guilty. In public they talked about being best friends, but it was without substance or evidence. The idea itself was nice but things were actually quite shallow. He never shared anything as personal as now. Maybe they were too young at that time to understand friendship. Relationships needed time, and that is what they didn't take advantage of. Does anyone at that age? They roomed together for a year and then she left back to her home in Belgium. She graduated and then couldn't get a work visa. She had no choice but to go back.

"It is funny," she pondered, "as little as we talked about your relationship with him, I knew you were in love. You have to know that the gay thing wasn't really weird for me. I just didn't understand it. The problem was more that I only learned to see you as gay. When we first met, you were just a smarty-pants that did well in school. Then you were just gay. You absorbed yourself in every part of the lifestyle…and left me out…and others too…I was left out Brad. Not only that, you rubbed it in my face. Maybe I have my own phobia about it. You know? Wow, I'm sorry if I am offending you."

"No, not at all," he replied as he played with the gauge on his sweater. She knew he was lying.

"What is he doing now? You have to finish." She stood up and walked the cups and saucers into the kitchen. She set them on the counter, pushing aside the elongated leaves of the Christmas cactus consuming the space.

"Elaina. There is more, much more," he emphasized. Brad looked to catch her as she came out into the living room. "I'm sorry that you know so little. Especially now."

She ignored the weak effort at an apology. "It is getting late, so if you want to keep me, you better provide me with something stronger than tea."

"I have some Scotch."

"Fuck yes my little gay boy!"

Brad thought her reference amusing.

Elaina relaxed back in her place, turning to see what the cats were doing. They hadn't moved, except Marty who turned his head over, stretching his legs out above him.

"How does he sleep like that?"

"Hell, I don't know." He pursed his lips and snickered through his nose. He was distracted, thinking what he was going to tell her next. He found himself standing in front of the old hutch in the living room against the partition separating the kitchen and the living room. Pushing several bottles around, the glass clanked as they were moved aside. Finally, he found what he was looking for.

He pulled out the bottle with the oversized black and gold outlined numbers against opaque paper, indicating '18' Years. It was a special bottle, not simply because of the age in the Barrel: It was the bottle of scotch his dad bought him for his twenty-first birthday. The seal was undisturbed.

Brad didn't hesitate as he peeled off the plastic and twisted out the cork cap. Brad took a deep breath and relaxed. This was the moment he wanted it for. He deserved it.

He put his nose to the top. It had a sweet but oak-like odor with a hint of seaweed. He turned into the kitchen and poured scotch into the appropriate glassware, saved for such an occasion. He added two cubes of ice to each. They cracked into the silence. He took his seat across from her and put the glasses on the coffee table.

"You still haven't told me anything about your dream. Kind of a mystery don't you think?" She reached to the coffee table, taking the cold damp glass in her hand, and brought the rim to her lips. She squeezed her eyes into slits and then took a sip. Brad looked at her and smiled, following her lead.

The malt flavor swam in his mouth, down into his stomach, and quickly into his head. He needed the intoxication. His mind escaped, remembering his father and the smell of dried tree bark caught in his flannel shirt after hauling wood. It was his essence, whom he knew in spirit had been watching over the night's proceedings.

"I keep having these dreams. It is the same dream actually, replayed over and over again, sometimes twice in the same night. I don't understand it. In the past I had it only once a month or so, but now it is nightly."

"Well, the only possibility is that you are trying to forget something." Her insight was striking, causing brad to guess how much she was holding back. Did Elaina know more and was humoring him, playing along?

"I need for you to know the rest of the story. I think it has to do with what happened after Jordan went to Mary's, and I've not spoken about it since." His voice became restricted.

"I think that if I told you the rest, it will all make sense. It will help me."

She looked at him seriously, unaware of the details. "Okay." She took another sip.

Brad understood his own passivity. He understood that he didn't face problems and wasn't facing life these days. Now was his opportunity to change it. The past hadn't gotten better by avoiding it. Working long hours, being distant from everyone, taking medication, and playing heavy cerebral games with himself left him isolated and alone.

Chapter Thirty-One

The screen door opened behind me as I sat on the top step with my suit cases behind me. I held onto my carry-on bag wrapped tightly in my arms like a security blanket embraced by an insecure child. The pain was excruciating, the situation dizzying. I was going to get sick, my mind left stunned, my body numb.

"Man! What are you doing?" Henri said as he cautiously approached, letting the door slam behind him. He sat down and moved in close sensing the gravity of the situation, only deepening the struggle irrupting inside my chest. Then I let it go, allowing him to pull me closer squeezing me tight. He rested his head on mine. He wept.

"He's gone, forever gone!" I groaned.

"Hey man, what is it, why aren't you on the plane?" he gently questioned.

"I'm not going." Sitting up, I moved away so I could look at him.

"That be clear my man." He leaned back, saddened, but not surprised.

"He talked to his mom," I said getting my composure.

"Jordan."

"Yeah, he wouldn't go to London, and wanted out, out of the relationship. He is leaving me to keep the relationship with his parents, his church."

"It is crazy, religion over love." he said shaking his head and looking down at his feet. "Were you guys having problems?"

"No, well, things got a little out of hand after his parents got involved this last time, but nothing more than usual I thought. We were in his dorm room and I answered the phone. It was her! He took the phone and it just got fucking weird from there Henri. Then he closed up. And this morning, he talked to Mary, you know, the gal we sometimes hung out with from GALA?"

"Okay…" He seemed confused, maybe that he couldn't place her, maybe wondering why she was involved.

"She went along, and even drove us to the airport, all along knowing that he wasn't going to get on the plane. He worked out staying with her until his mother gets here to pick him up some time in the next day. They all fucking betrayed me."

He sat in silence. His tenuous look told the story of a man who knew what to say, who had been betrayed and had the wisdom of a response, but knew the need for discussion and not answers.

"This is so fucked. She asked him about us on the spot. And he told her, and as expected she vehemently disapproved. He fell like a soldier in battle. He just crumbled right in front of me."

"Man, I don't get it," he said and then paused. "It is crazy really. Who cares what she thinks." He clearly didn't understand the powers that be.

"He does. It's the religion. The Mormon faith has no place for the homosexual. They don't accept it at all. Sure, they might placate on the surface…"

"So," he said sarcastically, "The puritans are at it again. Haven't you Americans learned from that shit? You started this country to get away from it, didn't you? Religious fundamentalism? Man! I wouldn't think he could be that weak. We are a stronger liberated generation! Why doesn't he get out and tell them to fuck off until they get their shit together?"

"Who the hell knows, but he can't. I've been asking myself the same question since I met him. Whenever his parents get involved, he just flips. They have some weird fucking power. He runs back to the church, and totally denounces that he's a fag."

"So, you've still not told me why he can't deal."

"I can only guess that the two are simply incompatible."

I wanted to cry again, seeing how powerful the church was and why I wasn't as powerful in his eyes.

He chose against us, me and him, Henri.

"Dude, you don't need that shit in your life. It's time you made your own decisions. You need to stop giving him the power to choose if you are going to be together. If he comes back, and you can bet he will, you can choose man."

"I can't choose my feelings, and I can't say I wouldn't go running back at this point."

"Then talk to him. You approach him and don't wait for him to come back holding the cards. Show him you have decision power. You need to let him know how you feel. He has hurt you. Brad my man," he said nudging me in the arm, "he has pissed you off. You need to tell him how you feel. You need to do it before it is too late.

He stood up, looking down at me. "Get yourself put together and we will be off. If this shit is going to have an end, being one way or another, you need to have a say without being a victim. Now is the time."

Henri lit a cigarette and took my suitcases inside. He pushed them just inside the door and I went into the bathroom. Looking into the worn mirror I gazed at my pale expressionless face, tucking my emotions into the opaque box in my head. The need to perform outweighed the hurt. The need to keep it together was my only chance in getting him back.

Before I knew it, I was jerked out of the trance and into the stiffness of reality with a pounding on the door. The mirror hadn't changed. My breathing was shallow, much shallower, a bead of sweat hung from my chin.

It was time to get into position, and stepping out, I searched for the cold pot of coffee from early that morning. I finished the room temperature warm liquid doctored with milk, dumping it down my starving throat. Flashes of the morning went past the visual space of my mind like a director visualizing a filmstrip. Was there anything in Jordan's behavior, any specific clip or scene that indicated or predicted why I stood drinking cold coffee and milk on the un-swept linoleum floor, now preparing for yet another confrontation?

We walked to Mary's hillside apartment with Henri talking about his night's drinking adventures, of which I detected from the odor coming off his breath all morning. It wasn't until we made the visual approach when the weight returned, the silence dividing us. I had no idea what to expect or what was to be said. There was no wisdom, advice, or example I could pull from with the intense tugging at my heart clouding the way.

Mary's Volvo sat in the parking space taking up part of the next while hanging over the walkway in front of her apartment door. Henri knocked. I pulled my jacket up close to my neck as the wind bit at my anxious sweat. Silence. No movement, no sound of feet on the floor coming at us. The sound of wind and the scent of the chilled air set in close. It was uncharacteristic for a June day.

The curtain behind the large window next to the door moved. Someone was there, seemingly avoiding us. I briefly saw her face and then as quickly as it came into sight, it was out again. It was the briefest of disguised innocence. The careful rustling of a chain and the snap of a lock gave way to the slow ushering of an opening door. Henri stepped in disturbing the cautious setting.

It was a small apartment with the kitchen connected directly to the living room, but smaller. A couch sat facing the door and curtained window off to the right. Jordan sat calm and secure and looked directly at me. It surprised me. It wasn't the passive dependent personality I had known. He looked without moving his eyes off me.

"I thought you'd come," Mary said, moving next to Henri and nodding at me. "You guys need to talk."

I stared back wondering where I was going to go. Emotions were capped off, held deep, locked hard and safe. He used a distinctively different approach, one with an unexpected beginning that would guide the conversation to a different ending. I didn't hate him. I knew him and was now not surprised by what he had done. London could wait. The challenge was working out the next steps.

Mary looked up at Henri and said in a whisper, "Let's go out back and have a cigarette." Henri agreed and followed her out the door. It shut, locking us into interaction, our eyes not leaving their position. I was bolted to the floor, still silent.

"I don't know what to say," I forced, pulling my eyes away, my throat tightening.

"Why did you have to do it this way Jordan? Don't you think I would have understood? I would have really. I can't believe you used Mary to go behind my back!"

As hard as I forced for composure, the tears made way down my face. He held his position. "Why are you doing this? After all we have been through?"

Then, forcing his head back, he groaned as he hit the wall intentionally.

"Jordan. Don't you hear me?" The pressure was building. "I'm spilling my guts. Please, don't ignore me." He refused to look up or speak. I started to rock on my feet. "What are you thinking goddamn it? At least tell me what is going on in that head of yours!" I blurted.

"I don't know," he replied in a tight jawed monotone.

I moved back and forth, building energy I couldn't contain. My eyes were now dry.

"I can't take this…why are you doing this to me? Fuck! Aren't you going to say anything?" I forced a step forward, stopping a few paces in front of him.

"I don't know what to say, is there anything to say to you Brad?"

He shifted his body, looking intently at his fingers on the hand he was picking at, pulling off strips of calloused skin. He fell into a trance, methodically picking at himself as if I was not there.

Then, what had started as a pinhole of emotional release from the depths of my core, now erupted into what equated to total destruction. The unthinkable was about to happen.

I got within range, standing over him now and yelled, "Jesus Christ, you fucking prick, stop ignoring me? I came to talk and you're going to fucking shut me out? At first you act all tough and now you're disappearing into some kind mystery fucking space! You're a piece of shit Jordan." He sat picking at his finger, even more intently looking for something to pull on while biting his lower lip.

"You're a fucking asshole Jordan, a fucking asshole that is choosing your "white shirt and tie church' bullshit over me! I hate you. I hate you for leading me into loving you and just fucking walking away again. You knew it from the beginning, didn't you? You've known it all along that you couldn't do it! I hate you!"

Pulling my hand back, without conscious effort or holding back, I swung. My hand hit him, blowing his blond hair like a puff of air over my hand. His head flew back hard with the blow. He didn't move but started to cry not looking back, his beautiful blond hair falling back over his eyes. I stepped back, trying to catch my breath and choking with the tears of fear, a sort very different than hurt.

"Oh my God," I cried. His face was taken over by tears, and a small stream of mucus ran out his nose. "I'm so sorry Jordan," I begged. He didn't respond. "I'm so sorry."

I left and found myself deliriously leaning up against Mary's car, wondering what had happened and how. I left, attempting to find my way home in my confusion and mixed up state. My mind swam. It was over. I knew that now. There was no turning back, no hope. Jordan was the Church's forever. The realization hit me in the gut, leaving me sick the deeper I realized the impact of what had happened only moments before.

Chapter Thirty-Two

For the rest of the day, I tortured myself over what I had done. I replayed scenes, flashes of hitting him, seeing his head forced to the side, watching his hair lift and then back down. If only I had restrained myself before the argument got out of control. I couldn't bear the thought of what he now felt. Was it hate? Disappointment?

Henri was with me that day, a true friend, not offering advice, but his calm consistent presence. He didn't say, but I knew he understood. He too was once so deeply in love, madly, to the point where he mattered less, but had also hurt them, striking the person he loved.

As zombies exist, so did I into the next day. I watched TV and waited for news of his safety. It wasn't until late into the evening when I got word. Mary called with the most awful news.

"Oh my God Brad. I'm so glad you picked up. Jordan is in trouble!" My heart pounded, my mouth moved away from the receiver. The only possibility was that his mother had already taken him by now. Or had she?

"What, what?" I urged.

"He is at the hospital in Lewiston. He tried to kill himself."

At first, I couldn't speak. What had I done?

"You need to get here Brad. Get here now! He needs to see you. We can't get him to talk. He is acting very strange and we can't shake him out of it. His parents...."

"Are they there?"

"Yes. And they haven't said shit to anyone. They sit with sticks up their ass like they are watching a fucking TV show."

"What?"

"Look, I'll explain later. We are on the psychiatric unit at St. Josephs. Do you know where that is?" She started to whisper.

"Yes."

"Visiting is going to end in an hour. Can you make it? He needs to see you."

"Yes!" With that, I hung up. The click of the receiver against the counter echoed in the living room. "I'll be there Jordan, as soon as I can, I will be there." The thought repeated in my head rhythmically.

I took the keys hanging from the hook on the backside of the door. They went to Henri's 1978 Cadillac. I paused only momentarily, and then decided. He would know it was urgent for me to commit such a violation.

The regional psychiatric facility was on the third floor of the building. Over the years, I heard many things about it, everyone has a horror story about someone they knew who had been there. Jordan was now a resident, leaving the stigma swimming in my head, jokes running in a stream, suddenly feeling personal and irritating.

I got out of the damp smoke scented car and looked for the entrance. Mary's car was hazardously positioned in the handicap space in front of the sliding glass doors. I walked into the lobby and found the hospital map obtrusively in the middle of an oversized sitting area, taking the stair well immediately to my right. I was breathless with anticipation moving up each flight before getting to the door titled, "Psychiatric Unit".

The doorway entered into a confined room. I was the only one there. In front of me was another set of doors. To my right was a speaker on the wall with a button and a sign that read, "*After 9:00 P.M., Ring for Assistance. Please Be Advised: Two Visitor Limit.*"

I pushed through the metal door, working to calm my breath. My eyes immediately found Mary. She was sitting by herself on a wide couch, across from a man and woman, clearly married, the woman resembling Jordan's finer features. It was his mother. I recognized her from the first day on campus at Geordie Hall. Mary must have sensed me. She quickly turned. A reserved but cautious smile formed on her face. I walked over and sat in a chair at the end.

"Hi," she invited.

"What is going on?" I asked in a deep breath.

"We are waiting on the doctor. Jordan's with him now. We're supposed to be able to see him when the doctor is finished, even if visiting hours are over."

Jordan's father avoided any acknowledgement of my presence. His mom held her purse tight to her chest, wrinkling her flower pattern blouse, and looked on with disapproval and concern.

"Oh, sorry to be rude," Mary said pointing at me. "This is Brad." She was looking at Jordan's Mother. She nodded her head.

Cautiously, I put out my hand, and with a tinge of acrimony I said, "Oh, I've heard so much about you. Nice to meet you." She met my hand with hers and sheepishly gave it a shake, then passively pulled back. An awkward silence followed.

"I need to have a cigarette. Want to join me?" Mary asked. It wasn't an invitation, but an order. I followed quickly behind her, Jordan's father still not taking notice of my presence. Before I knew it, we were back on the street.

"Oh my god. That was so fucked up! How long have they been here?"

"Since last night. It got completely out of hand. You...,"

"I can't fucking believe it! Why the fuck...I just want to...," I blurted, flabbergasted that they were sitting in the waiting room, the objects of my hate, and the cause of Jordan's pain.

"They are his parents Brad."

"Fuck that! Don't defend them Mary! Being the peace maker isn't called for at this moment," I spewed.

"Jesus, keep focused. Jordan is in it real bad," she said as she held out a lit cigarette. I calmed myself long enough to take a drag, then gave it back to her.

"What happened?" I asked.

"Well, he cried for about an hour. I decided to give him some space. Told him that I was going to go out to find us some burgers. Everything seemed just fine. And when I got back, he was gone."

"And...?" I led.

"Hey! Drop the fucking attitude. This is fucking serious shit. Knock it off and pull yourself together." She poked her cigarette at me. "Brad. None of us, including you, knows what your boyfriend is going through. We have to stick together. Fuck, it was a bad scene. The guy was freaky! When I couldn't find him walking around the neighborhood, I panicked."

"Where were his parents?"

"They came just before I took off to look for him."

"Did they help...I mean, did they help you look for him?"

"Yes. I told them how upset he was, how I left him for just a moment and then he was gone. Initially his mother blew me off, insisting he just needed space. I was about to get in her face when his dad nudged her in the arm. They got in their car and he said, 'Were going to search the surrounding blocks.' I told them I would go downtown. I got in my car and took off as fast as I could. I was the son of a bitch that lost him in the first place." She rocked on her feet and then continued.

"Something was wrong, really wrong this time. He wouldn't talk Brad. Just sat on the couch and didn't move. When he said he was hungry, I believed him. Then he just..." She paused.

"Just what? What happened? Where did you find him?" I pressed.

Mary ignored me, becoming fully absorbed in the story. She took long hard drags off her cigarette, her eyes fixated into the lines of the pavement as she traced her steps.

"I went directly to The Beanery. He wasn't there. Then I backtracked through campus. I looked in every memorable spot. He could have been anywhere. Then his dad passed me in their car. He waved me down. I pulled my car around and jumped out, running to the driver's side window."

"He looked up at me, with his eyes for the first time, no avoidance. He was worried. They were Jordan's eyes, a look I will never forget. He insisted I follow him. Confused, I asked what he was talking about. He said that he had a police radio in his car, pointed at it mounted on the dash. He heard that there was a jumper at the bridge in Lewiston. He was sure it was Jordan. How he knew, I didn't know, but I was willing to take the risk to follow him. 'You're the only one who can help. He will listen to you!' he insisted."

"What follows, you won't believe Brad. It was totally fucked up. We sped the forty-minute trip to Lewiston in thirty. I followed close, and then got in front to lead the way to the Lewiston-Clarkston Bridge. It was a small bridge, and not very high off the water, but Jordan always talked about sinking like a rock in water. He was deathly afraid of it."

"I pulled my car behind the crowd of swarming people. Police officers, Medical Technicians and onlookers stood at the police line as two guys in street clothes stood near Jordan. People were standing around chanting, yelling at him to do it. I was sick, unable to believe how fucked up the situation had gotten! I called out to him once, telling him to hang on. I tried to push through the crowd, but the force was too strong.

"He was on the bridge…"

"He was going to jump," Mary added. She dropped her cigarette, having smoked it almost to the butt and rubbed her stomach, continuing to gaze aimlessly into space, not fixated on any object, lost in a trance.

She continued, but changed her pace, holding something back. "I watched them attempt to talk him down. For a while, I thought he was going to really do it, you know, jump. He leaned forward real hard, and suddenly cops from the mass of people sprinted at him. They pulled him down violently, clearly pissed and taking it out on him. Jesus, they were rough on him. Then they took him to the emergency room. Another lady showed up to talk to him while I sat in the lobby. It was almost two hours before they finished. His parents didn't say another word to me. We waited, but there was nothing to say. They had placed him in custody and he was headed up stairs to the ward."

"Custody?"

"I don't know what it means except that he can't leave for the next couple of days, and thank God, he can't." Mary hesitated again, started to speak, but was interrupted. A woman came out from the unit and into the lobby. She said, "The doctor is going to let you visit now."

"Thanks," Mary said graciously. We followed her inside and back up the stairs.

I became possessed with reviewing Jordan's struggle over and over in my mind. He was crumbling like a house built on shifting sand. His identity was being blown into the air, only to land in fragments, a scattered person in the end. Would he return to Oakley with his parents and become a part of the Mormon collective consciousness? It was medieval torture. Guilt, an eternal guilt was eating him from the inside out, fed by the lingering rejection of his parents.

Now, I have heard recently that Mormons retort how much they love the homosexual but hate the sin. The notion is not only impossible, but absurd. Being gay is not the simplistic notion of lifestyle, born of the perversions of molestation or pornography. It is not satanic position. It is part of your soul, a beautiful expression of nature. Fundamentalism was the wind that tore at him, ripping his being to fragments and casting him about, grain by grain.

My anger shifted to the adults absorbed in their own selfish cognitions. Jordan sat in the hospital, on the other side of that door, going through a hell that made him wish he had jumped. Meanwhile, his parents sat up on their self-imposed royalty, looking down in disappointment and judgment. If they had cussed me out, or accused me of leading their son into hell, then I would have some form of battle to wage. But their axe was silence, the kind of condescending silence that stilted all questions and argument.

His mother leaned into her husband. "I don't suppose he is getting out tonight. What hotel are we staying at?"

"Let's figure that out later," he whispered back with a disgruntled tone.

She leaned into him closer. "We need to get him into the bishop as soon as we get back Mark." It was the first time I had heard his father's name. "I talked to him before we left, and he said that he could look into counseling through the churches' social services. We need to go as a family this time, don't you think? He has gotten too far away from us Mark." She spoke loud enough for us to hear, quiet enough to claim it was a private conversation. His father nodded agreeably.

"I don't imagine there will be a problem after he gets some good counseling. The bishop will be nice to work with."

Mary and I looked on as they spoke. They had an audience that for the first time, wanted to remain invisible. What else would they say if we weren't sitting there?

The door leading onto the floor made an electronic click and opened outwardly. A lady came out into the lobby and searched the faces before settling on Jordan's mother.

"When can we take him home?" she asked.

"He is in the custody of the county right now. It could be a couple of days." They looked up at her, struggling to remain in control.

"The fact that he is in custody," she continued, "helps us out a great deal. He doesn't want to be here, and remains very suicidal. He has a lot of support and we are going to start counseling in the morning with the therapist."

"We already have it worked out," his mother quietly stated, looking at her husband for affirmation.

"So, he will be going home with you then?"

"Yes." His father affirmed. "We are going to take him home as soon as he is released."

"I think that is best. He needs to be in a controlled environment for a while. The county has taken his freedom for now, and I don't think that freedom is something he can handle as long as he continues to be a danger to himself. Can you tell me what led up to this?" The tall woman, thin in stature took a seat next to Jordan's mother. Her name tag hung loosely on her shirt reading, "Clinical Nurse Director".

His father led, "He isn't fitting into that school."

"He said you haven't been getting along for a long time."

His mother flushed red with embarrassment.

"The doctor is going to start him on some medication. An antidepressant. Medication by itself is not a cure all. I'm glad to hear he is going to get some counseling when you return home."

"Yes," his mother added. "We want him home as soon as possible."

"Well, do you want to see him? He is getting dinner right now." Just then, the door to the ward opened. A guy stepped out and signaled to the nurse. After some whispering, conspicuously leaning into ears, she returned with a strained expression.

"Jordan doesn't want to see you today. Um, actually, he specifically doesn't want to see his boyfriend." She glanced at me, suddenly making the connection. "But, he will call you later."

Acting as if the reference was not said, Jordan's mother interjected, "We would like to see our son Ma'am."

"They're not family," his father added. My nostrils flared in disbelief. I churned with hatred. A fight was brewing and my restraints were being tested.

"I'm as good as family, and they know it," I said violently.

Yet again they looked at Mary and I, then the nurse, their silence communicating the churning distaste. It extended into eternity.

"I think the best thing for now is for you two," she said gesturing to them both, "to have a short visit without any complication. I can see a bitter history between you, and he is too fragile for that. It's not good, simply not good for him right now."

"Complication? I thought." Now what in the hell made me a complication?

They stood in satisfactory silence, his mother holding her purse tight to her chest, as if to protect it from thieves.

Mary put her arm around my shoulder, leading me to the exit. I stood in place, feet planted steady in cement, glaring at them all. With one firm jerk, she pulled me out of balance. "Tell Jordan that I love him," I said forcefully, leaning into his father's space, forcing him to lean back slightly.

You see? I couldn't win, and it was the reason I hated them even more, my head spinning with anger and hopelessness. God and the church and his parents, the nursing director and the hospital, stood with authority against me, me and Jordan. They won, attempting to collect the precious treasure on the other side of the magnetic door.

My eyes didn't leave the scene until we got out to the car. She opened the door and she pushed me in, not giving any time for last minute retaliation. Before I had time to understand why we were driving off, I started to cry, quietly to myself with my head turned into the passenger side window.

"Wait, Henri's car!" I said.

"We will come back and get it later."

"But..."

I sat back defeated. Mary turned the radio on and drove in silence, up the grade and back to Moscow. When we came into town, she turned onto Front Street and parked in front of The Beanery, the home of countless conversations and transitions over the years.

We took the usual place, a table in the back, away from the majority of people. Mary signaled for me to take a place in the order line, and claimed a table, taking off her flannel shirt tied around her waist, and put it on the back of her chair. She then met me in the line.

We ordered mochas, mine with four shots and hers with six. I sauntered to the table holding my drink, with Mary pressing hard behind me. An urgent attitude overcame her. I looked away.

"Brad, I want your full attention. You need to lose the self-absorbed bullshit. I've about had enough. There is more about the bridge that, until now, I've held back due to your self-centeredness. Frankly, I'm sick of it. Now, you force me to tell you, as much as it is going to hurt."

"Jesus Mary, what? Don't be a cunt." She glared sharply, restraining herself.

"You see," she said leaning forward, "It is so much easier for you to go on acting like an ass with Jordan's parents, believing Jordan doesn't want to be with you, sitting all the way home crying, self-absorbed in your sadness. You act like life is all about you. Jordan tried to kill himself Brad!

"What do you…"

"Shut the fuck up and listen," she said putting her fist between us.

"It was a bad scene. I got to the bridge, all those people standing around, at a good distance, but close enough for him to hear, urging him to jump. Sick fucks they were, totally sick. At one point he looked back and saw me, called out my name. There were two officers standing close to him. It would have only taken a quick reaction from them to grab his legs, but an even shorter second for him to let go of the cables and jump. One of them turned and asked me to come over."

"What? You?"

"Listen! You can't interrupt." Mary sat back hard in her chair. "I stood under him, looking up, scared as hell, wishing it would just end. Then he looked down at me, acknowledging me again with that fucked up smile of his. Then he said these words, and I don't want you to ever forget them."

"'Mary! Tell Brad that I love him, I love him with all my heart." His hands shifted position. He was going to let go. "Tell him it is not his fault." He looked down at me, allowing me to see the settled look on his face, but also the sadness that he had been carrying with him. "I love him Mary. That is why I can't go back. I can't go back to my parents, my church." He looked up, as if crying out to God. "I can't go back to face everyone in my ward. I can't go to singles groups or profess a testimony. It is all a lie."

'There was no fear in his face. "I love a man Mary. For that, I will never go to the heavenly kingdoms. I will always be stuck, without God." I wanted to say something, but before the words came, the officers seized the opportunity and called, 'NOW!'"

"As he came down, his body flew forward, his head hitting the railing he was standing on. He was knocked unconscious. They pulled him to the ground, holding his head, the paramedics quickly jumping in."

I now understood his choice to end his life, his final act of desperation. He had no choice. With every touch we shared came the shadows, the darkness of guilt. He was in turmoil, being himself meant spiritual death, his heart absent from peace. Mormonism was his culture, and culture you can't change.

Chapter Thirty-Three

Mary took me home and we sat with Henri, apologizing for first taking his car, and then leaving it. He didn't ask for details, instead asking about Jordan. Soon, being entirely exhausted, I fell asleep on the couch in the silence after the storm. I woke to the abrupt digital ring of the phone. I didn't answer, waiting for someone to pick it up. Warily looking around the room, I found that I was alone.

The phone fell silent for a moment, and then resumed its interruption. My body felt heavy, my stomach sick, but I forced myself off the couch, balancing myself with the coffee table. I found the "on" button with its annoying red blinking button and put it to my ear. Jordan, yes, it could be Jordan. I took in a deep breath. Could I tell him how much I loved him? Would I ask him to come back, hoping that the severity of his actions scared him enough?

The line was silent. I could hear faint talking in the background, but the mix of voices was too shadowed and unintelligible.

"Hello?" I said with a shaky voice. Then, more distant voices and no one on the other line. I was about to speak his name when I heard a light click and the activity in the background stop. I slowly put the receiver back to the charger. Maybe it wasn't him.

It rang again. This time I didn't hesitate.

"Hello? Jordan?"

"Jordan?" came the female voice on the other end, no shadowed voices or long drawn out silence. "No. Brad, are you okay?"

It was Lydia, the last person I expected to hear from. "Brad? Are you there?" I stopped breathing.

"Oh, yeah, sorry. How are you Lydia," I said, dazed and sick, realizing he had been left out of the most recent drama.

"Can I come over. I heard about Jordan. I've been really worried. Is he okay?"

"Okay, yeah, I do believe so. He is at the psychiatric hospital in Lewiston. I think he's doing fine. His parents are with him. That…"

"Hey, I don't want to do this on the phone. Can I come over?" She wasn't asking. There was a sense of urgency in her voice. I couldn't refuse. And, especially after how I treated her.

She was sitting in my living room minutes after hanging up. I started coffee. There was small talk, forced by the understanding that nothing meaningful could be said until I was able to focus. When I was finished messing around in the sink, with Lydia patiently looking on from the kitchen table, I sat down across from her, each of us nursing the hot liquid.

I told her about London. I told her about Jordan and me getting into a fight. I told her about the bridge and sharing the hospital lobby with his parents. I gave her the entire epic, trying to pick up where we left off. The words were vaguely empty, overshadowed by the tension between us. By the time I was finished, we were standing, holding each other, an embrace that sealed our friendship forever.

The ease to which we talked surprised me. I remarked on it as we sat eating dinner.

"How have we come to this place Lydia? I thought you were out of my life forever."

"Yeah. I didn't think it was possible either. I only regret not talking to you before. We were friends all along, weren't we?"

"Yes. But it was the way I treated you, not the other way around. I regret…"

"Do you hear what you are saying? You can't take responsibility for everything. In the last two hours I've heard you not only blame Jordan's fucked up faith, but also yourself. And what happened between us is the past. I want what we had. We had a friendship, that is what we had, and it was beautiful."

"And another thing," she continued. "I knew all along Brad. Maybe not at first. Dude, you put on a great act. But after we stopped fooling around, I started to understand you weren't attracted to me. I mean, it isn't like I didn't take it personal, but I tried to pass it off like you were going through some kind of phase."

"I'm really…"

"Knock it off with that. You didn't do anything wrong…Well, you could have been more direct about it, but I understand. I have to, cuz I care about you. My sister went through hell coming out, and I was there for the whole thing. She struggled with the Catholic Church, similar to Jordan I suppose."

She stopped and corrected herself. "No, I don't think it compares actually, the more I think about it. She was able to find some peace in it. Catholicism and Mormonism are quite different that way. I can see that now. She eventually got support from her congregation, even though she doesn't take communion anymore, out of protest really."

"Anyway, I'm just going on and on about things I don't know, but I do see that with Mormons, you either are or you aren't in the club, and you can't be in the club and believe that you are a well-adjusted person if you are homosexual. My God. What do they do with women who never get married? I suppose they become old hags that just read their Bibles and Book of Mormon every day of the week, glowing fake grins while making soups for weekly church events. Do they get to go to a higher heaven?"

"I want to try and see Jordan tomorrow. Would you come with me? I was thinking we could pick up my friend Mary and take her. She is really great. I…"

"I know her." The corners of her mouth innocently pulled up into a grin.

"You know her?"

"Yeah. She is the one who told me about his attempt."

"But how…"

"We took a rock climbing class together last semester. She kept mentioning you, and when I put two and two together, I started milking her for information. I've kept up on most all of it. It was kind of like reading a book. Couldn't wait until the next chapter."

"Oh my God." I sat with my mouth wide open. It turned into an uncontrollable laugh, but right then, I knew we were hopelessly connected.

"Anyway, before you go and laugh yourself into hysteria," she said as she giggled, "I agree to go. I can call Mary myself if you want."

Chapter Thirty-Four

I stayed up late that night hanging out with Henri. He also wanted to go to the hospital with us. His stable nature felt warm and I knew Jordan would enjoy him. Lydia called and confirmed the seven o'clock visiting hours. We took company with the porch, participating in small talk, thinking only of what was to come. We smoked cigarettes until my stomach couldn't take anymore, and then ended with a beer.

There was little doubt that Jordan's parents would be there, acting as the final power. I would stand tall, only by the sheer numbers behind me. It stacked up to be a sizable confrontation.

I felt boldly determined to make my statement. They were not going to keep us from him. Jordan was an adult and would choose his visitors. I talked tough over the intoxication of nicotine and alcohol and adrenalin. Henri supportively went along with energized self-talk, supporting me with each drag and puff of smoke.

Mary picked us up on time to make the forty-minute trip to Lewiston and also be early to visiting hours. Lydia was in the passenger seat, pushing her arm intrusively in front of Mary's face, waiving at Henri and I sitting on the top step. Mary jumped out of the car, jolting to a stop at eye level, putting her long lesbian finger in my face.

"Brad. You better snap out of it."

"What?" I defended.

"I can see that chip on your shoulder. You better remove it or you're not going to get past the door. I'm warning you now. Don't you dare make a scene?"

"You're going to let us do the talking, okay?" Lydia said leaning so I could see her from the driver's side window. Henri gave an affirming head nod.

"Fine," I droned. I got into the station wagon, and as I did, the smell of cigarette smoke overpowered me. The slight head twitch gave her away. Miss confidence had given into the anticipation.

Pulling into the hospital, there was no sign of his parent's car. The tension melted out of me. I started to talk uncontrollably as we made our way up the stairs, my companions giving a warning glance.

We stepped into the foyer, still no sign of his parents. Mary called for the receptionist through the hole in the glass window. She revealed herself from inside another office, stumbling on her oversized high heel shoes. The thin wire crosshatch reinforced glass was foreboding, magnifying her black rimmed glasses and polished steel braces. She appeared to be in her early twenties, wearing a long flower pattern dress. She used her finger to pick at her teeth, us being but five minutes early and clearly interrupting her dinner.

"Can I help you?" she said with an exaggerated sweet but course voice.

"We want to see Jordan, Jordan Anderson. He was admitted a couple days ago," Mary said, leaning close to the hole in the glass, causing the women to step back.

She put her hands down on her hips and looked down at the floor, confused by the question of who we were, and then smiled as she looked over at the four of us, stopping at Henri. "Oh yeah! Let me get the doctor. He wants to talk to you."

My chest felt tight with excitement. "Just take a seat. I'll go get him," she added, pointing to the waiting area, before turning on her heels.

We sat down, each taking up an entire couch meant for two. It was a haunted place, sitting in the same seats we were in at the beginning of his attempt. The seats where his parents sat remained empty. Their shadows remained.

The overhead intercom paged in a familiar voice, "Dr. Rob, please dial 221, please dial 221."

Within a few short minutes, a door at the end of the room opened. The relatively thin and short in stature man looked around at all of us with concern. Mary introduced herself, Lydia and then me, and then Henri, the most disheveled of the crew. He smiled politely, taking each of our hands cordially.

"I'm glad you came. Come this way." He led us past another door opening up into a long hall to the left. He took us down the hall and to the right, into a room with a sign on the wall indicating, 'Dr. Rob, Medical Director'.

"Take a seat." He gestured with an open hand at the small couch and love seat. He sat at his desk, turning his chair to complete the circle.

"Like I said, I'm glad you came. I'm afraid that things are not going as we liked."

"What do you mean," I panicked. Mary sat next to me and looked over in silent annoyance.

"Well, as you already know, Jordan was in the hospital on a protective custody. The police do this, and an evaluator, usually a psychologist, confirms the necessity of the hold at the time of admission. This morning, the second evaluator, or Designated Examiner, as they are called, saw Jordan."

"Why does he see two?" I asked.

"Well, I don't want to get into too many of the details," he said curtly, "but it is a second opinion in the process. If the patient clears, or says the right things, thus taking the patient out of the legal realm of the custody, then they are free to go. We encourage the patients to sign themselves in at that point and complete their care."

"Well, what happened?" Mary urged, knowing something had gone drastically wrong.

"Your friend left the hospital this morning about ten thirty."

"Holy shit!" I shouted standing up. "Why weren't we called?"

"He refused to put you on the visitors list or sign a release of information." He gestured for me to sit down. I ignored him. "So, what I'm telling you even now, I probably shouldn't. But frankly, I'm worried about him."

"Did he go with his parents?"

"No. They had a fight last night. The nursing staff called me and said they told him he was on his own. They went back alone."

"Who did he go with?" Mary pressed.

"He left by himself, said he was going back to Moscow. He left the hospital with what he came with. We called the police, and…"

"Didn't they put him back in?" I exclaimed with desperation. The severity of the situation weighted on me. He was caught once at the bridge trying to hurt himself. He wouldn't attempt to go there twice, too obvious. He was too smart for that.

"They don't have to do that. If they don't see an immediate threat, they don't have to hold him at all. My guess is they stopped him on the street and he was allowed to go."

"Oh my god," mumbled Lydia. "Has anyone heard anything since? Anyone call in…"

"No. All I can tell you, is if you know places he frequents, try to find him. And I doubt he stayed in Lewiston. I believe he is a serious risk to himself."

"What do you mean?"

"After his parents left, he stopped crying, smiled, seemed calm, was pleasant to work with. He became a hit with the nursing staff. Most protective custodies are a problem for us, not very easy to get along with. He looked fine, too fine if you ask me."

Without saying goodbye, we found our way out of the building and back into the car.

The drive back to Moscow was long and without words. As we descended into town, Henri took command. "Let's stop downtown. We need to split up. I will walk around Main Street and check out the usual places like The Beanery. Lydia, you come with me. Mary, drive around the surrounding streets and up around campus. He may be wandering up there. Brad, go home. He may be there waiting. If he is, stay put. We won't be far behind."

Mary dropped me off within three blocks of the house. She turned her wheel hard and drove off in a hurry. In a quick pace, I worked my way up the street and onto the porch. The house appeared quiet. Wind cut through the high oak trees. Birds made notice of my presence.

I went in, pulling on the loose spring door and through the entryway. The front door was open. I tried to remember if we had closed it, because leaving it open was common.

The living room was empty. I looked around for any sign of someone there. Nothing had been disturbed. Everything remained as it was before. I quickly went into the bedroom. Empty.

I quickened my pace, sure that I felt him there; maybe the hint of his odor, the scent of the skin just off his neck. I was not alone. I turned and entered the kitchen. Empty.

I went down the stairs into the basement. It was empty. My heart raced. Where could he be? Was I hysterical? I ran back up the stairs, hoping I could catch him trying to escape.

Then I saw him. In my haste I had missed him before. His sandy blond hair, dull and unattended, revealed him through the big window off the kitchen table. He sat outside, quietly sitting in the lawn chair. His head was relaxed, as if he were sleeping. Running out the back door, I quickly went to him. I stopped myself. As hard as it was to keep myself steady, I slowed my pace in my approach, fearful he would run off by my attack.

I wanted to take him in my arms. I wanted to hold him close and welcome him home. Taking the chair next to him, I sat down. His weary eyes met mine. They were dark with exhaustion. The blanket from the end of my bed draped over him, with only his head and the top of his shoulders showing.

"Hi there," he said with a cracked voice. His eyes drooped, and then lit up again.

"Jordan. What are you doing?"

"Just waiting for you." His head lifted off the back of the chair as he looked more directly at me.

"I've missed you." I started to get up. He shook his head.

"Where have you been?" I said, sitting back down, noticing warmth of the sun against the light breeze, not cool enough to require a blanket.

"Oh, just about."

"You and your parents had a fight last night?"

"Oh, so you've talked to the good doctor. He's homophobic you know. They are everywhere you turn." He closed his eyes and struggled to swallow, as if he had a sore throat.

"Yes. We had a talk," Jordan continued. "They don't like you Brad, my beautiful - beautiful baby. You know that though, don't you? They were going to take me back, and I almost went. I was going to leave the hospital and just go home, but they had to ask questions, questions about us. I told them Brad. I told them about us, and then us and sex. In the middle of all of it, they left. Yup, that is right Brad. They couldn't handle it. They thought of us together and couldn't handle it. Then..."

I wanted to know, but he was talking like a ghost. It horrified me.

"Jordan, you're tired. Let's go in," I said leaning over to his cheek. He turned away. I slowly sat back. A look of pain shot across his face. His breathing was shallow and then normal again. He struggled.

"Are you okay? Come on. You're worrying me. You don't look good Jordan."

"No worries man, my knight in shining armor, no worries anymore."

Something was deeply wrong. Not knowing what to do, fearful he was going to run, I went along.

"Then what happened next Jordan?"

"They started to leave when I told them that I hated them and Father God. My mom came up to me, didn't say a word actually, but looked at me disappointed. It didn't work. No, it didn't work this time, that eternal fucking slow gaze of guilt. No, I made decisions on my own this time."

"You're home now Jordan. You're home with me."

"Yeah, I guess you can say that." His eyes shut, and then squeezed tightly together, slightly arching his back. His face was becoming whiter by the minute, his voice weak.

"I love you Brad. But you know that don't you?"

"Yes Jordan, I do, and I love you too. Now come on, let's go inside. You're starting to freak me out."

"No, there is no need for that. You can't take care of me anymore like that Brad. I'm my own person now. Not your project, right? I'm making decisions on my own. I can't do it for my parents. I can't do it for you."

I didn't know how to respond. He punched me with his words. But he was right, I knew he was right.

"You've fooled yourself into thinking that you love me Brad," he continued.

"No…"

"Stop right there my dear Brad, my beautiful honorable knight. You don't love me. You just want to take care of me. But that will not be possible now. I'm taking care of me now Brad. I've made decisions that don't please you or my parents. They only please me. They are mine and mine alone."

His words were forced, effort needed to push forth his argument. He was slipping, but from what I didn't know. He was almost asleep, seemingly intoxicated. Then he slipped. It was my chance. Before he came back, I jumped up and pushing my arm under his knees, and the other his neck, and stood.

His weight was rubber; there was no tension in any of his muscles. His arm slipped from my chest. A wet sticky warm fluid soaked my shirt. I knelt back down. Just in front of me, where he had been sitting was the butcher knife from the kitchen sink. The arm of the lawn chair was covered in blood. His pants were soaked. I quickly put him down the rest of the way at the foot of the chairs, trying not to panic at what he had done, trying to figure out what to do next.

"NO", I whispered.

I pulled the blanket off his motionless shallow breathing body. Blood ran from deep lines running up his left wrist, dry crust haloing the perimeter. His body made a small jerk. Running inside, I frantically searched for the phone. I looked out the window to see if he was still there. He hadn't moved. I turned, cried out in panic, tears blinding me, aimlessly looking for the phone. It was on my bed, suddenly I remembered, from my conversation with Lydia the night before. I tried to dial 911. I dialed it wrong. I finally got it right. I went back to him, holding him to me, and waiting.

Part Four

"Standing at the Rail"

Chapter Thirty-Five

Brad sat looking off with a blank stare, tired in the final moments of the story. His thoughts swam in the shadows with insecurity and an odd sense of isolation. Elaina sat quiet, spurring his obscure desire to disappear into the walls. She looked down at her half-burnt cigarette, then up again, trying to get his attention with a long-exaggerated breath.

"I don't know what to say except that I'm really sorry Brad. What you have gone through is terrible. Absolutely wretched. How long has it been?"

Brad pulled himself out of his daze with a quick shake. "Just a little over two, two and a half years.

"It is a crazy story. Jordan had everything going against him."

"I blamed myself at first you know. I mean, I realize how irrational that is, but even now, just when I think I have gotten past it, it is right in my face. All of it! Sometimes I totally believe that if I got home a few minutes earlier, he could have been saved." Brad's said decisively. "But he was determined, and I'm not sure that it wasn't such a bad choice. He couldn't be helped, could he?" He looked at the dry bottom of his glass. He wished he had another, but didn't want to get up.

"Don't take this personal Brad, but who he needed most was his family. Religion should never separate people."

A flare of anger hit him in the chest. "You're exactly right. I blame the religion. Fundamentalism is a sickness," he blurted.

He was slightly embarrassed at his sudden loss of control. "I also blame them. They put their own prejudice behind it. How could any mother sit back and do nothing?

"Don't you blame him," Elaina prodded?

"Yes, I blame him. He left me behind to deal with this shit. It is weak, very weak. Hell, after all we went through together? Every fucking day I have to live with it while he is somewhere else out of his pain."

"Religion is meant to bring people together."

"Fundamentalism divides," Brad retorted.

"Yes, it does. It kills. I had no idea, and damn you for leaving me out," Elaina said as she threw her hands into the air, slumping into the chair and throwing her head back. The gray ash off the end of her cigarette fell into her lap. She brushed it off with her pinky and it disappeared between her hip and the leather.

She sat up again trying to calm herself with another deep breath. She put her cigarette out in the ashtray. Her mouth was bitter with tar. For the first time in several hours, she didn't reach for another. Looking directly at Brad, she raised her eyebrows to get his attention.

"After seeing Henri in Amsterdam, I was worried, but didn't imagine any of this. He looked very concerned and couldn't stand to leave you in Moscow. I knew whatever happened was important because he isn't one to exaggerate."

"I had Lydia and Mary. We supported each other, and honestly, I didn't think you would understand." Elaina looked confused, concerned, felt out of place.

"I didn't want to have to explain everything. The gay community stepped in and supported me."

"How did Lydia deal with it," Elaina said, avoiding the bait.

"Lydia was never the same. We have become good friends and I think we are close. But we really don't talk about it very much."

Elaina's face flushed red. She knew she couldn't make up the time and was hurt that they hadn't been closer. Brad left the tension hanging between them.

"You know Mr., it looks like on the surface that you are trying to move past Jordan's suicide, but don't you think that two years is a long time? You turned down a great job in San Francisco to stay working at the University. You just mope about. You're stuck. And where is this wonderful gay community? I don't see you with much support now!"

"Yes, and to set things straight, for the majority of it, I've been just fine."

"Yeah right!"

"Just wait a minute, I'm not finished."

She did her best to avoid an argumentative stance. His closed approach was making it impossible. He wanted sympathy, and she held it back.

Brad leaned forward looking narrowly at her, trying to control his annoyance. "But then, about two months ago, I started having that fucking dream. It is destroying me. I want to figure it out and get that image out of my head!"

In frustration, Brad put his head in his hands and looked down at the floor between his shoes. Elaina gave out a frustrated sigh.

"My God, you're deceiving yourself! Pull your head out of your ass!" She stood and moved in close, pushing in on his space. "You, and only you, have chosen to exist day-to-day as a damn ghost, acting like life isn't happening around you! Well, it is! That dream is telling you to wake up. It is time to cope!"

He shook his head, confused, slightly irritated at getting the deserving response. The more he avoided it, the more of his psyche it devoured. Consciously, he was choosing to forget about it.

"I mean," Elaina continued with a more relaxed tone, "It's obvious. You tell me you don't know where it comes from? I think you do. You just don't want to face it." She turned and sat back in the chair. It was warm and sticky and slightly uncomfortable.

Then Brad retorted with a sarcastic tone, meeting her face-to-face, "What do you mean? I'm sitting talking to you right now, aren't I? If you're so damn knowledgeable in dream interpretation, tell me!"

"Don't get that way with me! You know exactly what it means. You just need to dig a little more. Face it head-on. Drop the passive shit."

"Why are you attacking me when I'm clearly not ready for this? I told you the story to get it off my chest."

"Brad, you're tougher than that. Give me a rest! Stop that coy shit with me. I hope you don't expect me to sit back and watch you take the victim's seat that easily! Get it together and say it out loud! You tell me what this dream is about. You're not a psychologist, but you're not a dumb ass either!"

He pinched his eyes together, straining to say what was on his mind. "I don't know...maybe...that I wish it was me?"

"I certainly hope you don't think that dreams have to always be about you? Maybe you are Jordan in the dream? Haven't you considered that possibility?"

"No, it is me. They are my thoughts; I can feel it, as if I'm the one standing up there. There is nothing about Jordan in the dream at all," Brad continued, slapping his hand to his chest.

"Then, get to it!" She leaned forward now, was almost directly in his face, pushing him even harder.

He tried to avoid her and looked away. She turned her head to meet his. "So, it is you. You're standing at the rail. You're about to jump. You don't, instead you hold back, causing you to slip and lose your balance. Falling back you go, and you nearly get hit by a car. Don't you see it? You almost die in either direction, but the fact is that you don't! You hang on and then fall back from exhaustion."

"OKAY, So I don't die by falling into the river."

"That's right! You are too strong."

"I don't die from the car..."

"No, because you have a support system waiting for you."

"I live because I can't give up. I fall back into the world, but black out. I can't see anything remember? It is all black."

"Yes. You are alive, but not willing to accept that you can survive. You believe that taking on his trauma will make it better. Your guilt is driving you to hang on, but since you can't and fall back, you have to live. So, you choose to be blind to everything around you, a zombie."

"This is so confusing..."

"You need to wake up Man! You need people, and people need you! Don't you see it? You're wasting your life stuck in a blackout. You want to die but can't. You fall back and don't get killed. That's the difference between you and Jordan!"

"What?"

"Jordan had no option but to die. He had no place to run. Not even living in oblivion would have worked. He was forced to fight both sides. Either be himself and be a partner to you, or sacrifice it all to live a lie as a fundamentalist. He had no choice but to lean forward and die in the river!"

"Then why? Why did he have to be born into it? What God would put him on earth to test him like that? It is totally fucked. Give him a sexuality with which he can't live. Then give him a church that absorbs his identity, replacing it with their own. No loving God would give anyone that dilemma."

"That's my point. You weren't given his dilemma. That is my very point. No God would do that to anyone. It is the church that has it all wrong. Being gay is not an affliction, fundamentalism is. It promotes being a slave to perfection, secured by the power of shame. A gay person is not only imperfect in the eyes of any fundamentalist, but a perversion. You can't live life believing your core is nothing but a perversion."

"Yes, but, a fundamentalist says we believe in error, that 'gay' is our core biological nature. That is the fundamentalist loophole. They make everything a matter of cognition...choice. Once the homosexual understands 'correctly', then they can change."

"No Brad, we both know that fundamentalists of every kind believe that homosexuality is strong and virtually impossible to change. Remember? Mormons believe in celibacy as a way to keep them out of sin and involved in the church. They have long ago admitted that sexuality is stable. I mean, have you ever heard of anyone trying to take the feminine nature out of women, or the masculine nature out of men? Can you believe the uproar it would cause if we sent people away to counseling to reprogram gender? You are gay Brad. And even though you sometimes act a little masculine, you are still a poof!"

Brad snickered. Elaina was right. The realization hit him direct. Fundamentalism tries to have it both ways. The prejudice and fear of homosexuality was the cause. The Mormon Church didn't want to change its basic principles to accommodate homosexual members. They couldn't change their biological drives and settled on the doctrine of celibacy.

"Brad, fundamentalism destroys self-concept, much like the military blends away a platoon's individuality. There is no room for free thinking and possibilities. They are bound to the belief that who they are isn't important, that the desires of the church and the greater good, is what is right and holy. For the military, that greater good is the safety of the nation. For fundamentalism, it is the stability of the Church's belief system. And how much better could you subjugate people into your beliefs than to wipe away their choices through the guilt of black and white thinking. It is not only insanity, it is simply dangerous."

Marty and Sebastian looped their way through Elaina and Brad's legs. After hours of listening to human chatter, they were decisively bored.

"You see," Elaina continued, "Now that is pure love. They like you because you are there. You don't have to be anything but simply you Brad. They love you. And you love them back. What would your life be without them? I remember the day you brought them home. They put so much joy in that old house. And, simply because they love to be loved. I believe that is the kind of relationship God has with us. He isn't trying to change us. All expression of spirituality should love you just because you are you."

"Oppression is death," Brad interjected.

"It is. And as much as you are missing him and wish he could have chosen you, like you said before, I think he made the only choice he could make."

Brad looked down again, trying to hide his pain.

"He loved you Brad but didn't have any other choice. Whether he ended up being with you or the church, in both cases he would have lived life as a spiritual zombie. He was tortured."

Elaina stood up, walked past Brad and put her hand on his shoulder. "I need some fresh air. Let's take a walk."

Brad followed her to the door. He put on his outdoor clothing. After they were both ready, each looked pensively down at the cats, glancing curiously back in silence. They reverently admired their happiness, and the joy that it brought them in that moment. Walking down the stairs, the sudden blast of cold air from outside doorway sent a solid chill into their bones. Brad felt alive. He tried to remember the last time he felt so alive.

"Elaina." Brad stopped and turned to face her. "Thank you."

"Oh stop. I don't want to hear it, Mr., 'I need to always end everything on a positive note.'" Brad smiled, happy that she was next to him. She put her arm through the loop at his elbow and gave a gentle tug, briefly putting her head on his shoulder as they left Friendship Square.

"Elaina?"

"Yes?"

"On our walk, can we go up to the top of campus? I want to see the lights."

"Lights?"

"Yes, the lights. They make the air so orange with the snow. I want to see them."

"Sure. I bet it will look even cooler when morning comes."

Taking out her pack of cigarettes, she handed one to Brad and took one for herself. Cupping her hand around the flame, she carefully lit her cigarette and then his with the glowing end. The smoke tasted good mixed with the cold February early morning air. The coming light ran a light blue hue on the horizon behind them as they walked towards the university up Sixth Street. They walked into the disappearing stars of the west, holding each other arm and arm, admiring what they had, and acknowledging what would grow.

About the Author:

Jerod Killick is a writer and photographer from Vancouver, British Columbia. After studying as an undergraduate at the University of Idaho, he went on to complete a graduate degree in Clinical Psychology. Jerod has worked in acute psychiatric care, academia, health care operations management, and community psychotherapy as a private practitioner. He currently holds a position as a senior leader in mental health and addictions for Vancouver Coastal Health Authority.

www.ingramcontent.com/pod-product-compliance
Lightning Source LLC
Chambersburg PA
CBHW071248170626
46809CB00001B/123